THE BOOKSHOP
OF
HOPES AND DREAMS

(HOPE COVE BOOK 6)

HANNAH ELLIS

For Mario
with love

Chapter 1

The Rose and Crown wasn't one of Tara's regular haunts. But after the day she'd had, she just couldn't face sitting at home alone. There was a sprinkling of snow on the ground, and it seemed like a pleasant evening for an aimless stroll. When she passed the pub it seemed as good a place as any to drown her sorrows.

She'd only expected there to be a few old men nursing pints of ale. She'd been right about that. At least until Mr Blonde-Hair-and-Blue-Eyes appeared beside her at the bar.

"You look like someone's died," he said with a lopsided smile.

He looked to be about her age, somewhere around thirty. He was cute, and casually dressed in jeans and a dark T-shirt.

Leaning on the bar, Tara wiped the condensation from the side of her glass. The ice had melted, diluting the remnants of her gin and tonic. She didn't look at him as she spoke.

"Here's a tip. If someone's sitting alone in a bar, dressed all in black, looking miserable, maybe don't say they look like someone's died." She turned and locked eyes with him. "In case they've just come from a funeral or something."

He searched her face, a look of intensity on his. Then he took a deep breath. "Oh."

"Yeah."

"Sorry."

"Don't worry about it," she said. "It's the sort of inappropriate thing I say to people all the time."

"No, I meant sorry for your loss."

Her chin twitched and she took a few swigs of her watery drink.

The barman came over. The blonde guy ordered a pint of lager, then glanced at Tara.

"Can I get you a fresh one?"

"No." She swivelled on the stool to gaze out of the window. A pathetic amount of snow fluttered outside. "I should get home." But she didn't really want to go home. She glanced at the guy beside her. He really was very cute. Maybe a one-night stand would take her mind off things. Smiling, she put the idea quickly out of her mind and tried not to imagine what he looked like without his shirt on. "I suppose one more won't hurt. Same again, please."

Sitting at the bar wasn't particularly comfy, so Tara suggested they move to the cosy little nook in the corner. The high back in the booth meant she could rest her head back and relax. A fire crackled in the hearth beside them.

"I'm James," he said.

Tara's lips twitched to a hint of a smile. She hadn't even realised they'd skipped introductions.

"Tara," she said.

"And you had a bad day?"

"A bad day and a bad week."

"Whose funeral was it?" His eyebrows knitted together. "Or we can talk about something else if you want …"

"An old friend of mine," Tara said, staring into the fire. "Wendy. She and her partner owned a dog kennels in the village where I used to live. Me and some of the other local kids spent a lot of time playing there when we were growing up."

"I bet that was fun," James said.

"Yeah. It was." Tara sipped her drink. "Wendy was eighty. She'd been ill for a while so it wasn't a shock or anything." She paused and pushed her hair over her shoulder. "Actually, it still feels like a shock. I'm not sure why."

"It's nice that she made such an impression," he said softly.

Tara should probably change the subject. The poor guy had come in for a quiet drink and he was stuck listening to her problems. It felt good to talk, though. Especially to a stranger.

She stirred her drink with the straw, making the ice rattle against the glass. "I don't think I ever saw Wendy as a huge part of my life, but she was always there. I'd often call in for a cuppa with her and Annette when I was back in Averton. They were always good fun. When I was growing up, everyone else in the village seemed so similar. Then there were these two quirky old lesbians living in a farmhouse on a hill, doing whatever the heck they wanted."

"They sound great." He took a sip of his pint.

7

"I don't know how Annette's going to cope without Wendy. They were the most together couple I know." A lump formed in Tara's throat and she looked up at James. "I'm sorry. I don't know you and I'm telling you all this."

He shrugged. "That'll teach me to make stupid comments to women at the bar."

A slow smile spread over Tara's face. "What are you doing in the worst pub in Newton Abbot on a Saturday night?"

"Trying to find somewhere to have a quiet drink and clear my head."

Tara sat up straighter, wishing she'd changed out of the black dress she'd worn for the funeral. Not only was she completely overdressed but she was uncomfortable too. "You can tell me your problems if you want. It seems only fair after I told you mine."

"I'm not sure it's a problem," he said. "I inherited a property in Newton Abbot. And I'm trying to figure out what to do with it."

"What are your options?"

"Selling it seems to be the obvious thing to do."

"But?"

He sighed heavily. "Do you ever feel like you're at a crossroads and life could go one of two ways?"

"Not really. But I quite often feel like I'm at a dead end. Or going the wrong way on a one-way street."

He smiled. "I thought I knew what I was going to do. But now I'm tempted to do the exact opposite."

"Well, my friend Wendy used to say 'If you don't try, you'll never know.'"

"She sounds very wise."

"She had a saying for everything. A lot of them contradicted each other." Tara finished her drink and glanced out of the window again. The snow was coming down more heavily. "I should probably go home. Thanks for the drink."

"You're welcome." He stood when she did. "I'll walk out with you."

Outside the pub he zipped his coat up higher. "Do you need a taxi?"

"I'm going to walk," she said.

"Do you need me to walk you?"

"No." She chuckled. "I don't *need* you to walk me home."

"Okay." He flashed a boyish grin. "*May I* walk you home?"

She hesitated for a moment. It probably wasn't very sensible to let a strange man walk her home. She was usually a good judge of character, though, and he seemed like a decent guy. "You *may*," she said. "As long as you don't expect me to invite you in for a nightcap or anything."

"Definitely not expecting a nightcap," he said. They fell into step and walked down the main road.

"So what's it like to live here?" James asked.

Tara looked around. Newton Abbot was a small market town in Devon. There was nothing particularly special about it, but she'd always been fond of the place. "It's fairly quiet, I suppose. Depending on what you're used to."

"I live in Exeter," he said. "Not exactly a bustling metropolis but there's enough going on."

"There's probably a lot less going on here, but it has its charm."

"What do you do for a living?" he asked.

"I'm currently between a job that I hate and the job of my dreams."

"That sounds like a good place to be."

"Yeah." She puffed out a breath and it steamed in front of her face. "Until I can't afford to pay my rent anymore. Then it's not so great."

"How long have you been in the in-between place?"

Tara checked her watch. "Approximately forty-eight hours."

"I see." Shoving his hands into his pockets, he bunched his shoulders up.

"Wendy once told me life's too short to stay in a job you hate. When she died, it seemed like a good time to take her advice."

"That's a lovely tribute."

His smile was so warm it made her want to snuggle into him. She managed to keep a respectable distance. "Now I'm thinking she had some other advice about not leaving one job until you have something else lined up … and maybe something about sometimes sticking at a job you hate to keep a roof over your head."

"She definitely sounds contradictory."

They turned onto a side street. "It's quite a long walk," Tara said. "Don't feel like you need to freeze to death on my account."

"Is it cold? I was just thinking what a delightful balmy evening it is." His cheeks had turned bright red and a tiny snowflake clung to an eyelash. Tara shifted her gaze before she gave in to the urge to stroke it away. She braced against the cold and increased her pace.

"I'm sure you'll find a new job easily," he said. "What's the dream job you're looking for?"

"I've no idea. I feel like I'll know when I find it. Or more likely I'll go with Wendy's advice of doing a job I hate just to keep a roof over my head."

"A change is usually good," he said. "I'm sure it'll work out fine."

Tara clamped her jaw shut to stop her teeth chattering as the icy breeze stung her face. They walked on in silence until they reached her house.

"This is me," she said, hovering on the pavement outside the row of terraced houses. "I meant what I said about not inviting you in for a nightcap. I hope you're not offended."

"Not at all." He took a few small steps away from her. "I absolutely wasn't expecting you to invite me in for sex." He raised his eyebrows in mock horror. "Sorry, you were calling it a nightcap. I'd have turned you down anyway. For either!" He grinned cheekily.

Tara let out a laugh as she walked towards the door. As she turned the key in the lock she gave a small shake of the head. She hadn't thought she'd find anything to laugh about that day.

Chapter 2

Sunday mornings were always lazy. Tara had never been an early bird, and on the weekends she would often sleep until lunchtime. That Sunday she woke in a bit of a fog. It was partly the alcohol, but Wendy's funeral played on her mind too. Seeing Annette so heartbroken had been hard. The world felt a little dimmer without Wendy in it.

It was late in the morning when Tara finally dragged herself out of bed. Once she'd had breakfast, she fully intended to get out her laptop and trawl the job advertisements and update her CV. It seemed like a pathetic way to spend a Sunday. The fridge was depressingly empty. She stared into it for a moment as though food might magically appear, then she trudged back upstairs and threw on a pair of jeans and a jumper before hurrying out to her car. Oh, God. It was freezing and she hadn't even bothered to put socks on.

The roads were icy, and the car skidded a little before the tyres gripped the road. Parking the car on the main road, she made a dash for the supermarket and hastily picked out a bunch of junk food to get her through the day.

She'd just dumped her shopping on the passenger

13

seat when a familiar voice called out to her.

"Hey!" There was no one else around, but it took a second for Tara's eyes to land on James. He was standing outside the Reading Room, a run-down old bookshop just across the road.

"Hey yourself," she said, walking over to him. "So this is the property you inherited?"

He nodded as he gazed up at the building. "My great-uncle left it to me."

"That was nice of him. Were you close?"

"I barely knew the guy. From what I gather, Richard was a bit of a recluse. Did you know him, since you live round here?"

Tara shook her head. She remembered the old man who'd owned the shop and had heard about his death a couple of months before. "Sometimes he'd stand out in the doorway, but he wasn't the friendliest of people. I'm not sure how he stayed in business, to be honest. I never saw any customers in the shop."

"According to his accounts, he hadn't made a profit in years. The place was haemorrhaging money."

"Shame," Tara said. "It could be really nice."

"Do you think so?"

She stood back and looked at the shop front. "I have a vivid imagination."

"It definitely needs some work," he said. "And I don't know if there's any demand for a bookshop round here."

"But you're tempted to try?" she asked.

He nodded. "It feels crazy. I have no idea how to

run a bookshop. The rational part of my brain is telling me to sell it and carry on with my life."

"That sounds like the logical thing to do." Her eyes flicked over his shoulder, trying to get a look inside. It might be logical, but it would be a shame if he sold the place. If it was her who'd inherited a bookshop, she'd start renovating immediately. Tara wasn't a reader but even so, there was something so magical about bookshops.

"Were you on your way somewhere?" he asked.

She glanced down and realised she wasn't even properly dressed. Under her hoodie she still had her pyjama top on. And that was all. She hadn't even put on a bra. At least she'd managed to run a brush through her hair, but she didn't have a scrap of make-up on. Although she was fairly sure there'd still be remnants of the previous day's mascara somewhere around her eyes.

"I just nipped to the shop. My fridge was annoyingly empty this morning."

"All I can offer is coffee," he said. "And not great coffee at that. But you're welcome to come in for a nose around if you want."

"Is this the equivalent of you inviting me in for a nightcap?"

His laughter lit up his face. "You have sex on the brain, don't you?"

"I find it's good to get things out in the open," she said with a mischievous grin.

"Fair enough. I was inviting you in to see the inside of the shop, not my naked body."

"Go on then." Her gaze locked briefly with his as

he held the door for her.

Curiously, she stepped inside. How many times had she walked past the place without paying any attention? It had always looked so dull and uninviting. The inside wasn't any more appealing.

"It's … erm …" Stopping in the middle of the room, she looked around. Rows of metal bookshelves gave the place a clinical feel. The horrific pattern of the multicoloured carpet made Tara slightly dizzy.

"Awful?" James suggested.

"You can see why he didn't make any profit."

"I should sell it, shouldn't I?"

"No," she said automatically. "You should fix it up and make it a success. Working in a bookshop is a great job."

"Are you going to tell me it's your dream job and I should hire you as an assistant?"

She laughed, then her features became serious as she turned in a circle to scan the room. "Replace the carpets," she said. "Give the windows a good clean, and move the shelves back to let the light in. Put a new sign above the door, get rid of these cheap shelves and put in some wooden ones. It could be beautiful."

James leaned casually against the end of a row of shelves. "You really do have a great imagination."

"I do." When her gaze landed back on him, he was staring at her. Butterflies danced in her stomach. A loud knocking at the door startled her and drew her attention away from him. "Have you got a customer already?"

"No." He walked to the door. "It's my lunch."

The heavenly smell of takeaway pizza filled the room.

"I should probably leave you to it," Tara said as James closed the door behind the delivery guy.

"Probably," he said. "I don't like to share pizza."

"I can't say I blame you. If it was the other way round I wouldn't share with you."

"You don't look like someone who'd share their food." He smirked as he walked past her to the back of the shop. "Of course, if you had any tips about how to run a bookshop, it might earn you a slice."

"I've got loads of tips." She followed him with a big smile on her face. "I know all about it."

James placed the pizza box on the counter at the back of the shop and pulled over two rickety-looking wooden chairs. He took a slice of pizza for himself and immediately closed the lid.

Tara's mouth watered. "After you've renovated and made it lovely and inviting, you need to update the stock. Make sure you've got in a good selection of books. And make them look pretty. You know, have everything displayed nicely."

"Right." He took a bite of pizza and chewed slowly. "Where would I get new stock from?"

She rolled her eyes. "The suppliers."

He swallowed his mouthful then pushed the pizza box her way. She took a slice and sat down. It tasted so good it was an effort not to moan in pleasure.

"I don't even know which supplier Richard used."

"It'll be written down somewhere, I'm sure. Otherwise just do a search for the nearest supplier."

"Have you worked in a shop before?" he asked.

"Yeah." Well, she'd helped out in the local pet shop when she was thirteen and obsessed with animals. It wasn't paid. Honestly, she didn't help out at all, just hung out there every Saturday morning, looking at the bunny rabbits and guinea pigs. Close enough though.

"This wouldn't actually happen to be your dream job, would it?"

He was staring at her again. She swallowed hard. "I'm not sure you can afford to hire staff," she said, trying to keep the atmosphere light. Was he about to offer her a job because she'd spouted a few common-sense remarks about running a bookshop?

"It didn't make any money for my uncle," James said, as his gaze roamed the room. "But he had some savings. So I have a little bit to get me started if I did decide to give it a go."

She squinted and shook her head gently. "How come he left everything to you, if you barely knew him?"

"He didn't have anyone else. I remember coming over here sometimes when I was a kid, but then he and my dad fell out and they cut all contact. I'm not even sure what happened."

"That's sad." Tara looked hopefully at the pizza box.

"Help yourself," James said. There was silence for a moment. "Would you actually have any idea how to run a bookshop? Because I'm clueless. I could do with someone who knows what they're doing … and you did say you need a job."

18

Chewing slowly on the pizza, she put a hand in front of her mouth. She was buying time, trying to figure out how to answer. Why on earth was he offering her a job? And why did she have the urge to accept? It would all go badly when he figured out she didn't have the first clue about running a bookshop.

"I do need a job," she said. "And the location is convenient. I'm no expert, but I have some experience." Yeah, like she'd been in a bookshop before. "And I'm an avid reader." Oh, God. Why was she lying? It was ridiculous.

"Could you start tomorrow?"

She stared at him for a moment. "Not tomorrow, no." Tomorrow she had big plans to learn how to run a bookshop. "But Tuesday would be fine."

He held out his hand for her to shake. His palm was soft but firm, and his touch sent shivers down her spine.

"You're really giving me a job?" she asked.

"Yeah." He frowned. "Maybe we can have a trial period of a couple of weeks?"

She nodded. "After two weeks you'll never want to let me go."

Chapter 3

Dartmouth was only a half-hour drive from Newton Abbot. It was a cute little tourist town located at the estuary of the River Dart. Tara's mum used to take her there sometimes when she was a kid. They'd walk around the town and eat ice creams sitting by the harbour while they watched the boats come and go.

Tara parked on a side street and walked slowly to the Bookshelf. The quaint bookshop wasn't open when she arrived, so she loitered outside, checking out the window display. It was tastefully done, a neat and inviting selection of books set up in an orderly fashion. Tara peered through the window, trying to gauge what it was about the place that people liked so much. The Bookshelf had the best reviews of all the bookshops in Devon. It had been a surprise to Tara that people bothered to review bookshops, but apparently people liked to review everything these days and bookshops were no exception. It was cute enough, but Tara didn't see what was so remarkable about it.

"Good morning!" The cheerful voice made her jump. Tara felt as if she'd been caught scoping the place out.

"Morning!" she said to the smiley couple who looked to be in their fifties.

"Miserable weather, isn't it?" the woman said.

Tara glanced overhead at the grey rain clouds. "Yes."

"Coming in for a browse?" The man held the door for her, flipping the sign to "Open" as he did.

"Thank you." Inside it was bright and airy. Not at all like the Reading Room.

"Are you looking for something in particular?" The woman shrugged her raincoat off, revealing her floaty skirt and flowery blouse. The man was wearing corduroy trousers, and a waistcoat over a grey shirt. Tara could easily have picked them out of a line-up as a pair of bookshop owners. Maybe she'd suggest to James that they go clothes shopping.

"Erm …" Tara's eyes darted around. "I'm looking for some non-fiction. A how-to guide for running a bookshop. Do they do a *Bookshop Management for Dummies*?"

The frumpy owners smiled at her benignly. "You want to open a bookshop?" the man asked.

"Yes. Kind of. The thing is, I've got myself into a bit of a situation. I start work at a bookshop tomorrow and I might have lied a little in the interview. I said I have some experience when I don't."

"Oh, they'll train you up," the woman said. "Don't worry. You'll soon pick it up."

"Yeah." She bit her lip. "Except I'm expected to take on more of a management role. Almost consultancy work, really."

"Oh." The man sighed, then pulled a pair of glasses from his pocket and pushed them onto his nose. "That sounds like quite a situation you've got yourself into."

"Yes. I needed the job, you see."

"Is it an independent bookshop?" the woman asked.

"Yes." Tara nodded. "The owner has just inherited the place. He wants to give it a go but he doesn't know what he's doing."

"Hmm." The man glanced at his partner, then back at Tara. "Is it nearby?"

"It's over in Newton Abbot."

"It's not competition then, really." The woman looked pleadingly at the man. They seemed to be having some sort of telepathic conversation.

"Okay," he said with a sigh.

The woman clapped her hands together. "I'm Deirdre," she said. "And this is my husband, Darren. You're going to have the best day!"

"I'm sorry?" Tara raised her eyebrows in confusion. "I was just hoping to get a few pointers."

"No, no," Deirdre said. "That wouldn't do at all. What you need is full immersion. A day in the life of a bookseller. We'll have you all trained up by the end of the day. You'll have your new boss well and truly fooled, don't you worry."

"First things first," Darren said. "We like to start the working day with breakfast."

"Yes." Deirdre scrunched her face up when she smiled. "I like a wholemeal bagel with cream cheese. And Darren loves a chocolate croissant.

Don't worry about coffee. We've got facilities here."
She pointed to the coffee machine behind her.

Darren patted Tara's shoulder. "The bakery's a
few doors down. You can't miss it."

"Right," Tara said. "Of course. I'll be right back."
She was slightly dumbstruck as she walked down
the road. There was a chance she was getting herself
into an awkward situation. Maybe Darren and
Deirdre had seen their chance to have an unpaid
helper for the day. Oh well. Tara wasn't exactly in a
position to turn down advice, even if it did mean a
day's unpaid work.

There were already a few customers in the shop
when she returned. Deirdre and Darren were deep in
animated conversations. Tara slunk away to the back
of the shop and took a seat in a comfy armchair in
the corner. Comfy chairs were a great idea. She got
her notebook out and wrote it down.

The morning was hectic. Between customers,
Deirdre and Darren bombarded Tara with
information about setting up and running a
bookshop. To begin with she tried to write
everything down, but by lunchtime her hand was
starting to cramp and she wasn't even sure half of
what she was writing down was at all useful.

"So what's your favourite book?" Deirdre asked
when they tucked into sandwiches for a late lunch.
Tara had nipped out to the bakery again.

"I don't really read," Tara said, wincing slightly.

Deirdre stopped with her sandwich halfway to her
mouth. Gently, she set her sandwich down on the
counter. Then she took a slow and deliberate breath.

"What was the last book you read?" she asked calmly.

"I used to read those Secret Seven books when I was a kid." Tara chewed on her bottom lip. "Oh, and when I was a teenager I read some book that was being passed around school. Something about kids locked in an attic. It involved incest."

"*Flowers in The Attic*," Deirdre said flatly.

Tara beamed. "Yes!"

"Do you have at least a basic knowledge of the classics? If someone were to come into the shop and say they wanted the book with Atticus Finch or Elizabeth Bennett, you'd be able to help them?"

Tara shook her head. "The names ring a bell. What did they write?"

Deirdre just stared at her. Darren went over and gently rubbed his wife's back.

"Okay." Deirdre took a deep breath and glanced at her watch. "We don't have a lot of time, but I'll do my best. Let's start with the classics. Follow me." She went over to the bookcase at the back corner and began pulling out books. "Get your notebook," she said to Tara. "You'll need to write this down and go over it again later."

"I think she's a lost cause," Darren said loudly.

"I don't believe in lost causes," Deirdre called. The bell tinkled over the shop door and Darren enthusiastically greeted the new customers.

"I might be a lost cause," Tara whispered to Deirdre. "Maybe I should just confess that I don't know what I'm doing."

"You're resourceful and committed," Deidre said.

"Otherwise you wouldn't be here. I say give it a go. If it doesn't work out, it doesn't work out. You may as well give it a try."

Tara sighed. "I suppose so."

"Right." Deirdre lowered her voice. "*Lady Chatterley's Lover*. Bit of a naughty one this ..."

She spent the next three hours going through the racks, telling Tara the popular authors in each genre. She even summarised whole plotlines. Tara scribbled away and was glad when they had to take breaks for Deirdre to serve customers.

"What time do you close?" Tara asked, looking through the window at the early evening darkness.

Usually eight. If you want to succeed you need to be willing to put in long hours."

"Wow," Tara said. "What do you do about dinner?"

"We have a late dinner at home," Darren said.

"Okay." Tara was ravenous. Her head also felt like it might explode from all the information, but she didn't want to leave before they closed. Deirdre and Darren were a lovely couple. A lot of the customers were regulars and lingered in long conversations. It was a wonderful atmosphere, and she could see why they had such glowing reviews.

"We usually have coffee and biscuits around now," Darren said. "Keeps us going until dinner."

"That sounds great," Tara said, relieved.

By the time Darren switched the sign to "Closed", Tara was exhausted. And a little emotional. All she'd expected was to spend ten minutes asking a few basic questions, and instead she'd had a whole day of training.

Outside the shop, she gave Deirdre a big hug. "I don't know how to thank you."

"Come back and tell us how it all goes," Deirdre said. "I'll be thinking of you. I really hope it works out."

"And if not, maybe we can find a job for you," Darren said brightly. He gave her a big hug too.

"If you swot up on your reading list," Deirdre said, her eyes twinkling.

"I will," Tara said. She'd bought a stack of books too. It seemed like the least she could do, and she was very inspired to read some of the books Deirdre had recommended. "I'll definitely be back to visit."

Deirdre and Darren waved as they set off across the road. Tara inhaled a lungful of the sea air and pulled her phone out of her bag. She shot off a message to her friend Amber, asking her to meet her for a drink. Then she sent the same message to her friend Sam. They'd all grown up together in the village of Averton. The pair of them still lived there, as did Tara's mum. Tara had moved, needing to get away from the place after she'd finished school. Newton Abbot was only about ten miles away from Averton, so she was still nearby. And still spent far too many evenings in the local pub, the Bluebell Inn.

Tara beamed at her friends when she arrived at the lovely little pub that felt like a second home. "You both made it!"

"You call, we come," Sam said.

Tara eyed him suspiciously. "You were already

here, weren't you?"

He took a swig of his pint. "I called in for a quick drink after work."

"I wasn't sure if you'd make it," Tara said to Amber. "Are mums allowed out on Monday nights?" Amber's little boy, Kieron, was almost eighteen months. He was a cutie but full of energy and kept Amber constantly busy.

"I needed to get out of the house," Amber said wearily. "And I keep telling you, just because I have a child doesn't mean I can't go out anymore. Paul's quite capable of looking after him too."

Tara leaned forward and ordered a glass of wine from Andy, the barman. Then she turned back to Amber and Sam. "How's Annette doing?"

"So-so," Sam said. "She seems a bit lost. I went over yesterday and had lunch with her."

Sam lived next door to Annette, and he'd always been good at calling in and keeping an eye on her and Wendy.

"I still can't believe it," Tara said wistfully.

"We went to visit her yesterday morning," Amber said. "It's weird being up there without Wendy cracking her jokes."

"What's going on with you?" Sam asked, looking at Tara. "Did you really quit your job?"

"Yeah. I blame Wendy."

"Given the circumstances you can probably just say you changed your mind," Amber suggested.

Tara shuddered. She'd hated her job as a hotel manager in a nearby town. Andy set her wine on the bar. It was cool and crisp and went down a treat.

"I've actually found a new job," she said.

"How've you managed that?" Sam asked. "I thought you only started job hunting yesterday."

She nodded. "I've been offered a position in a new independent bookshop opening in Newton Abbot."

Amber and Sam both snorted with laughter.

"Sorry," Amber said quickly when Tara glared at them. "Are you serious?"

"Yes."

"You're going to work in a bookshop?" Sam asked.

"Yes!"

"Have you ever read a book?"

"Of course I've read a book." She gave him a playful nudge. "I don't know why the idea of me working in a bookshop is so funny. The guy who interviewed me was very impressed."

Amber winked. "I'm sure he was *very* impressed."

"What's that supposed to mean?" Tara asked.

"All men are impressed by you," Sam said.

"It's the hair," Amber said. "So wonderfully dark and glossy."

"It's also the legs and the chest." Sam tilted his head to one side. "You're very easy on the eye."

"You should have seen the state of me when he offered me the job. I'd rolled out of bed and hadn't even had chance to put a bra on."

"Oh, my God!" Amber screeched. She and Sam creased up with laughter.

"Get your minds out of the gutter." Tara smirked. "I just meant I pulled a hoodie on over my pyjamas."

"But you're still going to try to convince us he hired you based on qualifications and experience?" Sam asked.

"Fine. It wasn't a proper interview. I was in his shop and we were eating pizza. When he heard me talking about how I'd run the bookshop, he offered me a job."

"What do you know about running a bookshop?" Amber asked.

"I told him he needed to renovate, and order some books."

Sam raised an eyebrow. "And based on that you got the job?"

"He inherited the shop. He doesn't know anything about running a bookshop. I managed to blag it quite nicely. The main thing is I'm not unemployed."

"I'm sorry, but it doesn't really sound like a proper job." Amber patted Tara's arm condescendingly.

Tara shrugged her off. "It *is* a proper job."

"He wants to get laid," Sam said.

"No! It's not like that. He's a really nice guy. I met him in the pub on Saturday night and—"

"Hang on a sec," Sam said, interrupting her. "Am I connecting the dots correctly? You met him in the pub on Saturday night and had a braless interview with him on Sunday morning?"

"No!" Tara said again and laughed. "That's not the way it happened. It was all very innocent. Except that I lied about having previous retail experience. Anyway, today I spent the day with a lovely couple in a bookshop in Dartmouth. They taught me everything they know. Tomorrow I start my new job."

"It's going to be a disaster," Sam said.

Tara shook her head. "It's going to be brilliant. A whole new chapter of my life is beginning." She snorted. "*Chapter* of my life! Did you see what I did there?"

Chapter 4

Tara spent at least half an hour on Tuesday morning deciding what she should wear to her first day at work. After trying on several outfits, she settled on jeans and a blue V-necked jumper. Then she debated whether to wear her hair up or down. She tied it in a high ponytail, but changed her mind and pulled it loose just before she left the house. It didn't really matter how she looked anyway. There'd only be James there.

When she arrived at the shop, the door was locked and the place looked deserted. She banged on the window for a while. It hadn't occurred to her on Sunday to get James's number, and now she had no way of getting in touch with him.

She was about to give up and go home when he walked through the shop and opened the door. He was wearing jeans and a T-shirt, and his feet were bare. He dragged a hand through his messy hair.

"Did I wake you?" Tara said. "I thought you said to come at nine."

"Sorry." He glanced at his watch and opened the door wider. "I ended up crashing upstairs last night and I didn't sleep well."

Tara walked purposely to the counter at the back

of the shop and dropped her bag on the floor. "Well, I've got tons of ideas and I'm raring to go."

He didn't look anywhere near as enthusiastic as he slumped into a chair. "There might be a slight problem …"

"What's going on?" Tara suspected she was about to lose her job before she'd even started it. The day with Deirdre and Darren would be a complete waste. She briefly wondered if Darren had been serious about giving her a job. Maybe if she went and begged. Gazing around the shop, she realised how excited she'd been about doing the place up and making it warm and inviting.

James cleared his throat. "I spent most of yesterday going through Richard's paperwork and chatting with the accountant. And I don't think I can do this. It's far more complicated than I thought." He looked up at Tara and grimaced. "I thought I could clean the place up and order a load of books. It all seemed pretty easy in my head. But the business side of it is a lot of work in itself. And I'd have to put money into refurbishing. Then I'd have to pay for stock, and the accountant said I shouldn't expect to make any profit for at least six months, and realistically more like a year. It feels like the chances of this actually working out are slim."

Tara took a deep breath. He was probably right. She wandered to the back corner of the shop, blew dust off a bookshelf and frowned.

"I'd imagined turning this corner into a children's section." She looked back at him with a sad smile. "I thought we could make it really cosy with big bright

34

beanbags. And we could hold a story time for kids once a week. We'd fill the shelves with all the gorgeous kids' books. Julia Donaldson and David Walliams and all those wonderful stories. And the old classics too, like Enid Blyton and Roald Dahl ..." She paused as James came to stand beside her. "You can also make money selling merchandising products. Like the little Grinchalo cuddly toys ..." Tara froze. Did she say Grinchalo instead of Gruffalo? He didn't seem to notice, so she blundered on. "You could also sell greetings cards and mugs."

She moved to the main part of the shop. "With wooden shelving it would look great, and you can put some comfy chairs around the place. Make it really homely. You can even have a coffee machine so people will grab a drink and hang around longer."

James quietly followed her around the shop, and the more she spoke the more excited she got.

"I could do a really great window display to draw people in, and you can put a new sign over the door. We'd make it a real hub for the community. People will just love hanging out here, and while they're here they'll see all the lovely books and won't be able to resist. We could invite local authors to do events, and run writing groups and book clubs. And we could—"

"Stop talking!" James said, grinning at her. "You've convinced me. But please stop talking."

"Are you serious?" She stared at him. "You're going to do it?"

He shook his head. "*We're* going to do it."

***

"Shelves should be the first order of business, shouldn't they?" James rested his forearms on the counter as he peered at his laptop. He looked up at Tara. "I don't even know how to order shelves. Do I just measure up and order a load of flat-pack? Or do I need to get a builder to come and fit the place out?"

Tara grimaced. She had no idea. "Oh!" Her eyes lit up. "I know a guy." She slid her phone out of her back pocket. "One of my friends is a builder. He'll help."

James smiled and switched his attention back to the computer.

"Good morning!" Tara said cheerfully into the phone. "How are you on this wonderful Tuesday?"

"What do you want?" Sam said, his tone full of amusement.

"Where are you working today?"

"Over in Paignton. Why?"

"Can you nip out on your lunch break and help me with something?"

"I don't generally get a lunch break," he said. "What do you need help with?"

"We can't figure out how to do the shelving in the bookshop. How are we supposed to know what kind of wood is best? Should we just pick something that looks nice, or is some wood stronger than others? We have no idea."

Sam sighed heavily.

"Can you ask the foreman if you can nip out for an hour?"

"Tara," he said impatiently. "I am the foreman."

"Oh. Yeah, I knew that. Well done! So can you come over?"

There was a short silence. "You better have lunch for me."

"Yay! You're the best."

"See you soon." He hung up.

James was staring at Tara. "You got the guy to leave work to come over here?"

"He's one of my best friends. We've known each other since we were kids. Plus, I knew if I started talking about wood he'd get excited. He makes furniture and he's kind of a geek about it. You'll like Sam. He's a good guy."

"When's he coming?"

"I'm not sure," she said. "Soon probably. I'd better run out and get sandwiches. I promised him lunch. Do you want something?"

"No, thanks." He was gazing at his laptop screen like he had the weight of the world on his shoulders.

"Are you all right?" Tara asked.

He rubbed at the stubble on his jaw and nodded. "I think so. I can't believe I'm actually doing this."

"Stop worrying," she said. "This place is going to be amazing. And you'll make loads of money."

"I'll settle for not losing all my money at this point."

Tara returned from the shop armed with a bucket and cleaning supplies as well as a selection of sandwiches and snacks. Pausing outside the bookshop, she looked up at the sign above the door. The paint was peeling, and some of the letters were so faded it was difficult to read the name of the place. Tara had a hand on the door when she was distracted by a child's cry. A toddler pulled on his mother's arm outside the florist across the road. There were little teddies in the window, and the kid was determined to stop and look.

"Do you know what we need?" Tara said when she walked back into the shop. James stood up straighter and stretched his neck.

"Coffee machine?" he said wearily.

"No." She paused. "Well, yes. That as well. But what we really need is the most amazing window display." She put the cleaning supplies down at the back of the shop. "Something that people can't walk past without stopping to look. And we can make it really attractive to kids. Like a train in the window. So anytime kids are walking through town they'll ask to go to the shop with the train. And then the parents will see all the beautiful books and be drawn right in. What do you think?"

"I like it."

"I'm excited," Tara said happily.

"I can see that. What did you buy?"

"Cleaning stuff. And some food. Is there a kitchen back there?" She pointed to the door behind the counter.

"Yeah. Sorry, I should have given you a tour." He picked up the shopping bag and then held the door for her. Beyond was a small hallway with a few doors off it. "Here's the kitchen," James said, opening one door. Then he pointed over Tara's shoulder. "That's the bathroom and an office-slash-storeroom."

The kitchen was pretty small and needed a good clean. Tara put the sandwiches in the fridge while James unpacked the cleaning supplies. He plucked the receipt from the bottom of the bag, then pulled out his wallet.

"Oh, it doesn't matter," Tara said quickly.

"I'd rather this project only bankrupts one of us," he said, handing her the money.

"It's not going to bankrupt you." She gave him a friendly pat on the arm. "Stop worrying so much." She put the bucket in the sink and turned the tap on. "I'm going to clean the windows at the front. They're filthy."

In the hallway, she glanced at the stairs. "What's the apartment like up there?"

James shrugged. "A bit of a mess, like the rest of the place. Nice enough though. Two bedrooms. I'd show you, but since I'm now your boss, it seems slightly inappropriate to invite you upstairs."

"That's true." Tara grinned cheekily. "At least not on the first day of the job." Wow. Was she flirting with him? She had a feeling she might need to find a slightly more professional tone.

Focusing on earning her salary – and it occurred to her she had no idea of what that would be – she got to work on the windows. She wasn't too concerned about money. It felt good to be doing something she enjoyed.

"Are you going to live in the apartment?" Tara called across the shop as she cleared the debris from the window. There were two wonderful old bay windows, one at either side of the door. The wide window seats would be perfect for a display. They were currently covered in dust and a few random books.

"No," James called back. "I've got my place in Exeter. It's only a twenty-five-minute drive. I don't like the idea of living and working in the same place. And I definitely wouldn't give up my place until I knew this was going to work out."

"It will work out," Tara said. She wasn't sure he could hear her. Or if she was even talking to him. There was something about the place that had got under her skin. She wanted it to thrive.

Tara had just made a start on the outside of the windows when Sam pulled up in his van. "Hey!" she called excitedly.

"Hi." He kissed her cheek. "I can't believe you're dragging me into your weird scheme. What lies have you told this guy that I need to go along with?"

"I haven't lied." She lowered her voice and peered through the open doorway. James was nowhere to be seen. "I'm fairly sure he knows I have no experience." She frowned. "I accidentally said Grinchalo instead of Gruffalo. Seems like a clue that I'm a little out of place in a bookshop."

"Aw," Sam said. "I love *The Gruffalo*."

"Not something you expect to hear from a thirty-something-year-old builder," Tara said. "What is your reading level again?"

"Ha ha." He screwed his nose up and gave her a playful shove. "I was at Amber's place the other day and was looking at it with little Kieron."

"Whatever you say." She rolled her eyes.

"Hi." James appeared in the doorway. "You're the builder, I take it?"

"Sam." He extended his hand.

"I'm James. Thanks so much for coming over. I need all the help I can get."

"I'm not sure how helpful I can be," Sam said, stepping inside. "But I can probably give you some advice." He stopped and looked around. "Wow. It's a dump."

"Sam!" Tara slapped his arm. "We're trying to be positive."

"It's got potential, I suppose." He put a hand on one of the shelves and gave it a gentle shake. It wobbled precariously. "That's not safe," he said.

"We're getting rid of them," Tara said. "But we don't know what we should replace them with. I was thinking some nice light wood."

"Hmm." Sam frowned and walked to the back of the shop. He stopped and looked down at the dreary carpet. "What are you doing about the floor?"

"Not sure yet," James said.

Sam crouched in the corner and pulled at the carpet. "Do you mind if I ...?"

"Do what you want," James said.

With a tug, Sam pulled up a small section of the carpet. He sighed, then went to the shelves at the back wall and wiggled them. "None of these are secured," he said. "It's a health and safety nightmare. Can we get the books off and move them out of the way?"

Tara and James got to work helping Sam take the books off the shelves. They piled them all up beside the counter. James and Sam each took an end of the rickety metal shelves and walked them easily out of the way. "They're like something you'd have in your garage, not shelves for a bookshop." Sam shook his head and walked to the back of the room. "Grab the carpet at that corner," he said to James, pointing. They both pulled until a good portion of the wooden floor was revealed.

Sam crouched down to run a hand over the floorboards. "That's really nice flooring," he said. "It'll come up lovely if you sand it down and give it a coat of varnish."

"Yay!" Tara said. "See, it really has got potential. What about shelves?"

Sam scanned the room. "If it were me I'd get custom shelves. With a lick of paint on the walls, the original flooring and some decent shelving I think the place could be really nice."

Tara bit her lip and widened her eyes. "Will you build the shelves?"

"What sort of timeframe are you looking at?" Sam asked.

"We'd like to open in a fortnight," Tara said firmly.

"Would we?" James said in surprise.

"I think it's doable," Tara said.

Sam laughed. "It's not!"

"But if you help with the shelves ..." Tara

resorted to fluttering her eyelashes.

"I've known you far too long for you to get round me that way," Sam said.

"Please," she said beseechingly.

"I would." Sam rubbed his jaw. "But I don't have time. I'm in the middle of a big project."

"What about evenings and weekends?" Tara pleaded.

"I'm honestly snowed under," he said. "I've only got Sunday off, and I promised to help Annette out with some stuff."

Tara nodded. "Of course. I need to visit her too."

"Sorry," Sam said to James. "I could do it in a few weeks. I'm not sure you could get anyone to do it sooner than that."

"Don't worry," James said. "I'm not in that much of a rush. A few weeks would be great."

"Do you know anyone else you could ask?" Tara said.

"I could ask around on site, but everyone's inundated with extra work as it is." Sam blew out a breath. "Hang on while I make a call ..."

He pulled his phone out and wandered outside. James went over to look at the newly exposed wooden floor. They hovered around silently, trying in vain to listen in to Sam's phone call.

"Okay," he said cheerfully when he came back in. "I spoke to an old friend of mine. He can do it on Saturday."

Tara clapped her hands together and gave Sam a big hug. "You're the best."

"Ted's retired," Sam said to James. "So he can't

invoice you for the work. You'll have to give him cash."

James nodded eagerly. "That's fine."

"He's a perfectionist so he'll do a good job. He said he'll try and get someone to come with him, but if not you'll need to help him. It's a two-person job."

"Not a problem," James said.

"I need to go to the lumber yard sometime this week anyway," Sam said. "So if you want I can get the wood for you. I can get it cut to size to save Ted some work." He pulled out his phone and took a photo of the floorboards. "I'll get it to match the floor, or as close as I can." He stopped and looked at James. "Is that all right?"

"It's great," James said. "Thanks so much."

Sam put his phone away and pulled a tape measure from another pocket. He spent almost an hour measuring up and discussing the layout. Tara fetched him a sandwich and he ate as he worked.

Eventually, Sam seemed to have it all planned out. He moved toward the door. "So before Saturday you need to clear the room, paint the walls, then take the carpet up and sand the floors. I've got a machine I can lend you for that. I'll drop it in sometime." He squinted as though he'd forgotten something. "Put a coat of varnish on the floors too. And get it done as soon as possible so everything's completely dry before Ted comes."

"Will do," James said. "That's brilliant. Thanks again."

Sam checked his watch. "I've really got to run. See you later."

"Thanks!" Tara stood on the pavement with James, watching Sam's van disappear from sight.

"You were right," James said. "I like him."

Chapter 5

The rest of the afternoon was spent shopping for paint and clearing everything out of the shop. Tara and James took the old shelving apart and left it on the tiny patio at the back of the shop. Tara had plans to flutter her eyelashes at Sam again and get him to take it all to the tip in his van.

The books went into the apartment upstairs. It was tiring work going up and down the stairs with armloads of books. The apartment was pretty much like the rest of the place: dark and drab and fairly depressing. She could see why James wasn't keen to give up his place in Exeter just yet.

By the time she got home that evening, Tara was exhausted. She wasn't used to so much physical labour. It felt rewarding, and she soaked her aching muscles in a long bubble bath before crawling into bed.

The alarm went off before she knew it. She'd promised to get to the shop early so they could get on with painting.

Again, there was no sign of life when she got to the shop. At least she'd thought to get James's number. She jabbed at the phone screen until she found it.

"I dragged myself out of bed and you're not even here yet?" she said frostily. "I think you might need to buck your ideas up. This is *your* business. Why am I making more effort than you?"

"Sorry," he muttered, sounding half asleep. "I'm coming down now."

She hung up. It was a slight relief to hear he'd slept in the shop and she didn't have to wait for him to drive over from Exeter. She grimaced as she realised how snappy she'd been with him. It was a little inappropriate. He was her boss, after all.

"Sorry," he said again when he opened the door, dressed only in a pair of boxer shorts. Tara was momentarily speechless at the sight.

"Interesting painting attire," she said as she stepped inside.

He walked quickly back the way he'd come. "Give me ten minutes."

"I'll get breakfast," she said and headed back out of the door.

At the local bakery, she bought two coffees and a couple of croissants. She was sitting at the table in the kitchen when James reappeared. He slumped into a chair and reached for the coffee.

"No offence," she said. "But you look terrible."

"Thanks." He ran his hand through his hair. "I didn't sleep much. I looked up business courses online and signed up for one. I can work at my own pace and apparently after sixty hours I'll know the basics of setting up and running a business."

"So you started it last night?" she asked.

"Yeah. Think I fell asleep in front of the laptop

sometime around three."

"Oh, great. Now I feel bad for having a go at you."

He chuckled. "No. You were right. I asked you to be here early and I wasn't even awake. It's a bit rude."

"With good reason, though. I thought you were just being lazy."

"I wish." He rubbed at his eyes. "You know, a month ago I had a perfectly good job. They paid me money every month and I was never up until three o'clock in the morning worrying about work."

"What did you do before?" she asked.

"Software development and web design." He shrugged. "Not the most exciting job, but it paid the bills and was fairly stress-free. I had a lot of holiday time to take, so I'm using that instead of working my notice. But maybe I'll end up grovelling for my job back."

"You do want to do this, don't you? Have I railroaded you into it because I needed a job?"

"No." He stretched his legs out. "I think I needed a bit of railroading. And it's nice that someone else thinks the place has potential too. I want to give it a try. I just didn't realise quite how much work it would be."

"Once we're up and running it will get easier, I'm sure."

"I hope so." He pushed the chair back and stood up. "We need to get on with the painting. I've got an appointment at the bank this afternoon to set up a business account. I think I'd underestimated how much admin would be involved too."

"It will all be worth it in the end," Tara said as she followed him back into the shop.

Painting was satisfying work, and time went fast. They'd got a lot done by the time James left to go to the bank. He'd showered and put a crisp white shirt on with his clean jeans. She wished him luck and couldn't help but watch him as he walked out of the shop and to his car. A shirt suited him.

Tara had just finished painting when he arrived back. She was overjoyed to see the coffee machine in his arms.

"That's the first important purchase out of the way," he said.

Tara trailed behind him into the kitchen and sat and watched him set it up, while massaging the palms of her hands. She'd got a couple of blisters from gripping the paint brush.

"So what do we need to do next?" she asked.

"I think you can probably go home," James said.

Looking at her watch, Tara found it was later then she thought.

"What time do you want me tomorrow?" She remembered the message she got from Sam earlier. "Sam said he's going to drop the machine off for sanding the floors. He'll be here about nine."

"Good," James said.

"Shall I just come then?"

"I'm not sure I really need you if I'm sanding the floors. Come later if you want."

"Okay. Call if you think of something you need me for ..."

He frowned. "I feel a bit weird about you not having set hours, or an employment contract, and we didn't talk about how much I'm going to pay you …"

"We can sort it all out later," she said. "I trust you. I'll see you tomorrow."

"Tara!" he called as she reached the doorway. The look in his eyes was intense. "Thank you. For all your help with everything."

She smiled. "I think it's the first time I've had a job that I actually care about."

"Me too," he said, slouching against the counter. "It feels good, doesn't it?"

She nodded. "Very."

The next morning, Tara was rudely awoken by her phone. She squinted at the screen, presuming it would be James and that she wouldn't be getting the morning off after all. It was actually Sam.

"I'm standing outside the shop and there's no one here." He didn't sound overly cheerful.

Tara groaned. "I bet he's still asleep."

"Well that's nice," Sam said. "I'm doing him a favour and he can't even be bothered to get out of bed."

"It's not like that." Tara sat up and blinked her eyes. "He's really stressed and he's up until all hours trying to learn the business side of things. I'll call him now. He'll be down in two minutes."

"I'm already late for work," Sam said. "And presumably he wants me to show him how to use the thing too?"

"Please just wait. He's a good guy, I promise. Two minutes, okay?"

She hung up before he could argue. James's phone rang for a long time before he answered with a grunt.

"I hope you slept at the shop again," Tara said. "Sam's waiting outside. You need to go down and let him in, quick."

She held the phone away from her ear as he let out a string of expletives.

"James!" she shouted. "Put some clothes on before you open the door!"

When she snuggled back down under her covers, she was chuckling to herself. Poor James. He was going to burn out soon if he wasn't careful. Tara dozed on and off for a couple of hours, but her mind kept wandering to James working so hard to get the bookshop up and running. She felt some niggling guilt at being so pushy. If she hadn't been so enthusiastic he might just have looked around and decided to sell the place. Dragging herself out of bed, she got ready and went down to the bookshop to see how she could help.

"Looking good," she said when she walked in. She glanced at the floor, just to make sure he knew what she was referring to. He looked pretty good too in his faded jeans and blue T-shirt. The sweat marks should have been off-putting, but Tara found the overall look fairly dizzying. He turned the machine off and pulled the bottom of his T-shirt up to wipe the sweat from his forehead. The flash of abs sent her heart rate haywire.

"Want a coffee?" she called over her shoulder as she walked to the back of the shop.

"Just water, thanks."

When she returned from the kitchen, he took a break and leaned on the counter. "I can't believe I was still asleep when Sam got here," he said. "He was really nice about it but God knows what he really thought."

"He thought you were lazy and ungrateful."

James laughed. "I don't blame him."

"I put him straight," she said.

"Thank you."

"How's the studying going?"

"The more I learn, the more I realise how little I know about running a business."

"It's great that you're doing the course. Just don't forget to sleep too."

"I definitely plan on a full night's sleep tonight. And I need to make sure I go home, if only to get clean clothes."

She turned her nose up and sniffed. "Sounds like a good idea to me." She chuckled. "Aren't you tempted to move in here?"

"No." He shook his head. "There's a good chance I'm going to hate this place soon. I need to keep my house to retreat to."

"You're not going to hate the place," she said. "This time next week it's going to be completely transformed and you won't ever want to leave."

"Yeah. We'll see about that."

"I thought I might clean the kitchen today," she said. "Unless you had any other exciting plans for me."

"Not really. We could have a look at furnishings later. You were thinking beanbags and comfy chairs?"

"I think a children's corner with beanbags would be great. We'll need a rug back there too. And what about a rocking horse?"

"It's a bookshop, not a playground."

"True. It'd be cute though. A quaint cosy bookshop with a train set in the window and a rocking horse hidden away at the back of the shop. Kids would love it."

"Let's hold off on the rocking horse for now. The rest sounds good."

"You're the boss." She nodded. "I'll get on with the kitchen while you finish the floor. Then we can do some shopping!"

"Sounds like a plan." He rubbed the back of his neck and returned to sanding the floorboards.

The grating buzz of the sanding machine set Tara's teeth on edge. She closed the kitchen door and put some music on her phone to drown it out while she cleaned. When she'd finished she went in search of James. The floor seemed to be finished but there was no sign of him.

In the hallway, she called up the stairs to him but got no reply. The door to the apartment was ajar, so she ventured up.

"James?" she called again. He walked out of the bathroom with just a towel around his waist. She averted her gaze. "Sorry," she said quickly.

"It's fine." He ducked into the bedroom. "Come

in."

She apologised again when he came out of the bedroom. He'd put on a pair of jeans and was buttoning up the white shirt he'd worn to go to the bank.

"I really need to go home today," he said, undoing the cuffs and rolling back the sleeves. "This is the only vaguely clean thing I've got left." He picked up his laptop from the kitchen counter and went over to the couch. Then he patted the seat beside him. "Ready for some shopping?"

They spent a fun couple of hours choosing furnishings. They'd probably need more later but at least it was a start. Some of it would arrive on Monday, and the rest throughout the week. Things should really start to come together then.

"I think I'm going to head home," James said, closing the laptop. "Oh, and I have something for you …" He went to the kitchen and came back with a key. "I thought it made sense for you to be able to get in and out when I'm not here."

"Aw. You're giving me a key to your place. Things are moving pretty fast between us, aren't they?" The atmosphere between them was so relaxed that joking around felt natural. Except it hit her that James was her boss and she definitely sounded like she was flirting with him. "Sorry," she said. "I have a habit of making inappropriate jokes."

"Don't worry, I have a habit of giving my keys out to women I barely know. Works surprisingly well as a pick-up line."

Tara fed the key onto her keyring. "I'm going to

presume that's a joke too."

"I need to varnish the floor tomorrow," he said, getting the conversation back onto neutral ground. "And I managed to get a sign-writer to come at short notice. He'll be here at nine."

"Do you want me to be here to meet him?"

"Might be a good idea," he said. "I should probably invest in a ridiculously loud alarm clock."

"Maybe just go to bed at a reasonable time," she suggested as she moved to the door.

"I need to set up social media accounts and start advertising. Any chance you're good at that sort of thing?"

"Yes." She beamed. "I'll get on it tomorrow."

"Perfect. Thank you."

"You're welcome." She turned in the doorway. "Don't forget to sleep!"

Chapter 6

When Tara arrived the next morning there was a guy up a ladder repainting the sign above the shop. James was walking down the road towards her, tucking into a bacon sandwich as he went.

"So you're sticking with the same name?" Tara asked.

James's eyes widened and he wiped ketchup from the side of his mouth. "Do you think I should change it?"

"No." She felt bad at the look of panic on his face. "I wasn't sure if you might want something different."

"It's a bad name, isn't it? I never even thought about it."

"I think the Reading Room is fine."

The guy up the ladder cleared his throat loudly.

"Carry on," James said. "She just likes to confuse me and complicate things. Ignore her."

"Sorry," Tara said, chuckling.

James took her elbow and led her down the road. "We can't go in the front door. The varnish is drying."

"You already varnished?" She registered his white shirt, which was nowhere near as crisp or white as the first time she'd seen him in it. "Haven't you been home?"

"I almost went home." He led her down an alley a couple of doors down and then along the back of the building. "Then I realised if I wanted the floor to be finished before the shelves go up I needed to put the first coat of varnish on last night. I put the second coat on this morning." He held the back door open for her.

"Wow. You must be exhausted."

"Yeah. And I'm fairly sure I smell pretty bad."

"I won't get too close," she said as they reached the door to the apartment.

"I was thinking we could get started on a website and social media accounts, and then I definitely need to go home."

"I can get on with the website and stuff myself if you want. I can do it from home and check with you before anything goes live. Unless you want to do it. You're the pro at web design, after all."

"If you're happy to do it that would be great. I was thinking we'd do it together, but I also have a ton of other stuff I could be doing."

She flashed a cheeky grin. "Like washing your clothes?"

"Exactly."

She lingered in the doorway. "So you don't really need me here."

"Sorry. I could have just called you."

"It's fine. I'll see you on Monday."

"Yes. Got anything planned for the weekend?"

"Not much. Friday night is pub night. I always

meet up with Sam and a couple of others over in Averton. Not exactly a wild night out, but it's usually fun."

"Sounds good," he said.

"What about you?" she asked. "Any exciting plans?"

"About another forty hours of learning how to run a business, and building a load of shelves. Depends if you call that exciting."

"Oh, I forgot about the builder coming tomorrow."

"Yeah. Hopefully this place will look a lot different by the time you get here on Monday."

"I can't wait to see it. What time should I be here?"

He shrugged. "Nine?"

"Great. See you then!"

She spoke to James again an hour later when she had the first question about the website, and then about ten more times over the course of the day to get his input on various things.

She felt like she'd earned a drink by the time she got to the pub. As always, she got a taxi to Averton so she didn't have to worry about the car. Friday nights in the Bluebell Inn might not be a crazy night out, but she was fairly notorious for drinking too much and livening the place up.

Sam and Amber were already there. Tara got a glass of wine then joined them at the table in the back corner.

"Sam's been telling me about your hot new boss,"

Amber said.

"Those weren't my exact words," Sam said.

Amber chuckled. "He's been going on about James's hair and it made him sound hot."

"I wasn't going on about his hair." Sam rolled his eyes. "You asked what he looks like, and I said he has blonde hair."

Tara slipped into the chair beside Amber and shrugged her coat off.

"You said it was *silky* blonde hair," Amber said.

"It is," Sam said.

"Yeah." Tara took a sip of her wine. "When you say that it definitely sounds like you fancy him."

"Well, he's a little bit intimidating," Sam said, shaking his head.

Tara was amused by Sam. He was so sweet. It was amazing that he was single. "If it makes you feel better," she said. "I think he was intimidated by you. Ripping up the carpets and whipping out your tape measure. It was very sexy."

He took a swig of his beer. "How's it all coming on?"

"Good, I think. James is very determined. He's working like crazy."

"And does he still think you used to work in a bookshop?" Amber asked.

"I think I just said I worked in a shop. I can't really remember. He's not asked me about it anyway."

Sam looked at Amber. "She called it *The Grinchalo*."

"No!" Amber snorted a laugh.

"I got confused with *The Grinch* and *The Gruffalo*," Tara said with a giggle.

"How can you get them confused?" Sam asked.

"I'm not an expert in children's literature. Unlike some people!"

"Everyone knows *The Gruffalo*." He pulled a face at her as he stood. "I'm going to play pool."

Amber smiled as he walked away. "He's so sweet. And he's so good with Kieron."

"Has he been babysitting?" Tara asked.

"Yeah, just for a couple of hours when we were stuck."

"I can always babysit if you need someone. Why do you ask Sam and not me?" As soon as she said it she wished she hadn't. She knew the answer, and the inevitable conversation was boring.

"Because you don't like kids," Amber said.

"Why do you say that?" Tara said wearily. "There's something wrong with your hearing, because I swear whenever I say I don't *want* kids, you hear I don't *like* them. I like other people's kids. I just don't want any of my own." Somehow, Amber couldn't grasp this concept.

"I just always think you're not very interested."

"I'm interested in Kieron. And I'm more than happy to babysit."

"Okay," Amber said in a condescending tone.

Tara gulped at her wine.

"So the new job's going well?" Amber asked.

"Yes," Tara said. "Really well. I had a great week."

"And this James guy is nice?"

61

"Yes."

"And you fancy him?"

"No. Besides, he's my boss. I'm not going to date my boss."

"I want to meet him," Amber said.

"You will. Actually I need your help. We're going to do a story time every week. Can you invite your mummy friends?"

"Yes! Definitely. There's not enough to do with kids round here. You'll get loads of interest."

"I hope so."

"Can you just do one thing for me?"

"What?"

"Will you read *The Grinchalo*?"

Tara snorted and they dissolved into fits of laughter.

Usually, Tara was more than happy to spend her whole weekend lazing around the house. But that weekend she was restless. On Saturday she kept wondering how James was getting on with the builder and had been tempted to call over there. She'd resisted, but by Sunday she was desperate to get out of the house and ended up driving over to Averton. She headed straight for Oakbrook Farm. When she was growing up, she'd spent a lot of time at the kennels. She had many fond memories of Annette and Wendy's house.

She parked beside the old farmhouse and took a moment to inhale the fresh air and take in the familiar view. She'd played chase around the big old oak tree by the barn with Amber and Sam when they were children. And they'd known the hills and fields better than their own faces.

The kitchen smelled delicious when Tara stepped inside. Annette's face lit up at the sight of her.

"Please say you're cooking a roast?" Tara gave Annette a big hug.

"Tell her there's not enough to go round!" Sam called from the living room.

"Of course there's enough," Annette said. "Ignore him."

"Sorry I've not been sooner," Tara said. "How are you doing?"

"Surviving." Annette turned the heat down as something began to bubble over on the stove.

"Hi, Macy," Tara said as the little dog came sniffing round her legs. Then the dopey old golden retriever came over, wagging his tail. "Hi, Charlie!" She gave him a pat down.

"I heard you've got a new job," Annette said. "With a hunky boss."

"I did not say hunky," Sam shouted.

Tara chuckled. "I think Sam has a crush."

"And you too, maybe?" Annette asked. "It'd be nice for you to find yourself a nice fella at last."

"You want us all married off, don't you?"

"I don't understand why you can't marry Sam. That'd be all of you settled and I could go to my grave happy."

Tara couldn't quite cope with talk of graves. She was already feeling Wendy's absence. It was so strange without her in the house. She had no clue how it must feel for Annette.

"I'm not Sam's type," Tara said, raising her voice. "He likes blondes. *Silky* blondes."

"That joke's officially worn out," Sam said as he wandered in with a bottle of beer in his hand. He plucked a fancy ivory card from the fridge. It was a wedding invitation from their friend Max. He was getting married at a hotel in Hope Cove in a couple of months. Max had also spent a lot of time in Averton with them throughout their childhood; he was Annette's nephew and had visited often in school holidays. He and Sam had remained best friends.

"Are you staying in the hotel overnight?" Sam asked Tara.

"I guess so."

"You'll need to book it soon," he said. "I don't think there are that many rooms."

"I will." Actually, she wouldn't book the hotel because she had no intention of going to the wedding. She was keeping that fact to herself for the time being.

"So tell me about the new job," Annette said. "I'm so pleased for you. Wendy was always saying she wished you'd get a job you enjoyed."

"She's the reason I quit the hotel."

"I'm sure she'll be smiling down on you," Annette said.

Tara swallowed the lump in her throat. "I hope so. It's going well so far. Do you remember that old bookshop on Queen Street?"

"Yeah, that grumpy old guy owned it. What was his name?"

"Richard. He was James's great-uncle. The place is going to look amazing when it's all done up. I can't wait to see it now the shelves are in." She'd been itching to stop and have a look on her way to Annette's but she decided to wait until Monday.

"I'll have to come over and have a look when it's finished." Annette opened the oven and moved back as the heat wafted out. She lifted the chicken out and set it on the counter. There were roast potatoes too, and stuffing and vegetables. Silence descended when they sat down to eat. Annette's food was too good for conversation.

It was pleasant to while away the afternoon at Annette's place. When Tara got home that evening, her thoughts were on Wendy. She wished she could tell her all about the bookshop. And thank her for giving her the nudge she needed to make some changes.

Chapter 7

When she let herself into the shop on Monday morning, Tara felt a rush of emotions. It was incredible the change in the place. As she walked around, she trailed her fingers over the smooth wood of the shelves. They matched the floor, and the place looked so light and airy.

"What do you think?" James's voice startled her when he appeared through the back door.

"It looks fantastic." She turned in a circle, taking it all in.

"It does, doesn't it?"

"I can't believe how much you've achieved in a week."

"How much *we've* achieved." He bumped his shoulder against hers.

"We really could open up next week."

"Maybe," he said. "We've still got a lot of work to do."

"I can't wait for the furniture to arrive. And the beanbags."

"You're really excited about those beanbags, aren't you?"

"Yes!" She registered his stubble and the dark rings under his eyes. "Have you been remembering to sleep?"

"Occasionally," he said.

"How's the business course going?"

"Quite interesting actually." He wandered over to the brand-new counter at the back of the shop. The wood was the same as the shelves. "Last night I got to the module on hiring staff and managing employees."

"Oh, really?" She smirked.

"Yeah. There was a lot of stuff about interview techniques and what to look for in a CV. Apparently it's important to check references."

"What's your point?" she asked.

His nose scrunched up. "I think it's a good job I hired you before I read that section."

"I don't know what you mean. I think I interviewed really well."

"Hmm." He raised an eyebrow and looked around. "So what's left to do?"

"The rugs should arrive this morning," she said, "and the furniture. And I set up social media accounts and a website. You're dealing with the payment system ..." She glanced at him and he nodded.

"Sure you're not forgetting anything?" he asked. "Anything else a *book*shop might need?"

Oops. She'd been focusing on the refurbishments and had overlooked the small matter of books.

"Well, obviously we need to order books. I can give the suppliers a call later."

"So you know what to order?"

She stared at him.

"Do you know anything about working in a bookshop, Tara?"

She shook her head slowly.

"Ever worked in any kind of shop?"

"No."

"Do you have any idea how many books we should order, or which books?"

"No idea." She avoided eye contact and instead let her eyes roam the room. "I'd hazard a guess and say quite a lot."

"So neither of us knows anything about books?"

"Is there anything else we could sell that would fit on the shelves?" she asked.

James let out a humourless laugh and dropped his chin to his chest.

She gazed at him. "You never actually thought I knew anything about books, did you?"

He shook his head. "Even I know it's *The Gruffalo*."

"*I* know it's *The Gruffalo*! I was just excited and trying to impress you and I got mixed up."

He rubbed the back of his neck. "You impressed me anyway."

Their eyes locked for a moment and Tara's insides fluttered. She looked away.

"So how do we figure out what books we should order?" he said. "You don't happen to have a friend who's an expert on books who you could drag out of work to help us?"

"No." She laughed, and then her gaze snapped back to him. "Actually, I do!"

"I was joking," he said.

"I'll call Deirdre. I bet she can help."

"Who's Deirdre?"

With her phone to her ear, Tara didn't bother replying.

"Darren?" she said to the male voice who answered. "It's Tara. We met last week …"

"Tara!" he said happily. "We've been thinking about you. Deirdre kept saying she was sure you'd be back to visit sometime."

"I will." She smiled into the phone. "Definitely. I've had a busy week though."

"Hang on," he said. "I'm passing you over to Deirdre."

"I'm so glad you called!" Deirdre said. "How's it going?"

"Pretty well, I think. But we've come to a slight problem. We don't know which books to order, or how many."

"Yes, that's difficult at the beginning. The best thing to do is have a chat with the wholesaler and ask them what's popular at the moment. They're usually very helpful. If you tell them your situation they'll be able to advise you."

"I don't know how many books we need or anything. We've got a load of old stock from the previous owner, but I'm sure we need new stuff too."

"I'm sure you will." She paused. "Have you got a pen? Write this number down …" Tara did as she was told. "That's the wholesaler we use. Ask for Tony. He's an angel. Tell him you're a friend of mine and he'll look after you."

70

"Thank you so much."

"You're welcome. I've got to go, we've got customers. You'll let me know how you get on?"

"I'll be in touch," she said.

James had hopped up to sit on the counter. "Who on earth was that?"

"You know when I said I couldn't start work on Monday? I went to a bookshop in Dartmouth to ask a few questions about how bookshops work. I thought I'd be there half an hour, but I ended up there for ten hours."

James didn't say anything but looked at her intently.

A rumble of a lorry outside made her turn. "That might be the furniture," she said excitedly.

They spent the next hour unloading and unpacking. It was amazing to see everything slowly coming together. With the rug at the back of the shop in the children's corner, it looked really cosy.

Tara lounged in an armchair nestled at the end of a row of shelves. There was a side table next to it with an old-fashioned reading lamp. It looked very cute and quaint.

"Hi!" she called to James through the shelves. He was sitting in another armchair at the other side of the shop.

"Hi." A weak smile flickered on and off his face.

Tara went over to him. "Are you okay?"

"I have no idea what I'm doing." He swallowed hard. "And I'm spending a lot of money for someone who has no clue what they're doing."

"It's going to be fine."

He inhaled deeply. "I'm panicking."

"It's going to be great. I'm going to order books, and this time next week the place will be full of customers. There's nothing to panic about."

"If you say so." He didn't look at all convinced as he squeezed the bridge of his nose.

Tara was full of energy and maintained her positivity over the week. She ordered books and watched as everything came together. There was a hold-up with the beanbags, but the books arrived on Thursday morning at about the same time as the computer and some fancy equipment for scanning barcodes and recording sales.

When the delivery guy had gone they got to work opening up the boxes of books. At about the fifth box she opened, Tara stopped dead and took a deep breath.

"What's wrong?" James asked, standing over her.

"It's a lot of books," she said.

"If there are too many, it's your fault," he said lightly.

"I'm panicking." She swallowed hard and stared up at him. Suddenly, it seemed ridiculous to think they could open a bookshop. And she had a horrible feeling she'd talked James into it.

He crouched beside her and put a reassuring hand on her shoulder. "It's going to be great. We'll figure out where to put all the books and it will look amazing."

"And it's all going to be okay?" Tara asked with wide eyes.

He nodded. "So long as we don't panic at the

same time, it's going to be fine."

"Good." She reached into the box and pulled out a couple of thrillers with dark covers. "We need to decide an area for each genre. Then it's easy, right?"

He smiled gently and her panic ebbed away. They'd come this far; she couldn't fall apart now.

On Friday, James wasn't around when she arrived. She presumed he was probably still sleeping and didn't want to disturb him, so she went into the kitchen and got herself a coffee.

It was only ten minutes later when she heard someone in the shop and went to investigate.

"Hi!" James had his hands full of bags.

"I thought you were still in bed."

He cocked an eyebrow. "I overslept twice and you have me down as a lazy good-for-nothing?"

"Not at all." She grinned. "I was actually hoping you were still asleep. You've been working like a maniac." She eyed the shopping bags. "What have you got?"

"A project for you." He pulled a large box from one of the bags.

"A train set!"

"And an aeroplane." He pulled out another box. "You can hang it in the window. I thought we could go for a transport theme in one window and make it really attractive for the kids, like you said. I'm not sure about the other window."

"I was thinking a tree theme," she said. "I can balance the books amongst branches."

"Whatever you think," he said. "I'll leave you to get on with it. I need to meet with the accountant. I shouldn't be too long."

"No problem." She picked up the train set as James walked cheerfully back out of the shop.

When he returned a couple of hours later he looked a lot less cheerful. Tara expected him to be excited about the window display she'd created, but he didn't even seem to register it.

"Do you want a coffee?" He nodded toward the kitchen and she followed him back there. He sat down at the kitchen table. Coffee seemed to be forgotten, and Tara felt a sense of dread as she sat opposite him.

"What happened?" she asked.

He pushed his hands through his hair and squeezed his eyes shut for a moment. "The accountant thinks I'm the biggest idiot who ever lived."

Tara felt sick. "Why?"

"Because I'm blindly putting money into this place with no real business plan. He says I should be looking at what I really need rather than just jumping into things."

Tara had the feeling it wasn't the train set and toy plane that were too extravagant. "Did I order too many books?" She crossed her fingers that the bad business decision wasn't what she suspected it might be.

James dragged his teeth along his bottom lip and looked her straight in the eyes. "He's not sure why I need a full-time employee at this point."

Tara swiftly broke eye contact and nodded slowly. "Right."

"And he can't believe I employed someone without a contract or any sort of agreement about wages or hours. And there are about a hundred other reasons why I've been a complete idiot about the situation."

Her forced smile felt ridiculous. It *was* crazy the way he'd offered her a job, and the way she'd jumped at it. If she were honest, she'd known all along how insane it was. Maybe she'd just needed something to take her mind off Wendy's death. And maybe she needed to be involved in something that felt worthwhile for a change.

"You can't afford to pay me?" she asked. "I worked two weeks for free and now I don't have a job?" She didn't even care about working two weeks for free. It was the thought of not being involved in the bookshop anymore that she couldn't stand.

James reached across the table and covered her hands with his. It made it even harder for her to keep her emotions in check. "Of course I'll pay you for what you've done."

"But I need to start job hunting?"

He blew out a long breath. "I'm sorry. All I can afford is a part-time employee. At least until things get going."

"Okay." That wasn't so bad. "So I'll work part-time?"

"I wouldn't be able to pay you much, and you work so hard I'd feel terrible. You've been putting as much time and effort into this place as I have. It doesn't seem fair that I pay you a pittance."

"When business is booming you can give me a

raise."

He inhaled deeply.

"If you'd rather employ someone who knows what they're doing you can just say so." She swiped at a tear from the corner of her eye.

"I want you to stay," he said, squeezing her hand. "But I feel really bad asking you to."

"I want to be here."

"Are you sure?"

Tara had never been more certain of anything in her life. "Definitely."

"I promise you'll get a raise as soon as we start making some profit."

"I know." As they fell silent, all she was aware of was his hands covering hers.

She looked him in the eyes. "Why did you offer me a job?" It didn't make any sense. And even though he claimed to have no idea what he was doing, James obviously had a bit of common sense when it came to the business side of things.

He opened his mouth, then closed it again and pulled his hands from hers. "I don't really know." Standing, he smiled at her. "How did you get on with the window display?"

"I think it looks great," she said proudly. "The train was a brilliant idea."

When they walked to the front of the shop, a delivery van was pulling up outside. The beanbags had finally arrived. In really huge cardboard boxes. James dragged them inside, then got a knife to open the packages.

"Did you order huge bags of polystyrene balls?"

he asked.

"No." She grimaced. "That's how they come. You have to fill the beanbags yourself."

"Are you serious?"

"Yeah. But it's easy. You open the beanbag and pour the balls in. No problem. It'll take like five minutes."

He scratched his head. "There's no way it's a five-minute job."

"Maybe five minutes per beanbag. But it can't be difficult."

An hour later, James wiped the back of his hand across his forehead and glared at Tara. "What did you say about it not being difficult?"

She grinned as she looked at the five brightly coloured beanbags. They looked great, and it had been hilarious trying to fill them without spilling polystyrene balls everywhere. "If you could control your balls it would have been much quicker."

He stared at her. "Did you really just say that? You realise I'm your boss and that was completely inappropriate."

"Yeah." She flopped into the green beanbag, chuckling. "I realise that."

James sat cautiously on the blue beanbag, then wriggled to get comfy. "Are you sure some kid isn't going to unzip them and create a ball pit?"

"They're hidden zips!" Tara laughed. "Of all the things you could be worrying about now, the beanbags should be a long way down your list."

He raised an eyebrow.

"I'm joking. There's nothing to worry about."

They fell silent as they looked at the results of the last two weeks. The transformation was incredible.

"Wait there." James stood abruptly and disappeared out of the shop.

Tara sat bemused until he arrived back five minutes later.

"What have you got?" Tara peered at the bottle in his hand.

"Let's call it champagne."

"Fizzy wine? Classy."

"It's the best I could do. I'll find glasses." When he returned from the kitchen he looked a little sheepish. "I thought this was going to be far more sophisticated."

"Cheap fizzy wine in whisky tumblers! Yay!"

"It was that or mugs."

"Fair enough." She took a glass from him. "What are we celebrating?"

"Ha ha," he said dryly.

Tara took a sip. "We've done a good job, haven't we?"

"Yes." He nodded and leaned his head back onto the beanbag. "Tell me all the hard work is out of the way and it's going to be a breeze from here."

"Erm … I promised myself I wasn't going to lie anymore after my interview."

He rolled his head to the side. "I'm very glad you turned up that day."

"Me too." She held his gaze for a moment then glanced away when her heart began to beat a little faster. "When are we going to open?"

"I was thinking in a week."

She shook her head. "What about Monday?"

"It's Friday today," he said. "Monday seems a bit soon."

"Why? What else do we need to do? We could also open tomorrow ..."

"No way." He laughed. "Shouldn't we advertise? Have some sort of official opening? Or do we just flip the sign to 'Open' on Monday morning and that's it?"

Tara screwed up her features. "Maybe something in between. Since you're on a budget we shouldn't do anything too extravagant. But I think we could put some flyers around the town and have some cake and coffee. Keep it casual but a little more than just turning the sign to "Open"."

He nodded slowly. "That sounds good. But isn't Monday too soon?"

"The sooner you open, the sooner you can start making money."

"That's true."

"I'll organise cake and put some flyers up."

"Okay." He frowned. "We're really doing this?"

She clinked her glass against his. "We really are!"

Chapter 8

On Monday morning, Tara called into the bakery to pick up the selection of cakes she'd ordered. She arrived at the shop an hour before opening time, wanting to make sure everything was perfect. The brand-new bell above the door tinkled melodically when she walked in. There was no sign of James, so she put the cakes in the kitchen and switched the coffee machine on.

Back in the shop, she wandered through the shelves, making sure everything was as it should be. Her nerves settled as she stood among the books. It was peaceful and relaxing.

"You're here before me," James said when he walked in the front door five minutes later.

"It's easy to see who's more dedicated," she replied with a cheeky smile.

"I couldn't decide what to wear," he said. "I don't want to be too casual. But I don't want to seem stuffy. Jeans and a shirt works, doesn't it?" He held his arms out and looked down at himself.

"You look great," she said. He really did. The bright blue shirt suited him.

"You too," he said. "I'm trying not to freak out. I was having nightmares that no one would turn up."

"There's cake," Tara said. "People will definitely turn up."

"My sister, Kate, will come after she drops her eldest at school. She'll have the baby with her. Hopefully a couple of my friends will make it but most people can't get out of work. Who did you invite?"

Tara's eyes widened and she looked away. She'd put up flyers around the town, but she hadn't thought about personally inviting people. "I think my friend Amber will come," she said. "And Sam will try to make it."

"What about family?" he said. "Have you got any siblings you can force to come and support you?"

"No. There's only me."

"Parents then?" he asked.

"My dad lives in London," she said. "And my mum isn't very sociable."

"You invited her though? She might like to see where you're working and all the effort you've put in."

"I'll give her a call," she said. That'd also give her chance to call Amber and Sam. "Are your parents coming?"

"No. They live in France. Retired over there a few years ago."

"That's nice." She smiled. "I'm going to call my mum. I'll be back in a minute."

She stood on the street in front of the shop and called Amber in a panic, begging her to come. She didn't take much persuading. Sam wasn't quite as keen but said he'd try and call in.

Then Tara called her mum. Debbie worked as a mobile hairdresser and didn't have any clients that morning so was happy to drop by.

"Looks like my mum will come," Tara said when she re-joined James in the shop.

"Great." He was wandering the shelves just as she'd done.

"So we're all ready."

"Think so," he said. "I have a horrible feeling I've forgotten something."

"Don't start panicking. Everything looks perfect. We'll have loads of customers and they're going to love the place."

"I hope so." He leaned against the end of the row of shelves. "This all feels pretty crazy still."

"It is," she said. "But in a good way. Now, let's have a coffee and chill out before we're rushed off our feet."

"I like your optimism." He followed her to the kitchen, where she poured them both drinks. Then they set up a table at the back of the shop and spread out the cakes and urns of tea and coffee. Tara planned to always have tea and coffee available. James argued people would just come in for free drinks, but she was fairly sure she would sway him to her way of thinking eventually.

"Okay, it's ten," James finally said. "Time to open."

"It's three minutes to ten," Tara corrected him.

"I don't care." He walked purposefully to the door. "The waiting is making me nervous. I'm opening." At the door, he gave Tara a puzzled look.

"What happened to the 'Open' sign?"

She frowned and then her hand shot to her mouth. "I took it down when I was cleaning." She looked around but knew it wasn't just lying around somewhere. "It might have got mixed up with the books when we cleared everything out."

"So we're just opening the door?"

She bit her lip. "Sorry."

"I don't suppose it matters. We can stick a homemade sign up for now."

"It makes me wonder what else I've forgotten." Tara had a sudden feeling of dread.

"Nothing," James said. "And the sign doesn't matter. Neither of us are panicking today, okay?"

"Okay."

James propped the door open and took a deep breath. He definitely looked like he was panicking.

"I should have got some ribbon," Tara said. "A grand opening with a ribbon cutting."

"We said we were keeping it low-key."

"A bit of ribbon isn't extravagant."

"We'll look stupid when no one turns up and it's just us cutting a piece of ribbon."

"There'll be loads of people," she said cheerfully.

James stepped out of the door and looked up and down the road. "Not exactly a massive crowd so far."

"Don't be negative. I'm going to run to the shop and get ribbon. By the time I get back, there'll be customers."

"Don't leave me alone," he said with mock panic as she walked away.

"I'll be five minutes," she called back. Thankfully, she found ribbon in the supermarket and was back in no time. She tied a bow and strung the ribbon across the door, fixing it in place with tape.

"You're going to ruin the paintwork," James said.

Tara rolled her eyes. "Don't grumble. The paint's fine." She glanced over his shoulder. "Amber's here!"

"I thought I was going to be late," Amber said as she hurried over to them.

"Perfect timing." Tara gave her a hug and tickled Keiron's cheek before introducing her to James.

"Thanks for coming," he said. "I was worried no one would turn up. We have two customers so I can relax now."

Amber grinned. "Kieron's eighteen months. Can you really count him as a customer?"

"Yes!" James said. "He's doubling the numbers, so we're counting him. Besides, when he sees the children's corner he's going to be very excited."

"Tara told me all about it," Amber said. "I can't wait to see it."

"Have a look at the window," Tara said, pulling Amber's elbow to show her the display with the train and the aeroplane. Kieron waved his arms around excitedly, and Tara smiled widely at his enthusiasm.

"Told you kids would love it," she said to James.

"I didn't doubt it." He peered inside the car that pulled up. A woman stepped out and wrapped him in a hug, then instructed him to get the baby out of the car. She looked a similar age to James and her hair was the exact same shade of golden blonde as his, though hers fell in messy waves to just below her shoulders.

"You must be Tara," she said, surprising Tara as she threw her arms around her. "I'm Kate, James's sister. I've heard all about you."

"It's great to meet you," Tara said politely. "This is Amber."

Kate said a quick hello, then peered into the shop window. "It looks fantastic. I can't believe the miserable old man left all this to James." She raised her eyebrows at Tara. "I got nothing!"

"Well I am the eldest," James said, pulling faces at the baby in his arms.

"I think it has more to do with you being male," Kate said. "Here, let me take Billy before he pukes down your clean shirt."

"I told you we can go halves on the place," James said sheepishly as he handed the baby over.

"If you'd have sold the place like a sensible person I'd have happily taken half the money." She squeezed his arm. "You know I don't care. I'm really pleased for you."

"Thanks." James waved as another car pulled up across the road. He wandered over to greet the couple who stepped out. Sam arrived at the same time, and Tara gave him a big hug.

"I see cake inside," Kate called. "James, you need to cut that ribbon before I trample it down."

"I'm coming!" He moved away from his friends and picked up the scissors beside the door.

"Pose for a photo," Kate said.

James's face turned red. "Tara, come here."

"No," she said. "It's your venture."

He took her hand and pulled her over to stand with him, looping an arm around her waist.

"Speech!" Kate shouted as she snapped photos with her phone.

"This is your fault," James said, leaning in to whisper in Tara's ear. "If it weren't for the ribbon everyone would just go inside."

Tara laughed and moved closer, catching the scent of his aftershave. "Just thank them for coming and cut the ribbon." She tried to move away but he had a hand firmly on her hip, keeping her beside him.

"Thanks so much for coming," he said loudly. "Please come in and eat cake and buy books! The brand-new Reading Room is officially open." There was a small round of applause as he cut the ribbon. A few passers-by had stopped to look, forming a nice little crowd.

"To the cake!" Kate called as she hurried inside.

"She's funny," Tara said.

"Yep." James nodded. "She's great."

"We did it," Tara said, as people filed into the shop. "We're open for business."

As he pulled her in for a hug, a wave of emotion swept over her, and she lingered in his embrace. His cheek was warm against hers and his aftershave really was divine.

"Hi!" An eager voice interrupted them.

"This is Olivia," James said, introducing the short, blonde woman he'd been talking to before he was dragged away to cut the ribbon.

"We've heard all about you," she said to Tara.

A tall guy standing behind her extended his hand. "I'm Nick," he said. "I'm an old friend of James." He shook Tara's hand, then slapped James on the back. "It looks like you've done a great job with the place."

"Come in," James said. "Have a proper look."

Inside, Amber scuttled over and pulled Tara to one side. "He's lovely," she whispered.

Tara glanced over her shoulder. "James? Yeah, he is."

"You two would make the most beautiful babies."

"Amber!" Tara hissed. "He's my boss."

"I know, but the way he looks at you." She sighed dramatically. "He obviously adores you. Has he asked you out?"

"No! He's my boss."

"So?"

"It would be inappropriate."

"You must like him," Amber said.

"Why *must* I?"

"Because he's gorgeous! And he's really sweet. Plus, he owns a bookshop. He's a catch."

"Shut up!" Tara laughed. "I have to go and mingle. Try to behave yourself."

Moving out from behind the bookcase, Tara came face to face with James's friend Olivia.

"Hi," Tara said. "Did you try some cake?"

"Not yet." Olivia's smile seemed fixed and unnatural. "How did you and James meet?" she asked. "I was surprised to hear he'd employed someone. We thought he was going to sell the place, and the next thing he's telling us he's renovating and has employed some random woman."

Tara raised her eyebrows but otherwise ignored the jibe. "Well, he's done a great job, hasn't he?"

"It looks good. I'll give him that." She scanned the room. "Seems like a huge risk though."

Tara glanced over Olivia's shoulder. "Life would be pretty boring if no one took risks," she said. "I think he'll do well."

"He'd definitely have done well if he'd sold the place," Olivia said tersely.

"Hello!" Tara called to the new customers arriving. "Come on in and have a browse." She touched Olivia's arm, flashing an apologetic smile but secretly glad of the excuse to get away from her. Something about her put Tara on edge.

The atmosphere in the shop was wonderfully relaxed. Tara drifted around, chatting to various people, most of whom she knew by sight if not by name. She tried to stay close to the counter and kept an eye out for anyone wanting to buy anything. Quite a few people made purchases, and Tara felt more comfortable using the till the more she did it.

"What have you done with Kieron?" Tara asked when she found Amber browsing the children's section.

"James has got him," Amber said, not looking up from the shelves.

After a quick scan of the shop, Tara went over to the window and took Kieron from James. She wiped at the drool on James's shoulder. "You're supposed to be hosting not babysitting."

"He's fine," James said, making a face at Kieron. "We were looking at the train."

"You look a mess now." Tara rubbed at the wet patch on his shoulder again.

"I don't think anyone cares." He put a hand on the small of Tara's back and turned her gently toward the back of the shop. "Do you know the woman with brown hair, getting a coffee?"

"Yeah." Tara chuckled. "That's Belinda. She works in the chemist and is the biggest gossip I've ever known."

"I was in there a few days ago," James said.

"Did she ask you out?"

His gaze snapped to Tara. "How did you know?"

"She asks every guy out. Within a certain age range."

He frowned. "I thought I was special."

"Nope. Just male."

"I was actually a bit scared. She had me up against the wall."

"Did she now?" Tara winked. "That's a proper welcome to the town."

"You've got a filthy mind," James said with a smirk. "I meant she had me backed against the wall asking me a load of questions. Including if I had a girlfriend. And then if I wanted to go out for dinner with her."

"You didn't agree to go on a date with her, did you?"

He looked at her intensely. "No."

"Only because she's a nightmare," Tara said quickly. Had it come out sounding like she was jealous? "Sam went out with her once. She bullied him into it. It didn't go well."

"She talks a lot," James said, glancing away when Belinda turned around.

His friend Nick strolled over to them. "I'm going to have to go," he said. "This place is fantastic. Congratulations."

"Thanks." James shook his hand.

Nick glanced behind him and called out to Olivia. "I've got to get to work," he said. "Let's go."

"Okay, okay. Don't nag!" She rolled her eyes.

"How long have you two been together?" Tara asked, repositioning Kieron on her hip.

"Oh, we're not together." Olivia linked her arm casually through James's. "Nick and I work in the same building."

Tara smiled, slightly confused as to how they all knew each other.

Pulling on James's arm, Olivia kissed his cheek. "The place looks great," she said. "I'll be back to have a proper browse sometime."

As soon as his friends had left, James reached to take Kieron from Tara. "Belinda's coming over here," he said. "Sorry, Kieron, you're going to be my human shield." Turning, he nodded a greeting to Belinda. "I've just got to get this little man back to his mum."

Tara watched in amusement as he fled across the room.

"He's a bit of all right," Belinda said quietly. "Certainly makes the town a bit prettier."

"I have to serve customers," Tara said as she

spotted a middle-aged woman by the till with an armful of books. Belinda was harmless enough but she could talk all day, and all she ever did was gossip.

There was a steady stream of people in the shop, and time flew by. It was almost lunchtime and Tara's stomach was starting to rumble when she spotted James chatting to her mum.

"You made it!" Tara said, going over and giving her a quick hug.

"Of course. James was just telling me how brilliant you've been with helping him set everything up."

Tara waved a hand in front of her face. "I hardly did anything."

"That's a lie," James said. "I definitely wouldn't have opened today if it weren't for you."

"It's so wonderful." Debbie gazed down the rows of bookcases. "I'm going to have a look around."

"Help yourself to coffee," James called after her. He leaned close to Tara. "I thought you said she isn't sociable. She's very chatty."

"Sometimes she is, sometimes she isn't. She's a little unpredictable."

"It was a nice turnout anyway," James said. "Thanks for all your help."

"You don't have to thank me." She bumped her shoulder against his. "I only help because you pay me to."

"You do a lot more than you're paid to," he said. "And I really appreciate it."

Tara felt the heat creep up her neck. "You're

welcome," she said with an awkward smile.

Chapter 9

During the first few weeks of the bookshop being open, Tara and James gradually fell into routines. They agreed that Tara would work all day on Saturdays. She'd have Wednesdays off, and Sundays of course – when the shop was closed. The other days she worked five hours a day with various starting times. In practice, Tara ended up being there far more than that. Not because James asked her to, just because she loved being in the bookshop.

Her wages ended up being slightly more than she'd anticipated. It covered her rent, but not much more. For everything else she was dipping into her savings. Occasionally, she considered getting another part-time job to supplement her income, but she hoped James would soon be making enough profit that he could employ her full-time.

To that end, she threw herself into attracting customers to the shop. After talking to Amber, she decided to hold two story times each week. One in the afternoon for primary-school-aged children. And one in the morning for parents with younger children. Tara was nervous the first time she ran the story time. It was only reading stories to a bunch of toddlers and their parents, but she really wanted it to go well.

Amber reassured her afterwards that it was great, and James had seemed pretty impressed too. He'd been sceptical about the idea of story time generally, convinced that people would use it as a social event and not buy anything. Amber had argued that parents were usually quite happy to spend money on books for their children. Much more so than toys. She'd been right. Sales were always up on the days they had story time. Soon it was Tara's favourite part of the week. It was fun having the kids crawling around the beanbags and playing with the cuddly toys she'd put on the lower shelves.

During story times the shop was a hive of activity, but the rest of the week was much quieter. One Tuesday afternoon they had hardly any customers at all. James had disappeared to do paperwork and Tara was trying to find things to do in the shop to keep busy. Out of boredom, she wandered through to the kitchen. James was sitting at the table with papers spread in front of him.

"I thought you were upstairs," Tara said.

"No, I'm here." He tapped his pen on the table and glanced at his watch. "I'll come through and take over so you can go home."

"No rush," she said. "It's dead. Are you okay?"

"I'd be better if the shop wasn't dead. Sales could be better."

"It's early days." Automatically, she laid a reassuring hand on his shoulder. "Things will pick up."

"Hope so." When he stretched his neck, his cheek

brushed her hand, and Tara's heart rate went wild. She pulled away, realising she was being a little over-familiar with him. They spent so much time together and were so relaxed with each other that it was easy to forget he was her boss. Mostly, Tara just saw him as a friend.

The bell rang over the door in the shop and Tara headed back out.

"I'm coming now," James said. "You can go home."

"I'll just serve this customer," she called behind her. "Then I'm off."

A plump older lady was standing at the counter, smiling widely at Tara. "I was here last week," she said. "And I picked out this book just because I liked the cover."

Tara took the book from her and nodded approvingly at the coastal scene on the front. "Did you enjoy it?" she asked, wondering why she'd brought it back.

"So much." The woman's eyes rolled and she put a hand over her heart. "It's the best book I've read in ages. A bit of romance, a bit of mystery. I devoured it yesterday and today."

"That's great," Tara said.

"I didn't realise when I started it but it's part of a series." She gave Tara a huge smile. "I need the next book. I looked on the shelf but I couldn't see it. Have you got it in?"

"I can check." Tara scanned the book to bring up the information and found the next in the series easily. She squinted at the computer screen. "We've not got it in stock, I'm afraid. But I can order it for you. You could pick it up tomorrow lunchtime."

"That would be great. I was hoping to get straight into it this afternoon but I'll have to wait."

"You'll be happy to know there are six books in the series," Tara added.

"Oh, order them all for me!"

"Really?" Tara chuckled. "The book was that good?"

She did the eye-roll again. "So good."

Tara pressed a few buttons on the computer. "Can I take your name?"

"Barbara Fenton."

"If you call in after midday tomorrow they'll be waiting for you, Mrs Fenton."

"Call me Barbara," she said. "You've done a great job here. It was so miserable before. The old fella that ran the place was no help at all. I run a book club and asked him to order in the books we were reading but he refused. Said he didn't want to end up with a load of stock he couldn't sell. Grumpy old man."

Tara pushed her book back towards her. "Well, we're always happy to take your requests, so let me know if you ever want me to order anything."

"Would you really?" she asked.

"Of course." Tara handed her one of their bookmarks that doubled as a business card. If the books didn't sell they could send them back to the wholesaler. There wasn't anything to lose.

"You're a gem," Barbara said.

"You've got me intrigued now." Tara looked at

the book again. "I might have to get a copy myself."

"Borrow mine," Barbara said, pushing it across the counter.

"Are you sure?"

"Yes. Take it. You'll love it. But I warn you, you'll want to read the next book as soon as you finish."

"I'll give it a try and let you know how I get on."

"She's a local author too," Barbara said. "Lives over in Cornwall somewhere."

"I've been thinking about inviting some local authors to do events. Readings and signings and things."

Barbara's eyes lit up. "You should. It'd be fantastic."

"I'll start looking into it." That might be a good way to get more customers in the shop.

"See you tomorrow," Barbara said. "Thanks for your help."

"Thanks for lending me the book," Tara called after her. Opening the back cover of the book, she found a photo of the grey-haired author, Mavis Wright, along with a short biography which confirmed she lived in the area. On a whim, Tara did an internet search and found a contact form on the author's website. She decided it couldn't hurt to ask and sent off a quick message asking if she'd be interested in doing an event at the shop.

Instead of going home Tara took the book over to her favourite armchair nestled amongst the rows of books. Slipping her shoes off, she pulled her legs under her and opened up the book. She was vaguely aware of James coming back into the shop, and peeked through the shelves for a moment as he worked at the computer. Then she went back to the book.

About fifteen minutes later, James appeared at the end of the row. He stopped short and sucked in a quick breath. "I thought you'd gone home!" he said. "Have you been there all this time?"

"It's a good book," she said, holding it up.

"You just took about ten years off my life." He walked over and turned the book to look at the cover. "You know you could buy the book and take it home to read?"

"A customer lent it to me. I'm not sure what makes you think I can afford to buy books …"

He winced.

"Sorry." Tara reached out and squeezed his arm. "I was joking. Kind of."

"I feel really bad." James perched on the arm of the chair. "But you also don't need to be here so much."

"I know, but if I go home I'll feel like I should be job hunting."

James's eyebrows shot up. "Are you looking for something else?"

"Maybe another part-time job, that's all."

"You keep scaring me today. I thought you were thinking of leaving."

"I don't want to leave." She pushed her head back into the chair. "I want to stay here, reading this book."

"You do that then." He patted her knee as he

stood. "And I will figure out a way to pay you more."

"Please don't worry about it. You offered me a part-time job. I accepted it. My money problems aren't your concern."

He frowned and walked away. Five minutes later he was back with a cup of tea and a bar of milk chocolate. He set them on the little table beside Tara.

She gasped. "Now I'm never going to leave. Thank you!"

"You're welcome." James smiled as the bell tinkled above the door. Customers were a welcome sight.

As he walked away, Tara sighed and snapped off a square of chocolate. She hoped she'd be able to avoid finding a second job.

There was nowhere else she'd rather be.

Chapter 10

Amber had taken to calling into the shop on Monday mornings. She and Tara would have a coffee and a natter while Kieron toddled around. The shop was generally quiet first thing in a morning. They were sitting on the beanbags that Monday, chatting away while James walked Kieron around the shop, pointing out random things to him. Kieron didn't seem overly interested in hearing about popular book genres but James kept up a running commentary nonetheless.

"He's so sweet," Amber said quietly, with a nod in James's direction.

"Yeah." Tara couldn't deny that.

"What are you wearing for the wedding?" Amber asked.

Their friend Max was getting married that Saturday, and Amber was very excited.

"I bought a new dress," Tara said. It was quite ridiculous buying a dress when you had no intention of going to the wedding. She wasn't a fan of weddings. To save all the questions she'd RSVP'd yes and was planning to come down with a mystery illness on the day. Max was well aware of her plan and was fine with it. He was about the least judgemental person Tara knew, and one of the only people she felt she could be completely herself with.

"What's it like?" Amber asked excitedly about the dress.

"I'll show you a photo." Tara slipped her phone from her pocket. Even more ridiculous than buying a dress for a wedding you weren't attending was taking a photo of yourself in it so you could show your friend.

"Oh, it's gorgeous."

"Thanks." Tara took the phone back.

"Are you staying in the hotel?"

"No. I'll get a taxi back in the evening."

"I thought you were staying." Amber looked puzzled. At some point Tara might have said she was staying over. She'd lost track of her lies. "A taxi from Hope Cove will cost you a fortune. You should see if there are any rooms left. Or crash in Sam's room. He won't care."

"Maybe." She shrugged.

"How are you getting down there?"

Tara inwardly groaned. There was a lot of planning involved for this wedding that she wasn't going to. "I thought I'd get a lift with you."

Amber's eyebrows shot up. "You didn't mention it."

"Is it a problem?" Tara asked.

"No. But what if we'd been taking Annette or something?"

"Sam's taking Annette." She shook her head. "And I could still fit in anyway. I can also go with Sam if it's a problem."

"It's not a problem. I just don't know how you can be so disorganised."

Because I'm not bloody going!

"You're going to a wedding?" James hovered behind Tara while Kieron jumped repeatedly on a beanbag.

"Our friend Max is getting married on Saturday," Amber said. "Over in the hotel at Hope Cove. I can't wait. My mum's having Kieron for the night, and Paul and I are staying over."

"This Saturday?" James asked.

Amber nodded.

"You need the day off then?" he asked, looking at Tara.

Oh, great. She'd bought a dress and taken a photo of herself in it. But she'd forgotten to take a day off work for the wedding she wasn't going to.

Tara scrunched her face up as she stared at James. "I already asked you! You said it was fine."

"You didn't ask me," he said firmly.

"Oh, my goodness! I asked you last week. I knew I shouldn't have tried to have a conversation with you before you'd had a coffee."

"I have no recollection of the conversation."

Tara shook her head and rolled her eyes.

"It's fine anyway," James said.

"I know it's fine." Tara lifted Kieron into her lap, then glanced up at James. "You told me it was fine when I asked you last week."

"If you say so," he muttered as he wandered away.

"I can't believe he forgot a whole conversation." Tara frowned at Amber. "Men, eh?" She might have been a bit over the top, but she didn't want Amber to figure out she wasn't planning on going to the wedding. Amber definitely wouldn't understand. She'd no doubt tell Tara not to be so ridiculous. And to be fair, her reasons for not going probably did sound a bit ridiculous.

For one thing, the history between her and Max was slightly complicated. She felt strange about going to the wedding of a guy she used to sleep with. Not that Amber was aware of that fact. And there was no way Tara would ever tell her. The other problem was that weddings depressed her. Amber's wedding had left Tara feeling melancholy for about a month. The whole falling in love, getting married and having kids thing wasn't ever going to happen for Tara, and she'd rather avoid the stark reminders of that.

At least Amber didn't seem to suspect anything. She stayed a while longer, chatting away while Tara tried her best to nod along. It was hard to concentrate. She felt terrible for the way she'd spoken to James. He didn't say anything about it after Amber left, but the atmosphere between them felt slightly frosty.

It ended up being a weird week at work. James was aloof, and Tara was sure it was because of her lying about the wedding conversation. Or maybe Tara was overthinking things. Either way, the thought of him being annoyed with her bothered her more than it should.

On Saturday morning, Tara woke up feeling fairly

glum. She'd expected she would. It was almost tempting to change her mind and go to the wedding. She could get drunk and dance the night away. Except a whole day of pretending to be cheerful felt like a mammoth task. Best to stay home.

Amber was first on her list of people to call. In the end she just sent a message. There was less chance of getting caught out that way. Then she sat up in bed and called Max.

"I hope you're calling to say you've changed your mind and you're coming after all," he said.

"Sorry." She pulled the bedcovers higher. "I've got a stomach bug."

"I'd really like you to be here."

"Don't make me feel guilty. Are you excited?"

"Yes." He was grinning from ear to ear; she could hear it in his voice. "I can't believe I'm getting married today. It feels so weird. Everything's going so fast."

"Yeah. You'll have a house full of kids before you know it."

There was a short silence.

Tara laughed. "Lizzie's pregnant, isn't she?"

"Yes." He chuckled. "No one knows yet."

"That's amazing. I'm so happy for you." She really was happy for him, but the tears in her eyes definitely weren't tears of joy. She did her best to blink them away. "Congratulations!"

"Thank you. How are things with you? I heard a rumour you've got a new job and a hot new boss?"

"Sam's been filling you in then?"

"Something about him having great hair," Max

said, chuckling.

"He is pretty great actually, as far as bosses go."

"So you like him?" Max asked.

"Not like that. We're friends. And I love the job."

"I'm glad things are going well. How's your mum?" Max was the only person Tara had confided in about her mum's problems. Amber and Sam knew about it to some extent but mostly from village gossip rather than from Tara.

"She seems to be doing okay at the moment. But let's not talk about that. It's your wedding day! I'm really sorry I'm not there."

"Don't worry about it. Hopefully we can catch up soon."

"I hope you have an amazing day," she said.

"Me too. At the moment I'm getting phone calls from Lizzie every five minutes because her sister's split up with her boyfriend and is having a meltdown. Lizzie's worried the wedding photos will be ruined by the miserable bridesmaid."

Tara couldn't help but laugh. There was always some drama at weddings.

"I've told Sam to keep an eye on her," Max said. "I'm sure it'll be fine."

"Fingers crossed." Tara leaned back against the headboard. "Enjoy the day. And congratulations again!"

Tara ended the call feeling emotional. It was strange to think of Max getting married. They'd been friends for so long, and even though he didn't live nearby, he'd often turn up for a night in the pub with them. Max was easier to lead astray than Sam and Amber, and they'd had some crazy nights looking for other places to party when the Bluebell Inn was too tame for them.

Max had been off the radar since Lizzie came on the scene, and on the occasions that he had been back to Averton, it was all very sedate. There were no wild nights anymore. That was natural. Friendships were always evolving, and she and Max had gone their separate ways. She was happy for him, of course, but she also missed him.

Since she was claiming to be ill, she decided to act like it and lazed in bed for a long time before finally moving to the couch for a change of scene. She was happy to have a good book to keep her occupied. It was the fourth book in the series by Mavis Wright, the local author who Tara had emailed and invited to visit the shop. Unfortunately, she hadn't received a reply, but the books had her well and truly hooked. She'd been reading them in every spare moment.

Sam called her in the middle of the afternoon.

"Are you okay?" he asked.

"Yeah. Stupid stomach bug. I'll survive."

"I can't believe you're not here."

"How's it going? I heard you have to babysit the bridesmaid?"

"Yeah. I need your advice about that …"

"Aw, you like her?"

"Yeah. She's really sweet. And funny. And kind of ditzy but in a really cute way."

"Sam!" Tara laughed loudly. "You love her!"

"I just met her. Shut up."

"What do you want my advice on?"

"Well, she just split up with her boyfriend. Like yesterday or something. Do you think it's okay to make a move?"

"It's a wedding! It'd be rude not to."

"Good point."

"Take her down to the beach later." Tara moved onto her back and stared up at the living room ceiling. "Kiss her on the shore. Crazy romantic. She'll fall in love with you and you'll live happily ever after."

"Well, if the situation arises I'll kiss her and see how we go from there. She's really great. You'd like her."

"I'm sorry I'm not there to meet her." The lies were never-ending that week. She definitely wasn't sorry she was missing out on all the dancing and romance and everyone being in love.

"Sorry," Sam said. "Should I say it's the most boring wedding ever and you're lucky you're not here?"

"Yes. Thanks, I feel better now."

"I should get back to Josie." He sighed. "I've never danced so much in all my life. My feet are killing me."

"It must be love," Tara said cheekily. "Have a great night."

"Get well soon."

She smiled sadly as she ended the call. Dragging herself from the couch, she went to the kitchen and poured a glass of wine. It was pathetic, drinking wine in her pyjamas. Her mind drifted to James and the slightly awkward atmosphere between them all week.

Guilt niggled at her until she finally decided to do something about it.

Chapter 11

Quickly, she got dressed and walked out of the door. Fresh air was welcome, and she decided to walk over to the bookshop rather than drive. Plus, she'd drunk a large glass of wine fairly quickly so driving probably wasn't a great idea.

The bookshop was closed when she got there but a glow of light came from the back of the room. Tara let herself in and found James counting money in the kitchen.

His head shot up, then he snapped his gaze back to the notes in front of him. He let out a low growl as he lost count.

"Sorry." She grimaced.

"It's okay." He rolled his head from shoulder to shoulder. "How was the wedding?"

"I didn't go," she said sheepishly. James didn't look surprised. "I wanted to come and say I'm sorry."

"For pretending you'd asked me for a day off when you hadn't?"

"Yeah."

He shrugged.

"I was never going to go to the wedding but I didn't want Amber to know that. If she thought I hadn't taken a day off work she'd have known."

"It's not a big deal," he said.

Tara rocked on the balls of her feet. "I don't like you being annoyed with me."

"I'm not annoyed. I'm just tired and I need to count this money."

"I'll leave you to it." She hovered at the door. Somehow, she'd expected to talk to him and leave feeling better, but she felt worse. "I really am sorry."

For a moment his gaze locked with hers. "Do you want to get a drink?"

She screwed her face up, surprised by the question. "I'm not sure I'm fit to be out in public this evening."

"We could have a drink here," he suggested.

"Okay." It was definitely more appealing than getting drunk alone at home. "I can nip out and get something while you finish up here."

He smiled. She closed the kitchen door and went to the supermarket down the road. When she returned, to avoid interrupting James again she plonked herself into a beanbag.

"This is fancy," James said, picking up the bottle of bubbly when he wandered in five minutes later.

"You have to ask for the good stuff at the supermarket," she said. "They keep it hidden in the back. I bought glasses too. They didn't have champagne glasses but I thought wine glasses were better than the tumblers."

"Definitely an improvement." He popped the cork and poured them both a glass. "What are we celebrating?"

"One of my oldest friends getting married."

They clinked their glasses together. James shuffled to get comfy in the beanbag.

"I believe it's more traditional to celebrate at the wedding," he said.

"Yeah. But it's complicated."

"Because you're in love with him?"

She held his gaze and hesitated before answering.

"No. Maybe. No." She turned to face him. "Max and I were never meant to be. Do you ever feel like someone is almost perfect for you, but not quite? And maybe in another life you could have been with them?"

"Maybe." His eyes glazed over.

"Who is it for you?" she asked.

"I have an ex." He turned his head to her. "And everything was pretty great between us. But it never felt quite right."

"And did you ever think about just sticking with it, even though it wasn't quite right?"

"I stuck with it for far too long. Because it's really hard to break up with someone who's almost perfect."

"What did you say to her?"

"That I just wanted to be friends." He shrugged. "It was true. But I felt terrible."

Tara nodded. "Are you still friends?"

"No. She was pretty angry with me when we broke up."

"That's understandable."

"What about Max?" he asked. "You're heartbroken because he's getting married?"

"No. I'm happy for him. And I'm not in love with him. I'm just in love with the idea of him." She frowned. "We always had fun together, and I could talk to him about most things. It was always reassuring to know I could call him if I needed him. Now, I don't feel like I can. Which is how it should be. He's moving on with his life."

James looked at her intently. "I still don't understand why you didn't go to the wedding."

She sighed. "Because it would remind me that everyone else is falling in love and settling down." She gulped at the champagne as she felt herself getting emotional. "And I never will. I'll always be alone."

"That seems like the most unlikely thing ever," James said lightly. "Were you drinking before you came here? Because you're not making much sense."

"I may have had a drink," she admitted. "But all the nice guys like Max are getting married and having kids." She pointed a finger and almost spilled her drink. "The bride's already pregnant, by the way, so that proves my point."

"So far I seem to have missed your point entirely." He sat forward and topped up their glasses.

"My point is, everyone gets married and has kids. Those are the steps to a happy-ever-after."

"*You'll* live happily ever after." His voice was laced with amusement. "You'll find the perfect guy and have a bunch of kids, and I'll smugly say I told you so."

116

"I don't want kids." She sipped her drink and watched his reaction.

"Never?" he asked.

Tara cracked up laughing. "If I just didn't want them *yet* it wouldn't be an issue. Finding a guy who'd wait a while to have kids wouldn't be so difficult. How am I supposed to find a nice guy who doesn't want kids?"

Her smile faded and she leaned back into the comfort of the beanbag.

"You could try putting an advert in the waiting room of a vasectomy clinic."

James was completely deadpan until she started chuckling. Then they both sat up, trying not to spill as they laughed.

"I don't know why I didn't think of that," she said as she calmed down. "Thank you for solving all my problems."

Putting his glass down, he gave her leg a friendly nudge. "You'll find the right guy."

"All the best guys want kids." She gently kicked his foot. "When you were with the almost-perfect girlfriend, imagining your not-quite-perfect future, how many kids did it involve?"

He looked at her sadly. "Two," he said. "A boy and a girl."

"I can imagine that." Settling back, she stared at the ceiling. "You'll make a great dad."

"Maybe," he whispered.

There was silence for a moment, then Tara let out a shriek of laughter as her beanbag jerked and her champagne sloshed onto her thigh.

"Sorry." James had pulled at her beanbag so it was right beside his. "I didn't factor your drink into that move."

"Fairly sure I've had enough anyway." She set her glass down.

"You were too far away," he said as she got comfy again. "I felt like I had to shout to talk to you."

"I was about a metre away." She lay on her side to face him.

"Too far," he said.

"I don't like it when you're annoyed with me." Her eyes searched his face as the alcohol buzzed through her system.

"I'm not annoyed with you," he said.

"You were," she said. "Rightly so. I made you look stupid in front of Amber. I'm sorry."

"That wasn't what bothered me," he said. "I was annoyed because I knew there was something going on with you and you obviously didn't feel you could talk to me about it."

"Well, you're my boss. It wouldn't really be appropriate to tell you my problems."

He nodded. "You treated me like your boss, so I treated you like an employee."

"Okay." She swallowed hard. "You made your point."

"I wasn't trying to make a point. I just don't always know how to act around you."

"I prefer it when you treat me like a friend and not just an employee."

"Me too."

With her face close to his, her heart rate was steadily increasing, and as their eyes locked she had the sudden urge to kiss him.

"I should go home," she said, standing. "I've had too much to drink and I'm an emotional wreck."

He stood up too. "Shall I walk you home?"

"No. Thanks." She gave him a quick hug and tried to ignore the heady scent of his aftershave as it invaded her senses. "I'll see you on Monday."

Tara was only a few metres down the road when James called out to her. He was pushing his arms into his jacket, and locked the door behind him.

"What are you doing?" Tara asked.

"You said I should treat you like a friend. So I'll walk you home, if that's okay?"

"That's okay," she said as he fell into step beside her.

With his hands in his jacket pockets he offered her his elbow, and she linked her arm through his. "So, I was in the pub the other night and Belinda from the chemist came in and cornered me."

Tara chuckled. "Did she ask you out again?"

"Yes. She's pretty persistent. And somehow I ended up buying her a drink, and now I feel very uncomfortable about it."

"You should," Tara said. "If you bought her a drink she probably thinks you're officially a couple. She'll be expecting you to propose any day now."

"Don't tease me," he said. "She makes me nervous."

They chatted and joked easily and arrived at Tara's house before she knew it.

He wrapped her in a big hug. "Promise me you're not going to go in and sit drinking and feeling sorry for yourself."

She blew out a breath. "That was my plan."

"Don't. You have no reason to feel sorry for yourself. One day you'll fall in love and everything will work out perfectly."

Tara frowned. He was wrong, but he was sweet to try and cheer her up. When he smiled at her, butterflies filled her stomach and she found herself wanting to kiss him again. She shouldn't have drunk so much alcohol.

"Thanks," she said, backing away.

"If anything," he said. "You should feel very lucky. A lot of people would be really envious of you."

"Really?" she asked with a grin. "Why's that then?"

He shrugged. "You have an amazing job … and a great boss. Things could be worse."

Tara laughed as he turned to walk away. They called goodnight to each other before she let herself into the house. She didn't reach for the wine. And she didn't crawl into bed to cry herself to sleep.

Instead, she got into bed feeling quite content with the world.

Chapter 12

When Tara walked into work on Monday morning, she followed the music drifting from the kitchen and found James standing by the coffee machine. He was humming along to the radio with his back to her. Tara leaned against the doorframe, quietly watching him. Her mind whirred back to Saturday night and how close she'd come to kissing him.

Now she imagined how it would feel to walk over and snake her arms around his waist. Her heart beat faster as she thought of him casually turning and kissing her lips.

James was startled when he finally caught her watching him. He swore under his breath.

"Sorry," she said, feeling herself flush.

His face relaxed and he reached to turn the music down. "I didn't hear you come in."

"Just arrived," she said.

"How was the rest of your weekend?"

Tara moved around him to get herself a coffee. "Fine." She put the mug under the machine, feeling awkward as she waited for it to fill. "Thanks for Saturday night."

"Did you keep drinking after I left you?" he asked with a smirk.

"No. I went straight to bed," she said proudly. Her smile faltered. "Amber will probably call in this morning. I told her I had a stomach bug on Saturday."

"Good to know," James said. "I'll try not to say the wrong thing."

"Sorry." Tara winced. "I shouldn't involve you in my personal dramas."

"Don't worry about it." He headed to the shop and she followed. "We agreed we were friends, after all."

She gave him a small smile as her thoughts drifted again to Saturday night and being so close to him on the beanbags.

"There's an email for you, by the way." James logged on to the computer and opened the email account for the bookshop. "From Mavis Wright? About an author event."

"No way!" Tara moved to peer over his shoulder, trying to ignore the scent of his aftershave. The urge to lean closer and bury her face in his neck was fairly inappropriate. She concentrated on the email.

"She's the author of the books that Barbara from the book club recommended. The series I've been reading."

James nodded. "It seems like she's keen to come and do a reading and sign books."

"That's brilliant." Tara's eyes trailed over the email. She'd just about given up on ever hearing back from her. In the email Mavis apologised for the delayed reply and explained that she'd been travelling. Automatically, Tara put a hand on

James's arm as they huddled together round the computer.

"I should reply," she said, moving James to the side. "Or should I call?" She pointed at the screen. "She said I could call her. It's a bit early though. Maybe I should wait until later."

James looked at her in amusement and she gave him a friendly nudge.

"What are you going to say?" he asked, leaning on the counter.

"That I love her books and she can come whenever she wants!"

"Maybe you should try to sound a bit more professional," James said. "And have some idea of what you'll discuss with her. Like, will she be expecting a fee? And how many people do you think we can get to come? Stuff like that."

Tara stood up straighter. He made a lot of sense sometimes. "I might mull it all over and call her this afternoon."

"Good idea," he said with a smug smile.

She sat down in her favourite armchair and pulled her phone out to do some research on author events in bookshops.

Amber arrived ten minutes later. Tara excitedly told her about the email from Mavis Wright as soon as she came in the door, which delayed the inevitable subject of Max's wedding. When Amber filled her in on the big day, Tara tried her best to sound sad to have missed it. On some level she *was* sorry she missed it. It would be nice to be emotionally stable enough to go to a friend's wedding without worrying it might cause a nervous breakdown.

Just talking about the wedding caused Tara's spirits to dip, though that was mostly because she felt guilty for lying to Amber. It played on her mind after Amber left. Thankfully her phone call to Mavis Wright perked her up again.

Mavis was a wonderfully positive person and Tara thoroughly enjoyed chatting to her. They arranged for her to visit the shop on a Thursday afternoon in a few weeks' time. Mavis would read an excerpt from her most recent book and then spend time signing. Tara would do a bulk order of the title being promoted and also a selection of her other books. And of course there'd be coffee and biscuits for refreshment.

The rest of the week went in a bit of a blur. Tara threw herself into organising the event. After a phone call with Barbara from the book club, she was confident of a good turnout. That was the main worry out of the way. She also spoke with someone at the local community centre and arranged to borrow chairs. It was fun to have a project, and she enjoyed designing posters and flyers to advertise the event.

"I could probably have saved the printing costs," Tara said as she hung the colour poster in the shop window on Friday afternoon. It was almost closing time and she was looking forward to meeting up with Amber and Sam in the Bluebell Inn that evening. "I was chatting to Belinda from the chemist about Mavis Wright coming to the shop, so that's probably all the advertising we need. Everyone within a ten-mile radius should know about it by now."

Chuckling, she turned and caught James staring at her with an odd look on his face.

"What?" she said.

"Do you want to go out for a drink with me?"

Her eyebrows shot up and she opened her mouth without managing to form a reply. "Tonight?" she finally said. "I can't. I'm meeting Amber in the pub."

"Tomorrow, then?"

Tara moved swiftly past him. Her heart was racing. "Don't you see enough of me at work?" she asked, trying her best to sound breezy.

"No," he said flatly.

Stopping by the counter, she forced herself to look at him. His features were soft but serious.

Tara reached for the computer mouse for something to distract her. "I know we agreed that we're friends but—"

"I wasn't asking you as a friend." He moved closer, his gaze intense.

"I can't go on a date with you," Tara said quietly.

"Why not?"

"Because you're my boss." Her stomach went all fluttery when she looked at him, and a part of her desperately wanted to go on a date with him. It wouldn't end well though, and she hated the thought of ruining their friendship, not to mention their working relationship.

"It doesn't mean you can't go on a date with me."

He leaned casually against the counter.

"I don't want things to end up awkward between us," she said. "I like my job."

"It doesn't have to be awkward. We can date, and if it doesn't work out, we go back to how things were."

"You make it sound very easy," she said.

"It is." His twinkling eyes were almost too hard to resist. All Tara could think about was kissing him.

"I don't think it's a good idea," she said firmly. "I can't date my boss."

He puffed out a breath. "What if I quit?"

"It'd probably be easier to fire me," she said with amusement.

"I considered that," he said. "Would you go out with a guy who'd just fired you?"

She shook her head and checked the time. "No."

"That's what I thought. So the only option is for me to leave."

"No," she called as she headed into the back to get her jacket. "The only option is for us to not go on a date."

"I don't like that option," he said when she returned.

"See you tomorrow," she said.

"For drinks?"

"No." She glared at him. "For work."

He followed her to the door. "I can see I asked at a bad time. I'll try again when you're in a better mood."

"I'm fairly sure that's harassment in the workplace. I could report you."

"Or you could go for a drink with me," he suggested with a boyish smile.

She lingered at the front door for a moment. "I can't," she said quietly.

He nodded, and she hated how vulnerable he looked. As she walked away she wished it had been easier to turn him down.

When she walked into the Bluebell Inn Tara was in a daze. James was invading her every thought, and she struggled to concentrate on anything else. They'd become close over the past months, but she'd been fiercely avoiding imagining him as anything other than a friend. It was much harder now he'd asked her out. She couldn't help but think about how different her evening could have been if she'd accepted. Or even how different her life could be. She imagined him walking into the Bluebell Inn with her. How would it be if they were together and did all the things normal couples did?

She'd hadn't had a lot of boyfriends, but when she had, she'd never invited them into her circle of friends. They'd always been kept on the sidelines. Her relationships had been separate from her friends and family. But in this case there wouldn't be a relationship to keep separate. James was her boss, and there was no way she would risk her job for a relationship that would never last. And she was sure it wouldn't last. She thanked Andy when he handed her a glass of wine, then went over to join Sam and Amber.

"What's going on?" she asked as she sat down.

"Sam's in love with the bridesmaid," Amber said.

Taking a sip of his pint, Sam didn't bother to deny it. When Tara glared at him, he shrugged. "I like her. Her name's Josie, by the way. Can we stop referring to her as the bridesmaid?"

Amber beamed at Tara. "Josie's moving in with Annette and opening up the kennels again."

"No way." Tara's eyes widened. "Are you serious?"

Amber nodded.

"That's amazing." Tara gave Sam a friendly shove. "You're so gonna get laid."

He rolled his eyes.

"Well you must have made a good impression," Tara said. "If she's decided to move to Averton."

"Turns out she has a boyfriend," he said, "so it's just awkward."

"What was she doing flirting with you if she has a boyfriend?"

"She thought it was over but ..." He shrugged again.

"Where's she moving from?"

"Oxford," Sam said.

Tara sipped her drink. "Long-distance relationships never work. They'll split up in no time. Then you can swoop in. Do the friendly neighbour thing in the meantime."

Amber glared at Tara.

"What?" she asked innocently. Her face fell as she remembered that Sam's last relationship had fallen apart due to what was supposed to be a short stint at long-distance. She smiled sheepishly and looked to

Amber. "So what's she like?"

"I didn't speak to her," Amber said. "She only had eyes for Sam. And he completely monopolised her for the entire day."

"That's true." Sam's face lit up, then he gave a short, humourless laugh. "I can't believe she's got a boyfriend."

"I'm telling you," Tara said. "It won't last. When does she arrive?"

"Sunday," Sam said.

"I'm going to go round to Annette's on Sunday," Amber said. "I want to meet her."

"I might come too," Tara said.

"You can't both be there," Sam said. "It'll intimidate her if there's a big welcome committee. And you can't tell her I've been talking about her."

"Fine." Tara sighed. "I won't come over. But I want to meet her soon."

Sam nodded then headed to the pool table.

"He's really smitten," Amber said.

"I hope she doesn't break his heart," Tara said. "But it's good that Annette will have someone keeping an eye on her. And opening the kennels again will be good for her."

"I think so too," Amber said.

Tara gazed across the pub at Sam. "I have a feeling about this Josie. I bet Sam ends up marrying her." She held her hand out. "Tenner?"

"I'm not putting bets on Sam's happiness." Amber shook her head. "And I'm surprised at you being so positive. You're usually much more doom and gloom about relationships."

"Only about my own," she said.

"How's James, by the way?"

"Fine." Tara took a long swig of her drink. She really didn't want to talk about James. To change the subject, she asked about Kieron; that always kept Amber talking for a while. Tara nodded along with the conversation while her mind drifted to James. Why did he have to ask her out? Now he'd complicated things, and she really wanted an easy life.

As her thoughts ran away, Tara drank too fast. When Amber got chatting to one of her neighbours who was sitting at the next table, Tara went over and joined Sam by the pool table. The drinks kept flowing and she moved around the pub, chatting to various people.

By the time she fell into bed that night, the room was spinning and she finally gave up on her mission to avoid thinking about James.

Chapter 13

Over the following two weeks, James asked Tara out for drinks several more times. She kept turning him down, but she wasn't sure how long she could keep that up.

"I can't believe he asked you out," Amber said, leaning back in her chair at the Bluebell Inn. "Actually I *can* believe it. That's not really surprising at all. I can't believe you turned him down."

"Of course I turned him down. He's my boss." Tara hadn't actually meant to tell Amber about him asking her out, but Amber had got suspicious when she noticed an atmosphere between them. When questioned, Tara had accidentally let it slip.

"You work in a bookshop," Amber said. "And it's just the two of you. It's not like you work in a corporate environment. There's no reason you can't date James."

"Apart from the fact that things will be very awkward when we break up." She rested her elbow on the table and propped her head on her hand. "I don't want to lose my job."

"You wouldn't lose your job," Amber said, clicking her tongue. "And you two are perfect for each other. You wouldn't split up." The door opened. Amber leaned to look around Tara. "Oh! She's here."

"The famous bridesmaid," Tara said flatly. She turned to look at the petite young woman with brown hair and big eyes. "Ugh, she looks so perky. Totally Sam's type."

When Amber raised her hand to wave her over, Tara pushed it down again. They were partially hidden by a group standing at the bar, so Josie didn't see them when her eyes roamed the pub.

"I invited her," Amber said. "We can't ignore her."

"We're not." Tara's gaze followed Josie as she headed for the bar. "Sam's right there. I want to watch for a minute."

When Sam caught sight of Josie his face lit up.

"They're so going to get married and have ten kids." Tara stuck her hand out to Amber. "Twenty quid."

"Why are you always trying to make bets on our friends' lives?"

"Because there's not enough entertainment round here." She fell silent as they watched Sam and Josie chat at the bar. Sam turned and pointed them out to Josie, and Amber waved and went over to them. She arrived back a moment later and introduced Josie to Tara. Sam had gone over to play darts.

Tara hadn't known what to expect from Josie, but she was pleasantly surprised. She'd made a few judgements based on the fact that Josie already had a boyfriend but had clearly been flirting with Sam. But it actually seemed very innocent. Josie told them how her relationship had been falling apart for a while but it was hard to finally end things. It definitely didn't seem like there was any ill intent.

"Tara's boss asked her on a date," Amber said, redirecting the conversation from Josie's love life.

"Where do you work?" Josie asked.

"In a bookshop in a small town nearby." Tara registered the surprise in Josie's features. She hadn't managed to adopt a bookish vibe yet. Plus, the drinks were flowing nicely and she suspected Josie had her pegged as a party girl.

"What's your boss like?" Josie asked.

Tara shrugged. "Perfectly pleasant when he's not asking me on dates."

"Just go on a date with him," Amber said. "Otherwise I'll have to stop visiting you at work. The sexual tension between you is getting awkward."

"There is no sexual tension." Tara spluttered out a laugh. It was a lie, but she didn't think it was quite as obvious as Amber made out. "He asks me out, I say no. That's all there is to it."

"He sounds creepy," Josie said, frowning.

"He's not," Amber insisted. "James is lovely. Put the poor guy out of his misery and go on a date with him."

"No." Tara laughed.

"You probably shouldn't," Josie said. "It sounds like it could get messy."

"I like you." Tara smiled as she stood. "You make far more sense than Amber. I'm getting us shots.

Who's up for tequila?"

"No." Amber groaned. "And if Josie had met James she'd agree with me about him."

"Three tequilas it is!" Tara strutted over to the bar. It was refreshing having someone new with them. Josie changed the dynamic, and she seemed very chilled out. Hopefully, she'd hang out with them more often.

***

As it turned out, Josie slotted straight into their little group. On Monday morning, she arrived at the shop to join Amber for the coffee and chat session. It was lovely to see Josie's reaction as she wandered round the shop, taking it all in. She was very impressed by the window displays.

The three of them lounged on the beanbags while Kieron toddled around the place. James introduced himself to Josie and then disappeared upstairs, leaving them alone.

Josie wiggled her eyebrows. "You forgot to mention he's hot."

"She should go on a date with him, shouldn't she?" Amber said.

"Definitely," Josie said. "The way he looked at you made me want to leave you two alone."

"Well, he's my boss. He shouldn't look at me like that." Tara tried to sound stern but all she could think about was the way her stomach filled with butterflies whenever he looked at her.

"Tara thinks it's harassment," Amber said,

amused.

"He's gorgeous," Josie said.

Tara sipped her coffee. "That doesn't excuse the flirting. If he was fat and balding you'd agree that his behaviour was unacceptable."

Josie wriggled to get comfy in the blue beanbag. "I don't know how you can resist him."

Standing, Tara went and straightened out the children's books. "He's my boss," she said. How many times did she have to say that? And would anyone ever accept it? James didn't seem to see it as a reason for them to not date. Part of the problem was that she wasn't firm enough in her reply. It was hard to be firm when she so desperately wanted to go out with him.

Tara changed the subject, asking Josie about her boyfriend. Surprisingly, she'd split up with him over the weekend, and was eager to talk about it. And about Sam.

When Amber and Josie left, Tara flopped back onto a beanbag.

James came in. "What's up?" he asked, hovering over her.

"Nothing," she said with a sigh.

He sat down. "Josie seems nice."

"She's sweet," Tara said. "It seems like she and Sam are going to get together."

"And you don't approve?" he asked.

"It's none of my business."

"So why are you suddenly so down?"

"I don't know." She rested her head back. Listening to Josie talk about Sam had definitely left her feeling low. She envied Josie's excitement and her unwavering positivity. Even though she'd just split up with her boyfriend, Josie was still optimistic about relationships. It was naive and unrealistic, but Tara was envious nonetheless.

"How about I take you out for a drink tonight to cheer you up?" James asked.

Tara stared up at the ceiling. It was so tempting to say yes. Her heart hammered in her chest when she looked at him. It would be so easy to say yes. And so lovely to spend an evening with him.

She decided it was best to ignore the question. Really, she should tell him no once and for all. Make it very clear it wasn't going to happen between them instead of half-heartedly giving him the brush-off.

"I need to call Barbara," she said. "See if she has any idea how many people from the book club will come to the signing next week."

James's eyes followed her as she went over to the counter and picked up the phone. It was off-putting, so she wandered into the kitchen to chat to Barbara.

Tara's bad mood lingered for the rest of the day and she was frosty with James. At least he was sensible enough to give her some space. They remained in work mode for the rest of the week. She focused on her job and spent a lot of time going over the plans for the author event the following week. James didn't ask her out again and she was glad. It was so much easier when they kept their relationship on a professional level.

***

Tara was a nervous wreck when the book signing came around. It had been a lot of work organising it and she was desperate for it to be a success.

"It'll be great," James whispered as the door to the shop opened in the middle of the afternoon. "Stop panicking."

Tara recognised Mavis Wright from her photo and went over to greet her.

"This place is adorable." Mavis wore a bright blue suit and looked to be in her sixties. Her shiny grey bob was perfectly styled.

"This is James," Tara said as he came over. "He owns the place."

Mavis's eyes trailed over him unapologetically. "You're fairly adorable too," she said, offering him her hand.

He chuckled as he shook it. "Thanks? We're excited to have you here."

"Look at that!" Mavis sucked in a breath as she walked over to the display Tara had made of her books. It filled a whole table in the middle of the room. Among the books was a photo of Mavis and a short biography. "I love it," she said, beaming.

"All Tara's work," James said.

"Everything looks fantastic." Mavis scanned the room again.

"I thought you could sit at the table to do the reading." Tara pointed through the chairs they'd set up at the back of the shop. "We're not quite sure how many people to expect but I think it should be a good turnout."

"Perfect," Mavis said. "I'll probably abandon the

table. I like to move around. I tend to play for my audience. Apparently authors are supposed to be introverts but I missed the memo."

"Whatever you want to do is fine with us," Tara said, amused.

The bell tinkled as the door opened again.

"Hi!" Tara smiled brightly at Barbara. She introduced the two women and told Mavis that it was Barbara who'd recommended her books to Tara.

"I'm a huge fan," Barbara said. "Would you mind if I get a photo with you?"

"Of course not," Mavis said.

Barbara passed her phone to Tara and the two women huddled together for the photo.

Then Mavis got her phone out and passed it to Barbara. "Now, would you mind taking a photo of me and this cute pair?" She pulled Tara and James either side of her in front of the display of books. "Smile nicely," she said teasingly. "I only put pretty pictures on my Instagram feed."

Tara and James laughed as Barbara snapped a couple of photos. The bell rang over the door, interrupting them. As customers began to trickle in, James got to work handing out coffees while Mavis wandered round taking more photos. Tara stayed with Mavis, who asked her a string of questions about the shop. It was fun telling her how she'd randomly met James and they'd renovated the shop together. Mavis was fascinated and peppered her with questions.

The shop quickly filled up and soon all the chairs were occupied. Tara was thrilled with the turnout.

When it seemed like people had stopped arriving, she went up to the front and introduced Mavis. There was a round of applause as Mavis came and stood in front of her audience.

Tara slunk away to the back of the crowd and then moved to the door when a large group of young people walked in. They lowered the average age of the crowd considerably.

"We've got a book reading happening today," she said apologetically. "It's just starting."

"That's what we're here for." A petite blonde smiled at Tara. "Mavis is hilarious. We skipped lectures for this."

Tara bit her lip as she tried to hide her surprise. "Come in, then." She held out an arm. "I'm afraid we're out of seats."

Mavis stopped mid-sentence as the students filed in. "Better late than never!" she said. "Heavy night last night, was it?" She rolled her eyes and looked to the front row. "My groupies. They follow me everywhere. If they weren't all so cute I'd be looking into restraining orders!"

The latecomers called out friendly greetings, then silence fell and Mavis carried on. She had a wonderfully chatty, jokey style and had the room in raucous laughter a few times. Her books were tinged with humour, but the way she read the excerpt so dramatically was wonderful. Then she animatedly told stories about how she'd got inspiration for her books. A lot of it was centred around her ex-husband, who she'd written into a book just for the pleasure of killing him off.

After her little talk, Mavis hung around for a long time, signing books and chatting to people. The whole afternoon was wonderfully busy and Tara had a great time, mingling and discussing books. By the time Mavis came over to say goodbye, Tara felt like they were old friends and hugged her tightly as she thanked her for coming.

Once Mavis had left, the customers gradually dispersed too. The shop was in complete disarray, with chairs all over the place and coffee mugs abandoned throughout the shop. Closing time had come and gone, and as the last customer left, Tara flicked the sign to "Closed".

She let out an exaggerated sigh before she burst into spontaneous laughter. "That was amazing."

James looked up from the computer. "We sold more books than we usually sell in two weeks!"

"Really?" Tara had left James to serve customers and hadn't paid attention to how much people were buying.

"We should definitely do more author events," he said.

"I'm so happy it worked out," Tara said, feeling giddy. "I was really nervous, but it couldn't have gone better."

"She's a character, isn't she?"

Tara's shoulders shook as she chuckled. "It was like a stand-up routine! I haven't laughed so much in ages. I didn't know what to think when all those students turned up."

"It was great." James's features turned serious. "Thanks for organising it."

Tara's phone beeped. It was a message from Josie, saying she was sorry she hadn't been able to make it but she was glad it had gone so well. "That's weird," Tara muttered. "Josie's asking if we're trending yet. And she's put a hashtag with *cutest bookshop in Devon?*" Tara came out of the messages and inhaled sharply when she registered all the notifications on her phone. "Oh, my goodness."

"What?" James asked, hovering beside her.

Tara flicked between the various social media sites.

"What's going on?" James asked.

"Look at us!" Tara held the phone out to show him the photo of them with Mavis Wright. "She has a massive following on Instagram. All of social media, but especially Instagram. It seems that as well as being a novelist she also has a really popular blog. Her online presence is huge."

"I thought you'd researched her. You didn't know this before?"

"I just looked at her books." Tara was still scrolling through her phone. "I had no idea she had a blog. This is fantastic publicity."

James had pulled his phone out and was reading through the comments on the photo. "I'm going to print the picture out and hang it on the wall. We can start a photo wall of all the authors who visit the shop."

"I feel like I might have set the standard too high. I'm going to have to choose the next author carefully, aren't I?"

"Yes. They also need to be a social media

influencer. No pressure!"

"I didn't know how exciting it would be to work in a bookshop." Tara couldn't stop smiling. "I thought it would be a lovely relaxed job. I had no idea you could get such a buzz from it."

"It was quite a day," James agreed.

"I feel like celebrating," Tara said. "Shall we go over to the pub?"

"Yes." He nodded. "We definitely earned a drink."

Chapter 14

They sat at a picnic table in the little beer garden at the back of the Jolly Farmer. Spring was in full force and the air was wonderfully warm. It was a pleasant way to spend a Thursday evening. Tara was fixated on her phone when James brought two beers out. She barely looked at him as they clinked the bottles together, and snorted with laughter as she read one of the comments on the photo of them with Mavis Wright.

"There are a lot of comments about you." She held the phone out to James.

He squinted to read the slightly risqué remarks about him, then raised his eyebrows. "So her followers are a load of pervy women? I feel like I should be offended."

"Not all *women*," Tara said cheekily. "Apparently you appeal to a lot of men too. And I don't know why you'd be offended; they're only saying nice things."

"It feels degrading," he said, stifling a smile. "Can you comment and tell them it's what's on the inside that counts?"

"Yes." She turned the phone back to her and pretended to tap on the keypad. "I'll tell them you might look nice but you're a very grumpy boss with a wild temper."

Laughing, he grabbed the phone.

"I was joking," she said. "I wasn't writing anything. It's fun reading the comments though."

James took a swig of his beer and turned his face to catch the last rays of sunshine. "I like owning a bookshop." His phone buzzed on the table. He glanced at it but continued. "I feel like I've been constantly worried that it's going to fail, but today I started to think it might actually work."

"I have a good feeling," Tara said. She pointed to her phone. "With this kind of exposure business is bound to pick up."

"I really hope so," James said. It hadn't fully registered with Tara quite how much pressure he was under. Setting up a business was a lot of stress. His phone buzzed again.

"Secret admirer?" Tara asked.

"No. My sister, Kate. I told her you'd invited an author to the shop and she's asking how it went." He scanned the message on his phone. "Now she's teasing me for the comments on Facebook." He put the phone aside, then reached for it when it buzzed yet again. "Now she's reminding me about tomorrow night." He blew out a breath. "I don't know why she thinks she has to remind me of everything. Little sisters are a pain."

"What's happening tomorrow?" Tara asked.

"My brother-in-law's birthday. A group of us are going out for a meal and drinks. Bernie's also my best friend. We met on the first day of school."

144

Tara's eyes widened. "Your best friend married your sister?"

He nodded. "Yeah."

"Was that weird?"

"Yes." He grimaced. "It's great though. They're an amazing couple."

He went on to tell her about his niece and nephew while Tara made light work of her beer. They drank another round as they rehashed the day and laughed over social media posts. When James walked her home, Tara automatically linked her arm through his, then wished she hadn't. Every time she got physically close to him, she felt out of control.

As soon as they reached Tara's place, she slipped her arm out of his and took a discreet step away from him.

"Do you mind if I come in for a minute?" James asked.

Inwardly, she sighed. Why couldn't they go out for a drink without things getting complicated? "I'm probably going to go straight to bed," she said. Oh, flipping heck. Did that sound like an invitation?

He chuckled then bit his lip. "The beer went straight through me, that's all. I wasn't angling for a *nightcap* or anything."

Tara let out a laugh and opened the door. "Bathroom's at the top of the stairs," she said.

While James rushed upstairs, Tara went through to the kitchen. Maybe she should offer him a drink. It had been a fun day and she didn't really want it to end. Her mind raced as she heard James coming back down the stairs. Was inviting him to hang around a good idea, or a very bad idea?

"Thanks," he said as he stood in the doorway. He walked slowly into the kitchen. "I like your place," he said. "Your kitchen's nicer than either of mine."

"You sound very posh talking about your two kitchens."

"I am quite fancy." He smirked. "Thanks again for today. I'll see you in the morning."

"Yeah." Her heart was beating erratically. She didn't want him to leave. "See you tomorrow."

After giving her a peck on the cheek, James headed for the door. Tara followed him, smiling from the doorway as he set off back down the street.

He was her boss, she reminded herself sternly.

On Friday, Tara was still on cloud nine after the successful event with Mavis Wright. A few customers came in specifically asking for her books. They'd sold out, but Tara had put a big order in and promised to keep books aside for them when the new stock arrived. She decided to keep a display table with Mavis's books for a few weeks. Seeing as Mavis was doing such a great job of promoting the shop for them, it seemed like giving her books pride of place was the least they could do.

Tara had just switched the sign on the door to "Closed" that evening when her phone rang. It was Josie.

"Are you in the pub already?" Tara asked. "I'm just about to leave work."

"I'm on my way now," Josie said happily. "You didn't see it, did you?"

Tara frowned in confusion. "See what?"

"Mavis Wright wrote an article on her blog about the bookshop."

"Really?" Tara asked.

Josie sighed dramatically. "It's beautiful. Stop what you're doing and read it."

After she ended the call, Tara kept her phone out to look for the blog post. It wasn't difficult to find. Mavis had tagged them and Tara's phone had exploded with notifications again.

"Apparently, Mavis wrote something else about the shop," Tara said as she walked into the kitchen. The look on James's face stopped her in her tracks. He had his phone in his hand.

"What's wrong?" she asked.

"I just read it," he said quietly.

Tara's heart thumped. Why did he look so serious? "She didn't say anything bad, did she?"

James shook his head and his gaze shifted back to his phone.

Confused, Tara opened the blog post. The article was entitled "The Bookshop of Hopes and Dreams: where you don' t have to open a book to find a romantic story".

Tara put a hand to her mouth and wandered back into the shop. She lowered herself into an armchair, and she felt light-headed as she read. Everything Tara had told Mavis about her and James was now available for anyone to read. It was their whole story, from the night they'd met in the pub to restoring the shop and how determined they both were to make a success of it. Mavis had embellished

147

it with her own take on their relationship. Once Tara had finished reading it, she read it again. Then sat feeling sick.

When she finally ventured back into the kitchen, James was standing in the exact same position, slouched against the counter.

"Did you tell her all this?" he said, glancing at his phone.

"Kind of," Tara said in a panic. "But not like that. I told her how we met and everything, but she made it sound different." She made it sound as though Tara was in love with James. "She twisted things. I should call her and tell her to take the post down. She can't go around publishing nonsense about people."

James puffed out a humourless laugh.

"What?" Tara said as he stared at her.

"I was wondering whether I should risk asking you out for dinner, but it feels like you shot me down before I even had a chance to ask."

His jaw was tight and his brow creased as his gaze dropped back to his phone.

"Yes," she blurted out.

James looked up at her questioningly.

"Yes, I'll go for dinner with you." Tara's palms were sweaty and her head was spinning.

"I wasn't asking as a friend," he said cautiously.

"I know that. I'll go on a date with you." She realised it sounded like she was forcing herself. "I mean, I want to go on a date with you."

"Okay," James said.

"Tomorrow." Tara swallowed hard. "Let's go out

for dinner tomorrow night."

James nodded.

"Good." Tara's gaze was locked with his and she felt rooted to the spot. "Have a good night tonight."

"You too."

She backed out of the door and fled into the shop. It took a few deep breaths to get her heart to stop racing. Slumping against the counter, she automatically looked down at her phone. Her eyes ran over the blog piece once more, lingering over a remark about the chemistry between her and James. The awkward thing about the article was that it was absolutely spot on.

Tara was about to leave and go home, but she stopped with her hand on the front door. It was an effort to keep her breathing under control as she turned and walked quickly back to the kitchen. James still hadn't moved.

His head shot up as Tara quickly crossed the kitchen. Standing right in front of him, Tara took hold of his shirt collar and pulled gently until their faces were almost touching. When her lips grazed his, her breath caught in her throat. He tasted like coffee, and the smell of his aftershave was sweet and wonderful. His lips parted as she kissed him. Her stomach fluttered wildly when his arms snaked around her waist, pulling her closer. She pushed her hands into his hair and their kisses became more urgent.

They were both breathless when she finally pulled away. Her fingers gently caressed his neck as she stood with her cheek against his, trying to catch her breath.

"So the article wasn't complete nonsense?" James said, his lips twitching into a smile.

"No," Tara said quietly. Taking his face in her hands, she kissed him one more time. Then she stood up straighter.

"See you tomorrow?" James said as she took a step back. His eyes sparkled as he gazed at her.

She nodded quickly. "See you tomorrow."

Chapter 15

"Let's get it over with." Tara draped her jacket over the chair in the back corner of the Bluebell Inn. Josie, Sam and Amber grinned up at her. "You can have five minutes to tease me and then we're changing the subject."

"Is it true," Sam said seriously, "that going into the bookshop might be hazardous to my health? Because of all the electricity in the air?"

Tara rolled her eyes and sipped her wine.

"I love that line," Amber said wistfully. "She summed you and James up so perfectly. I wish I could write like that."

"She's definitely good at making up stories," Tara said.

Josie spat out a laugh. "It's all true. I thought you might drop the innocent act now that it's not just us who's noticed the sparks flying between you two."

"What did James say about the article?" Sam asked.

Tara thought of the look on James's face as he read it. Her mind drifted to kissing him and she shifted in her seat. "He didn't say much. We only just saw it at the end of the day so there wasn't much time to discuss it." Her three friends stared at her.

"What?"

"Can't you just get together with him?" Josie said.

"Did something happen?" Sam asked, giving Tara a funny look.

She frowned. "No. What are you talking about?"

"You're very smiley this evening," Sam said.

"No, I'm not," she insisted.

"Stop smiling and we might believe you," Josie said.

Tara forced her lips into a straight line, then cracked up laughing. "You're all making me laugh!" She stood quickly. "I think we should do shots. Who wants one?" She was met with groans. Josie looked as though she could be persuaded. She usually could.

As she went to the bar, Tara realised Sam was right; she couldn't stop smiling.

"You're in a good mood," Andy said when she ordered drinks.

"I've had a good week," she said. She thanked Andy as she paid him, then returned to the table and deposited a shot of tequila in front of Josie. They clinked the glasses together and downed them in unison.

"What's going on with everyone else?" Tara asked.

"Sam's taking me to a car boot sale on Sunday," Josie said, far too enthusiastically.

Tara laughed loudly. "That's romantic!"

Josie leaned closer to Sam. "I'm excited."

"I can see that," Tara said. "I just can't figure out why."

"I've never been to one," Josie said. "I'm hoping to find more furniture to put in the barn for the dogs."

"You're still doing that?" Tara asked.

"Yes," Josie said. "I'm not stopping until the dogs have absolute comfort!"

Sam kissed the side of her head in what Tara thought was a slightly condescending gesture. Apparently Josie thought the same because she nudged him away, chuckling. "You all think I'm crazy, don't you?"

Tara and Amber exchanged a look, then nodded. It was lovely how easily Josie had slotted into their group. It felt like she'd always been friends with them.

"Lizzie and Max are coming over for dinner on Sunday, too," Josie said. "Annette's cooking for us all."

"Sounds like a busy day," Amber said.

Tara caught Josie and Sam exchanging a look. "You two are sickening," she said. "You're not allowed to have silent conversations. If you've got something to say you need to share it with the group."

Josie let out a long sigh. "Sam thinks Lizzie's pregnant. He thinks they're coming over on Sunday to announce the news."

"Aw," Amber said. "That would be nice."

"Sam's decided this by monitoring Lizzie's alcohol intake," Josie said with a flicker of a smile.

"I'm fairly sure I'm right," Sam said.

"You're not," Josie insisted. "I know my sister.

She'll have everything meticulously planned. There's no way she'd get pregnant before the wedding."

Sam gently nudged Josie with his shoulder. "I can't wait to say I told you so about this."

Tara watched their banter with amusement. It was all the more entertaining because she knew Sam was right. She also happened to know, from a recent phone conversation with Max, that they were expecting twins. Max was over the moon and Tara loved hearing him so happy. She stood to get another drink before anyone questioned why she was grinning from ear to ear.

The evening went by in a happy blur. Tara was in a great mood. Her thoughts were never very far from James. She was determined to put all her niggling doubts aside and enjoy her date with him the following evening. It would be great to spend time with him and not worry about hiding her feelings. The more she had to drink, the more optimistic she felt about the situation.

When she arrived at work the following morning, she was late and hungover.

"Sorry," she said sheepishly as she walked in.

"That's not good," James said as he glanced up at her.

She checked the clock. "I'm not *that* late."

"You're pretty late," he said lightly. "I was hoping I could disappear for a nap when you got here, but you don't look like you're in much better shape than me."

"I was planning on napping on a beanbag," Tara said. "Did you have a good night?"

"Yeah." He yawned. "There was just too much alcohol involved. How was your night?"

"Same as always. I had a good night. Has the shop been busy this morning?"

"Six customers so far." He squinted and stood straighter. "Which means the bloody bell has rung twelve times. Why did I get such a loud bell?"

"I've often wondered the same," Tara said. For a moment they just stood smiling at each other, then Tara moved away, walking through the shop and looking for something to do. There was nothing, so she made them both a coffee. A few more customers came in as the morning went on.

"Hungry?" James asked when there was a lull.

"Yes." She was starving.

"What sandwich do you want?"

"Cheese and pickle," she said automatically. They'd got into the habit of having sandwiches for lunch and kept supplies in the kitchen. Cheese and pickle was her favourite but usually James refused to make it, so she was surprised at his lack of resistance.

The shop was quiet when James came and told her lunch was ready. Tara headed out the back to eat in the kitchen with him.

"What's this?" she asked, frowning as she took a bite of her sandwich.

"Cheese sandwich," he said, smirking but not looking at her.

"That's not what I asked for!"

"Really? That's what I heard."

She gave him a playful kick under the table. "You're mean."

"You know I'm not going anywhere near Branston pickle. I'm not sure why you thought I was more likely to with a hangover." He stretched his leg out so it rested against hers.

"So I've got a boring cheese sandwich while you've got ..." She looked at his bulging sandwich, which was spilling bits out every time he took a bite. "What's in there?"

"What's *not*?" he said as he chewed. "Ham, cheese, mayo, salad, tomatoes. It's amazing."

Tara stuck her bottom lip out until he held the sandwich out for her to try.

"That's way better than mine." She covered her mouth with her hand as she chewed.

After taking another bite, James swapped their plates around and tucked into her cheese sandwich instead. She was acutely aware of his leg against hers as she ate.

There'd been no mention of their date that evening. Tara wanted to bring it up but felt suddenly self-conscious. All she had to do was ask if they were still on. It shouldn't be so difficult.

When she finally spoke, her voice came out sounding slightly strange. "Are we still going out tonight?"

He nodded. "Where do you want to go?"

Before she had chance to answer, the bell rang. James rolled his eyes and stood up. Leaning across the table, he took a big bite of her sandwich and grinned mischievously.

They had a steady stream of customers over the next couple of hours. Tara was chatting to one of the ladies from Barbara's book club when James interrupted them to tell Tara her phone was vibrating with a call. She waved him away, happy to ignore it. Once he'd pointed it out, the noise of it vibrating under the counter was more obvious. It stopped for a few minutes then started again.

"Sorry," Tara said, leaving the customer to browse. It was her mum calling. Instead of answering, Tara buried the phone under a pile of papers.

"You could answer it," James said.

"It's only my mum," she said wearily. "I'll call her back later."

Tara had a bad feeling. When the customer left, she retrieved the phone to find it still ringing, and a feeling of dread swept over her.

"I'm just going to take this quickly," she said to James. The bell rang over the door. Tara smiled at Barbara walking in, then went into the kitchen. Hopefully it would only be a quick call.

"Hi," Tara said. The lack of reply was unnerving. "Mum?" She could hear her breathing. "Are you okay?"

"Yes." She was crying and her voice was muffled.

"I'm at work," Tara said, wanting to be sympathetic, but praying that her day wasn't about to unravel.

"Sorry." Debbie's voice was high-pitched and full of emotion. "I just wanted to ask if you want to come for dinner tonight, before you go to the pub."

"I go to the pub on Fridays." Her mum knew that really. "It's Saturday today."

"Okay," Debbie said weakly. There was a short silence, then a loud sniff. "I wanted to say I'm sorry."

Tara slumped into a chair and leaned her elbows on the table. She squeezed her eyes tight shut.

"I keep thinking back." Her mum's voice was shaky as she sobbed. "I was a terrible mother, wasn't I?"

"No." Tara's eyes filled with tears. "Don't say that."

"There's so much time that I don't even remember," Debbie said desperately. "I don't know what happened, and I don't know who was looking after you."

"You were always a good mum. There's nothing to apologise for. Hang on ..." She moved the phone to her shoulder as James appeared in the doorway. He looked like he'd been about to ask a question but paused.

"Are you okay?" he asked.

As she nodded, a tear spilled down her cheek. Ignoring it, she looked at him questioningly.

"Barbara said she ordered a load of books but I can't find them."

"They're in the storeroom. Bottom shelf on the right. There's a whole box of them."

"Thanks." He smiled sadly.

"I'll just be a minute," she said.

"Take your time."

Tara returned the phone to her ear. "Mum?" The line had gone dead and there was no answer when she tried to call back. She stayed at the table with her head in her hands. After a few minutes, James rapped gently on the doorframe.

"Is everything all right?"

She swiped at the tears on her cheeks and avoided eye contact. "Would it be okay if I nipped out for an hour or so?"

"It's fine." His features were etched with concern. "Is everything all right with your mum?"

"I think so. She's not feeling great. I'll just drive over and check on her quickly. If you're sure that's okay?"

"Of course." He ran a hand down her arm as she passed him. She had the overwhelming urge to lean in and rest her head on his shoulder. Tiredness consumed her, as though her body could predict how exhausting the visit to her mum would be. After giving James's hand a quick squeeze, she grabbed her bag and hurried out of the shop.

Sometimes her mum would get upset but then be fine again half an hour later. Tara hoped it was one of those times. Deep down she knew it wouldn't be.

Chapter 16

Tara's phone rang just as she parked the car in front of her mum's house. It was tempting not to answer. Phone calls from her dad never left her in a good mood.

"Hi," she said, pushing her head back against the headrest.

"Hello, love. How are you?" Her dad's voice was awkwardly upbeat as always. He always sounded terrified of saying the wrong thing. Inevitably he would always say the wrong thing.

"I just pulled up outside Mum's house."

"Good." He sighed. "She called me earlier. I was worried about her."

Tara gave a dry laugh. "I'm sure she's fine. I had to leave work to come and check on her, so feel free to carry on with your life."

"I'm sorry."

Pain shot from Tara's palm and she realised her fingernails were digging into her skin as she clenched her fist. Taking a deep breath, she flexed her fingers. She'd been cold and distant with her dad for so long that it had become a reflex. It was the only way she knew how to be with him.

Her dad cleared his throat. "Your mum and I were

161

talking about meeting up sometime in the next few weeks. Maybe you could join us?"

"I've got a lot on at the moment." Her hand made a fist again.

"I heard about your new job," he said. "It sounds great. Did you get my email?"

"Yes," she said through gritted teeth. He emailed her regularly, telling her about his life and asking about hers. She almost never replied. "I better go in and check on Mum."

"I'd really like it if you came to visit sometime," he said quickly. "Ben and Natalie would love to see you too. They still talk about that summer you stayed for a week."

That visit had been about ten years ago. The summer after Tara had finished school. She'd enjoyed it too. It was the most time she'd ever spent with her half-brother and sister. Ben was five at the time and Natalie was seven. In Tara's head, they'd remained that age. After that visit she hadn't been back much. A couple of weekends here and there. If she'd realised how hard her week away would be on her mum, she'd never have gone. Her mum had peppered her with questions afterwards. She'd wanted to know everything. But she cried when Tara told her about Dad's new family and his life without them. Even as she sobbed, she forced Tara to tell her all about it.

"I'll think about it," Tara said tersely. They both knew she wouldn't visit. It was too hard. "I've got to go." Opening the car door, she said a curt goodbye and ended the call.

She didn't bother ringing the doorbell but let herself in with her spare key.

"Hi," she shouted. Debbie was in the living room, sitting on the couch with her head in her hands. The place was a mess. Tara stood in the middle of the room, looking around. The coffee table was littered with dirty coffee mugs and crumb-covered plates. There were photographs strewn across the floor and broken glass in the corner. She went and picked up the broken photo frame and pulled out the old family photo. Six-year-old Tara beamed at the camera.

"What happened?" she asked as she collected up the shards of glass.

"I'm sorry." Her mum's face was streaked with tears and her eyes were bloodshot.

"Don't worry." Tara went to the kitchen and put the glass shards in the bin. Back in the living room, she picked up the photographs and returned them to the shoebox Debbie kept them in. It looked like she'd flung it across the room. Then Tara took a seat beside her mum. "Are you okay?"

"I just keep thinking about everything and I feel terrible. You went through so much and you were so little."

"I'm fine." Tara draped an arm around her mum's shoulder. "You were a great mum. Stop worrying so much."

Debbie bit her lip. "But you spent so much time looking after me."

She still did, Tara thought sadly. "I never minded looking after you." Tara began collecting up the dishes from the table. "And I turned out okay, didn't

I? No harm done. Why don't we get tidied up a bit? You'll feel better then."

Her mum shook her head miserably. "I had no energy the last few days. I had to cancel all my hair appointments because I couldn't manage them, now I need to call and rearrange them but it all feels too much."

"I'll clean up then, and you can make a start on rearranging the appointments."

"There are eight appointments to rearrange." Debbie put a hand to her mouth as a sob escaped.

Tara put the plates down and reached for her mum's hand. "Just focus on one. Okay? Call and make a new appointment with one client. That's all you need to do."

With a deep breath, Debbie moved to her computer in the corner. Tara got on with cleaning up. It was late in the afternoon when Tara checked the time. She'd managed to coax her mum into rearranging five appointments, and she told herself that was an achievement for Mum. Part of Tara wanted to make the calls for her, but she'd tried that approach in the past and it hadn't been good for her mum's confidence.

When she looked at her phone, there was a message from James asking if she was okay. She replied saying everything was fine and apologetically told him she wouldn't make it back to work. He sent a message straight back, telling her not to worry about it and asking her to call him when she got home. Tara stared at the screen, her fingers hovering over the keypad. She should say something about their dinner plans. But she wasn't sure what to say. Without replying, she pushed her phone into her pocket and went back to her mum.

"Tracie and Lisa are awake now." Debbie tapped away at the computer. The women she'd met in an online support group were scattered across the globe and operated on different time zones.

"That's good." Tara had mixed feelings about her mum's support network. On the one hand she was sure physical human interaction would be better for her. But on the days her mum couldn't make it out of the house and had no one else to talk to, Tara was thankful she at least had people to message and feel connected to.

"I spoke to your dad earlier." Her mum looked at her warily.

"Me too," Tara said. "He called just before I got here."

"That's nice." Her focus went back to the computer and she typed as she spoke. "We should try and meet up with him sometime."

"He divorced you," Tara said with barely veiled anger. "Which means you don't have to see him."

"We had a lot of good times." Debbie looked up from her keyboard. "Before things went wrong."

"I don't remember much before we moved here," Tara said bitterly. That was a lie. She remembered plenty. She just wished she didn't. "Shall I make you some dinner?" Tara checked the time and thought again about her own dinner plans.

"No, thanks. I'll get something later. You go, if you need to." She was engrossed in her messaging, and Tara felt slightly irritated that her mum was suddenly more interested in her online friends. But it was also a relief that her mum had other people to lean on. "Thanks for coming over." Debbie stood and gave her a tight hug. "I love you."

"Love you too." Tara clung to her mum for a moment, then quickly walked out when she released her. "I'll call you tomorrow," she shouted behind her.

As she drove home, Tara went through the usual range of emotions: anger, irritation, sadness. It was all very familiar. The shop was already closed when she passed, and Tara slowed to peer through the window. There was no sign of James. She was tempted to stop and go in. What she really wanted to do was grab a book and curl up on a beanbag. James would no doubt make her a cup of tea and sit beside her. She imagined him making jokes to cheer her up.

Thinking about James only made her feel worse. She had to call him and cancel their dinner plans. As soon as she got home, she pulled her phone out. She paced the living room for a few minutes, then sank onto the couch to call.

His voice was comforting. "Is your mum all right?"

"Yes." She hugged the phone to her ear. "She's okay. Was the shop busy this afternoon?" Small talk would put off the inevitable conversation about dinner. She didn't want to disappoint him, but she couldn't go.

"Not really," he said. "I wasn't rushed off my feet."

"That's good." She let out a long breath and leaned on her knees. "I can't make dinner tonight."

"Okay." There was a brief pause. "Shall we rearrange for another night?" His voice was unemotional but Tara was filled with guilt.

She wanted to tell him she couldn't go out for dinner with him ever. It seemed so harsh over the phone. Plus, there was a chance she was just feeling emotional and would see things differently in a few days.

"Let's talk on Monday," she said.

"I'm worried about you," he said gently.

She screwed her eyes shut. "I'm fine."

"Call if you need anything."

"Thanks." As she hung up she wished he wasn't so nice. It just made everything harder.

***

"You're early," Tara said to Amber on Monday morning. They arrived at the shop at the same time. Tara had hoped to have a chat with James as soon as she got to work, but it'd have to wait.

"Kieron was up at five," Amber said through a yawn. "We needed to get out of the house."

"Five o'clock is insane." Tara tickled Kieron's cheek. "That would kill me."

"It's not fun," Amber agreed.

When they went inside, James scooped Kieron up for a hug. Kieron immediately wriggled to get down again and headed over to jump on a beanbag.

"How does he get up at five and still have so

much energy?" Tara asked in awe.

"I have no idea." Amber hung her head. "It's really unfair."

"Sounds like you need coffee," James said, raising an eyebrow. His gaze landed on Tara. "I'm going to disappear upstairs for a while. I've got some paperwork to get on with."

"No problem." It was normal for him to make himself scarce while the girls were around on Monday mornings. They only ever stayed for an hour at the most and there were rarely any customers at that time. Josie arrived completely flustered not long after James went upstairs. She'd been offered an acting job back in London and was torn over whether or not to accept it. It took Tara's mind off her own problems for a little while as they discussed the pros and cons. Josie also told them that Lizzie was pregnant. Tara acted suitably surprised at the news.

James reappeared after Josie and Amber left. "All quiet again?"

"Yeah." Tara sat on the green beanbag with a fresh cup of coffee.

"What's wrong?" James picked up the blue beanbag and deposited it beside Tara before sitting down.

"Josie's been offered her dream job in London."

"Wow." James's eyebrows shot up. "What about Sam?"

Tara shrugged. "I don't think she should give up on an amazing opportunity for him. Besides, Sam's besotted with Josie. They'll figure it out." She hoped so anyway. Given Sam's history with long-distance relationships he might not be overly keen. He loved Josie though; he'd support her.

Silence stretched out. Tara knew they needed to talk about what was going on between them.

"I'm sorry for cancelling dinner on Saturday," she finally said.

James nodded slowly. "I get the feeling you don't want to rearrange."

"I don't think it's a great idea." She placed her mug on the floor and sat up straighter. "Working together and dating seems like a recipe for disaster."

"On Friday you thought it was a good idea ..."

"Not really," she said weakly. "I read Mavis Wright's article and got caught up in it. I shouldn't have kissed you."

James looked at her intensely. "You don't really believe that?"

"It's too complicated. I like working with you. I don't want to mess that up."

"I don't see why it would."

"Because when things inevitably go wrong, it will be awkward working together."

James dropped his head to his hands and rubbed at his eyes. "What makes you think things wouldn't work out?"

She paused, trying to figure out a way to explain how she knew things wouldn't work out between them. He wouldn't understand. "I just see you as a friend," she finally said.

He gave a short, humourless laugh. "So all this time I've been imagining things between us? It's all one-sided? I like you, you don't like me?"

"I like you," she said. "Just not in that way."

When he reached for her hand it sent shockwaves through her whole body. Her instinct was to snatch her hand away, but his touch felt wonderful. If she wasn't careful, she'd lose her resolve. Calmly, she stood up.

With perfect timing, the bell rang over the door and a customer stepped in. Tara hurried over to greet the middle-aged woman, happy at the interruption.

The atmosphere was tense for the rest of the day. James made her a sandwich at lunchtime but left her to eat in the kitchen alone. They barely spoke all day, just moved around each other in an uncomfortable silence.

"Is it okay if I finish now?" Tara asked in the middle of the afternoon. She'd got into the habit of working longer hours than she was supposed to, but given the tense atmosphere she decided to make the most of the fact that her job was only actually part-time.

"Yeah." James didn't look up from the computer.

After grabbing her bag, Tara said a hasty goodbye. She was almost at the door when she turned on her heel and walked back to him. James stood up straighter, his features set into a frown.

"It's already awkward," Tara snapped. "It's awkward because I won't go on a date with you, so what would it be like if we dated and it didn't work out?"

He glared at her. "It's not awkward because you won't go on a date with me. It's awkward because you're lying about how you feel."

"Right." She put her hands on her hips. "So you know how I feel better than I do?"

"I know how it felt when you kissed me." His features softened. "I don't understand why you're pretending."

"I'm not pretending." The words didn't even ring true to her, so there was no way she was fooling James. "I don't want to keep having this conversation. I'm going home."

James walked around the counter as Tara set off for the door again. "What exactly are you so scared of?"

She stopped dead. Her whole body tensed and she had the urge to run at him and shove him as hard as she could. She took a deep breath. She also had the urge to close the shop and tell him all the things that terrified her. All the reasons why she knew it would never work out for them and why she wouldn't risk getting her heart broken again.

Her gaze locked with his. "I'm scared I'm going to have to find a new job because you won't take no for an answer."

James looked like she'd slapped him. She hated the hurt in his eyes. After a moment he turned his attention back to the computer, and Tara finally left the shop.

Everything felt impossible.

Chapter 17

Tara stuck to her part-time hours the following week, and the weeks that followed. Business had taken a turn for the worse. The weather was great, so it might have had something to do with that. With fewer customers, Tara found herself alone with James more often than she would like. After the day she'd stormed out, he hadn't mentioned anything more about them dating. Things weren't the same between them and she missed the relaxed atmosphere.

Outside of work things felt fairly strained too. Josie had moved to London. Even though she'd only been in Averton a couple of months, Tara missed having her around, and the dynamics in their group had shifted when she left. Probably because Sam hadn't handled the situation very well. Tara was furious with him. Somehow, she'd assumed he'd be supportive of Josie's career opportunity. Instead he'd given her an ultimatum: if she left, things were over between them. Josie had chosen to leave and Tara couldn't blame her at all.

In fact, Tara had made her thoughts on Sam's behaviour very clear, and as a result they were barely speaking. The last couple of times she'd seen

173

Sam in the pub, he hadn't spoken to her other than a curt greeting. He must have been missing Josie, and Tara caught herself feeling sorry for him a couple of times but quickly went back to being annoyed with him.

It was a drizzly Saturday when the perky-looking blonde woman walked into the shop late in the afternoon. Tara recognised her but couldn't quite place her. The woman glanced around the shop as she walked straight to the counter.

"Is James around?" she asked.

"Yes." Tara tried to remember where she knew her from. "I think he just nipped upstairs."

"We met before," she said. "At the opening. I'm Olivia."

"Oh, yes. I remember. I'm Tara." They stared at each other for a moment. "I'll give James a shout." She found him in the kitchen.

"What's up?" he asked.

"Your friend Olivia is here," she said. There was a flash of surprise in his features before he nodded and went into the shop.

Olivia greeted him with a kiss on the cheek. "I was just in the area," she said. "So I thought I'd call in and say hi."

"It's good to see you," he said. "Do you want a coffee?"

"That would be great."

Tara walked through the shop. She stopped by the window display and moved a couple of things around. When summer had arrived, Tara had spruced up the displays. She'd decided to keep the overall themes the same but change them slightly for each season. People would often stop and gaze at the displays, and it always gave Tara a thrill.

At the back of the shop, Olivia was loudly telling James how great the place looked. Her gentle laughter echoed around the room and grated on Tara's nerves. Through the shelves, Tara stole glances at them. Olivia had a hand on James's arm as she beamed up at him. She looked desperate and pathetic.

When Tara had rearranged most items in the window, she wandered through to the kitchen. It annoyed her to see Olivia laughing and joking around with James. Tara used to be like that with him too, but now they operated on a strictly professional level.

She forced herself to go back into the shop when the bell rang, hoping it was Olivia leaving rather than a customer arriving. Tara sighed at the sight of Belinda from the chemist walking in. James and Olivia were still chatting in the kids' corner. It really wasn't Tara's day.

"Do you ever hear anything from Josie?" Belinda asked after a quick greeting. Her eyes lingered on James and Olivia for a fraction too long when she noticed them.

"I get the odd message," Tara said frostily. "Why?"

"I saw Sam the other day and he looked heartbroken. It must be so hard for him. I offered to take him for a drink to cheer him up but he said he's busy. I guess he's throwing himself into work to take his mind off Josie." She clicked her tongue. "I still can't believe she just left like that. Poor old Sam."

"She didn't just …" Tara trailed off and leaned on the counter, glaring at Belinda. "Did you come in to buy something or just to gossip?"

"I'm worried about Sam," she said with a look of mock concern. Glancing over her shoulder, she exchanged a look with James. It made Tara want to grab her by the arm and drag her out of the shop.

"You're not concerned," Tara said loudly. "You're a gossip. Sam's fine. He doesn't need you commenting on his life to everyone you meet."

"I can see you're in a great mood," Belinda said with a dramatic sigh.

"Did you want to buy something?" Tara snapped.

"Service with a smile as always!" Belinda turned to James and rolled her eyes. "Have a nice weekend." She waltzed out the door.

There was a hint of a smirk on James's lips as he looked at Tara.

"I can see why the shop's so quiet," Olivia remarked. "It's not the best customer service." Tara scowled and turned her attention to the computer. Now she felt like dragging Olivia out of the shop too.

"Belinda's the town gossip," James said lightly. "She works in the chemist and spends her lunch breaks going round the other shops in town prying into people's lives."

"Even so," Olivia said. "If you work in a shop you should really be professional, regardless of whether or not you like the customers."

"She's not really a customer." James took Olivia's coffee mug from her. "I should probably get some work done."

"Are you coming out tonight?" Olivia put her hand on his arm again. "You've not been out with the gang in ages."

"This place keeps me pretty busy."

"You work too hard," she said. "Come for drinks tonight."

"Maybe," he said.

She pushed up on her toes and kissed his cheek. "See you later then!"

Tara's lip curled automatically and she kept her attention firmly on the computer screen. She mumbled "Goodbye" as Olivia left.

"What's going on with you?" James asked after he'd taken the coffee mugs to the kitchen.

"Nothing. Sorry. I shouldn't have snapped at Belinda."

He came and stood beside her and leaned on the counter. "You don't usually let her get to you."

"I don't like her talking about Sam." She stood up straight. She'd been staring at a blank computer screen for quite a while. "I'm worried about him too. But I'm also annoyed with him."

"What happened?"

Since their topics of conversation had been strictly business over the last weeks, James hadn't heard the whole story, only that Josie had left. "Josie wanted to take the job, and Sam said if she left their relationship was over." Tara sighed. "I had a go at him in the pub one night. Told him he was an idiot. He's barely spoken to me since."

"Did you try apologising? I'm sure he'd be fine with you."

"The trouble is I still think he's being an idiot!" She puffed out a laugh.

James smiled. "You can think he's being an idiot and still be friends with him."

"You're probably right," she said.

He checked the time. "Do you want to go and call him? Maybe you can go for a drink with him and clear the air."

The shop was quiet but Tara didn't feel like leaving. "I'll give him a call later," she said. "I'd rather hang around here if that's okay?"

"Of course."

Tara glanced at the door. "Why's the shop so quiet?"

"I don't know," James said with a shrug.

"It's been quiet all week."

"It's probably just the time of year."

"I hope so." She frowned. There wasn't actually anything for her to do, so hanging around for the rest of the afternoon felt a bit pointless. "Do you need me to do anything?" Maybe she'd have to go home after all.

"No." James glanced at the empty shop. "There is one thing you could do …"

"What?" Her forehead creased.

He placed his hands on her shoulders and walked her through the shop. When he got to the thriller section he stopped and scanned the shelves.

"What are we doing?" Tara asked.

James looked serious as his eyes scanned the books. Finally his features relaxed and he pulled a book from the shelves and passed it to her. It had come in as new stock the previous week, and Tara had been immediately attracted to the cover. She'd spent a while examining the book and reading the description. Before things had got weird between her and James, she'd spend any spare time in the shop reading, but she'd stopped doing that in her bid to keep things professional at work. She turned the book over.

When his hand landed on her shoulders again, she laughed but let him lead her to the armchair at the other side of the room. The weight of his hands was comforting.

"Sit," he said. "Read. Stop worrying!"

"Thank you," she said as she curled up in the chair.

He raised his eyebrows. "Don't bend the spine."

"James," she called as he walked away. "The shop's doing okay, isn't it?" There was something about the way he'd looked when she mentioned the shop being quiet. Like he was worried.

"It's fine." He nodded quickly. "Nothing to worry about."

She didn't quite believe him, but if there was a problem he obviously didn't want to discuss it.

Tara soon got wrapped up in the book. There were no customers for the rest of the afternoon and it worried her. Saturday was usually their busiest day.

"We've got the next author event in a few weeks,"

Tara said as she got ready to leave. "Hopefully that will give sales a boost."

"We'll survive." James followed her to the door and turned the sign to "Closed".

"Enjoy your night out," Tara said.

"What night out?" he asked slowly.

"I thought you were going out with Olivia?"

"Oh." His eyebrows shot up. "Yeah. Thanks."

As Tara made her way home, she wished she hadn't mentioned Olivia. Hopefully she hadn't sounded jealous. What did she care if he was going out with Olivia? There was a group of them going anyway; it wasn't like he was going on a date with her. Not that Tara cared.

When she got home she forced herself to put James out of her mind. Her thoughts landed on Sam instead, and she got her phone out to call him. She'd feel better if she cleared the air between them.

"How are you?" she asked when he answered.

"Fine."

The conversation probably wasn't going to be as easy as she'd thought. "Are you still angry with me?"

"Yep."

She rolled her eyes and paced the living room. "I didn't even say anything that wasn't true. You *did* mess things up with Josie."

"Is this your idea of an apology?"

"No. I don't think I have anything to apologise for. I just wanted to check you're okay. Do you want to go out for a drink?"

"No," he said flatly.

"You're very stubborn sometimes."

"I just don't feel like going for a drink."

"Fine. Call me when you do feel like it."

"Okay." He hung up.

Tara flopped onto the couch, furious with him. As the anger slipped away, she just felt sad. Before she knew it her mind was back on James, imagining him out with Olivia.

It really wasn't the best Saturday night.

Chapter 18

It was a couple of weeks later when Tara saw Sam again. He hadn't been in the pub and she was worried about him. When he walked into the shop on Saturday morning, Tara looked up in surprise.

"Hi," she said.

He looked fairly sheepish as he walked over to her. "I'm sorry."

"Me too." She gave him a big hug. "Are you okay?"

"Not really." He caught sight of James in the children's corner and said a quick hello. James greeted him politely and went back to putting new stock on the shelves.

"What's going on?" Tara asked.

Sam shoved his hands into his pockets. "Josie's coming to visit and I have no idea what to do."

"When's she coming?" Tara asked excitedly.

"Today." He paced a few steps. "She's on her way now."

"No way," Tara said. "She'd have told me."

"She just called Annette last night."

"Hang on." Tara went into the kitchen and retrieved her phone. There were messages from both Josie and Amber arranging to meet up over the

183

weekend. "You're right," she said, reading through the messages as she went back to Sam.

"I wasn't making it up!" he said. "What am I going to do?"

"What do you mean?"

"I want to get back together with her."

Tara sighed. "You were awful to her. Have you spoken to her since she left?"

"No."

"At the risk of offending you again ... you're an idiot."

"I realise that." He ran his hands through his hair. "But what should I do, grovel? Beg her to come back?"

"I don't see how begging her to come back is going to help. You refused to support her career. If you want to get back with her you need to start being supportive."

"So I tell her we can have a long-distance relationship?"

Tara shrugged. "That seems like the least you can do."

"What else can I do?" He stared at her for a moment. His shoulders drooped. "Move to London?"

"How much do you want to be with her?"

"A lot." He scratched his jaw. "Fine. I'll move to London. I hate London, by the way. I don't like cities."

"Slow down," Tara said with amusement. "All I'm saying is if you really want to get back with Josie you need to be willing to do whatever it takes.

And she's not going to forgive you overnight."

"You think she'll forgive me though?"

"Maybe. Try not to be too intense this weekend. Just act normal and let her see how much she misses you."

"Good plan." He wiped his hands on his jeans. "I'm a nervous wreck."

"You'll be fine."

At the door, Tara gave Sam another hug, happy that things were back to normal between them.

"Are you really giving relationship advice?" James asked, an amused look on his face.

"I was actually having a private conversation with my friend."

"It wasn't that private, or you wouldn't have had it in front of me."

Tara rubbed at a mark on the countertop. "Do you want to share *why* you don't think I should be giving relationship advice? Just because I'm single doesn't mean I can't give a friend some advice when he asks for it."

"It has nothing to do with you being single," James said with an annoyingly smug look.

"What then?" The mark had vanished but she continued to rub at the spot nonetheless.

"Never mind." He walked over to the counter and picked up a flyer advertising the author event they were holding the following week. "Are we all set for this?"

She stared at him. "Why shouldn't I give Sam advice?"

"I didn't say you shouldn't give him advice," he

said flatly. "I just find it surprising, since you're scared to be in a relationship."

Tara opened her mouth to argue but stopped, realising she had no argument. James had hit the nail on the head. She was terrified of being in a relationship. But with good reason.

Swallowing hard, she looked at the flyer in James's hand. "Everything's organised." She rubbed at her temple. "I need to nip out for some painkillers. Do you need anything?"

"No," James said. "Are you okay?"

"Just a headache," she said. "Won't be long."

The chemist's was annoyingly busy. It was a stark contrast to the empty bookshop. Tara had to wait a few minutes in the queue, and she was heading to the door again when she saw Belinda restocking shelves.

"Hi!" Belinda said cheerfully.

Tara forced a smile. "How are you?"

"Fine. Everything ticking over okay at the bookshop?"

"Yep. It's quiet but we think it's the time of the year." She didn't know why she was talking to Belinda. Usually, she was much more guarded with the gossip queen.

"I heard James saying the same. Hopefully it picks up soon."

"Yeah." Tara lingered, wondering what James had said. Was he seriously worried about business?

"He was in the Golden Lion last week," Belinda said. "With the annoying blonde."

"Olivia?" Tara asked too keenly.

"Yeah." Belinda frowned. "Are she and James an item?"

Tara shrugged. "Not that I know of. But he's my boss. He doesn't have to tell me who he's dating."

"It's a shame business is bad, anyway," Belinda said idly. "He sounded stressed. Hopefully you don't lose your job."

The thought of losing her job made Tara feel panicky. In the past few weeks she'd done some half-hearted job searches for something part-time to boost her income. If she was honest, she was still clinging to the hope of a pay rise at the bookshop, but that seemed less likely with every passing day.

"I've been looking for something else actually," she blurted.

"Really?" Belinda's eyebrows shot up.

"Yeah." Tara decided to take advantage of Belinda's gossipy tendencies. It was far easier than trudging around local businesses herself. "Just something part-time. I could do with some extra money. Do you know of anything?"

"No." She squinted as she mulled it over. "I can keep an ear out."

"That would be good," Tara said. "Thanks."

It felt weird asking Belinda for help, and Tara wandered back to the shop feeling fairly down. She should probably tell James she was looking for a part-time job before he heard it from Belinda. But when she got back to the shop, he told her to go home early, and she didn't argue. The headache was getting worse and she just wanted to lie down.

At home her thoughts lingered on the fact that

James had been in the pub with Olivia. She knew Olivia had been calling him too, having clocked the display on his phone a couple of times when it had rung beside the computer. Maybe they were dating. It was none of Tara's business, but she couldn't stop thinking about it.

James's relationship status also seemed fairly trivial when Tara pondered the drop in customers in recent weeks. She wondered how long the shop could survive if business continued to be so slow. After all the work they'd put in, the thought of it failing was heartbreaking. Especially after they'd got off to such a good start. Hopefully things weren't as dire as they seemed.

***

It didn't take long for Belinda to spread the news of Tara's job hunt. When Tara arrived at work on Monday morning, James was in the kitchen with his head in his hands.

"I heard you're looking for another job," he said.

"Yes." Tara dropped her bag on a chair. "I told you ages ago I'd need to find a second job at some point."

He looked tired as he rubbed at his eyes. "Sorry."

"What are you sorry for? This was always the plan. I've just been putting it off."

"Would you rather work here full-time?"

She searched his face to see if he was serious. "Yes," she said slowly. "But you can't afford to pay me …"

He dragged his fingers through his hair. "Things are going pretty well. I was intending to ask you in the next couple of months anyway. But we can make it immediate."

"Really?" She pulled out the chair opposite him. "Because things have been so slow. I was worried about the state of your finances."

"It's not so bad." He smiled, obviously realising how unconvincing he sounded. "I looked through the old accounts and August has always been slow. Richard never did well, but the summer was always the worst. As soon as the schools go back and the weather turns things will pick up again."

"So we're hoping for bad weather?"

He chuckled. "Yeah."

"I can keep working part-time until things pick up again."

He shook his head. "You can have a pay rise immediately. It's long overdue."

"Thank you." She was torn between not wanting to add to James's money worries and not wanting to find another job.

"You really don't need to thank me," he said wearily.

Before Tara could reply, her phone beeped. She read the message from Amber saying that Kieron had a cold and they wouldn't be over for a coffee. She then got a message from Sam, who was apparently outside the shop.

"Sam's here," she told James as she headed for the door.

"How come you open up so late?" Sam asked as

she unlocked the front door and ushered him in.

"Because nobody wants to buy books early in the morning. I guess you don't either?"

"No."

"I presume you want more relationship advice?" Tara caught James's eye and smirked. "But I'm not sure I'm the right person to ask."

"I might get coffees," James said, smiling and heading back to the kitchen.

"Did you see Josie?" Sam asked.

"Yeah, I saw her yesterday." Tara had enjoyed catching up with Josie at Annette's place.

"Did she say anything about me?"

"No." Tara pursed her lips together. "I don't think your name came up at all."

Sam sat down on a beanbag. "I saw her on Saturday," he said sadly.

"And?"

"And I'm an idiot. She's doing so well. I don't want to mess things up for her. Plus, I don't think she'd take me back."

"You really love her, don't you?" Tara plumped up a beanbag and took a seat.

Sam nodded as James reappeared with coffees.

"I don't know what you should do," Tara said as she took a mug from James. "And apparently I shouldn't be giving relationship advice anyway."

James smiled. "I never said that."

"You implied it," Tara said lightly.

"What do you think I should do?" Sam said, looking to James.

His eyebrows knitted together. "I think sometimes

persistence pays off."

Sam nodded slowly while Tara looked incredulously at James. Was that remark aimed at her? She stared at him for a moment, then shifted her gaze to Sam.

"Persistence could also land you with a restraining order," she said.

Sam sipped his coffee and looked thoughtful. "James is right; you shouldn't give relationship advice."

"I can't believe you said that," James said after Sam left for work.

"What?"

"'Persistence can get you a restraining order'!"

"It's true," she said, grinning. "Sometimes it's good to know when to give up."

He inhaled deeply. "I take it that's aimed at me?"

Tara went to the computer to check the emails.

"Sorry," James said. "I've taken the hint. I'm just glad we can be friends."

She looked up at him. "Me too."

And she *was* glad. But there was an ache in her chest at the thought that he'd given up on them ever being a couple. It was stupid, because she knew it was never going to happen. But there was something about him saying it that made it feel so final. And it made her wonder what was going on with him and Olivia.

Thankfully, there wasn't much mention of Olivia in the months that followed. Life seemed to balance out. Josie returned to Averton and moved in with

Sam. It was great to see him so happy again. Fridays at the Bluebell Inn returned to being the usual fun evenings.

Tara's mum was back on an even keel, and even though Tara knew better than to think it was the new norm, it was always great to see her more stable. She visited her mum most weekends and the place was always neat and tidy, and there was food in the fridge, which was a sign that she was doing well.

Work was good too. James was right; as soon as the schools started up after the summer break, business picked up. Story times were busy again and they held a couple of author events in the autumn that went well.

On the first of December, Tara arrived at work with a buzz of excitement.

"You're doing the window displays today?" James asked as she played Christmas music through her phone.

"Yes!" She took the bag of goodies she'd bought the previous week over to the window. "I'm so excited. I love this time of year." She pulled a string of tinsel from the bag and draped it round James's shoulders.

"You're very cheerful," he said.

"Because I get to cover my window displays in snow and Christmas decorations! How could I not be cheerful?" She turned the music up a fraction. "Go away and I'll give you a shout when it's finished. You'll be amazed."

"I'm sure I will." He walked off and she got to work on the display. The train was transformed into the Polar Express, complete with a little Santa figure to sit on top as its driver. There were reindeer and snowmen, and she gave the window panes a frosted effect with a smattering of fake snow. It was a lot of fun to do and she was really pleased with the end result. A few passers-by stopped to look while she was working on it. One little boy stood with his mum for ages, and the look on his face filled Tara with joy.

It was almost lunchtime when Tara finished and went to fetch James.

"Close your eyes," she said excitedly.

"Really?" He tilted his head to one side.

"Yes." She stood in front of him to block his path. "Close them."

He sighed then did as he was told. Tara took his hand and led him through the shop, trying to ignore the way her heart rate quickened.

"Can I open them?" he asked when they stopped.

"No," Tara said, realising it wasn't the best view. "You need to look from outside. Like the customers see it."

"Are you trying to freeze me?" he asked when she opened the door and they were enveloped by an icy gust of wind.

"It'll only take a minute." She shivered and pulled him outside. Her hand was still holding his when they stopped on the pavement. "Okay. You can look now."

His eyes snapped open but he didn't react, just stared ahead.

"What do you think?" she asked.

He loosened his grip on her hand, then entwined his fingers with hers. Tara's stomach felt as though she'd taken a sudden dip on a rollercoaster. Her instinct was to let go, but instead she tightened her grip.

"I love it," he whispered.

"Come and see the other one." She pulled him to the other window. The usual tree branches had been spruced up with some fake snow and blue and silver baubles.

"I like it," James said then released her hand and moved back to the other window.

"I can see which you prefer," Tara said.

"That one's for adults," he said with a boyish grin. "This one's magical."

"Come on." She held the door open. "Before we freeze."

"I can't wait for Christmas now," James said as he walked inside. "Which reminds me. What do you think I should do about opening the shop over Christmas?"

"I don't know." She followed him to the back of the shop. "What were you thinking?"

"I suppose I'll either close between Christmas and New Year, or open for reduced hours."

Tara's knee-jerk reaction was that they should open, but she wasn't sure why. It probably made more sense to close. She suspected her reasons for wanting the shop to be open were linked to the way she'd reacted to holding James's hand rather than any logical business decision. If they didn't open between Christmas and New Year it would be almost two weeks that she wasn't at work. Almost two weeks of not seeing James.

"It probably makes sense to open," she said, feeling utterly pathetic. "You can see how it goes and make an informed decision next year."

He frowned. "I kept telling myself it probably isn't worth opening."

"You might be right." Her stomach knotted at the thought. "Do whatever you think."

"I think you're right," he said. "I should open. If it ends up being a waste of time at least I'll know for next year."

"Yes." She felt a ridiculous rush of relief at not having the time off.

"We won't both need to be here," James said, breaking her bubble. "And you're definitely owed some holiday time."

She stared at him, unable to find any words. There was no way she could argue her way out of that without sounding like a crazy person. Or a person who enjoyed their boss's company too much.

Suddenly, she was far less excited by the thought of Christmas.

Chapter 19

December flew by. Tara loved the buzz in the air in the run-up to Christmas. She chose Christmas-themed books to read at the story times, and the kids got more excited the closer it got to the big day. The customers seemed to be in a better mood, and work was more enjoyable than ever. The trouble for Tara was that she loved the run-up to Christmas far more than Christmas itself.

The tradition was to spend the evening at the Bluebell Inn on Christmas Eve. That was always fun. After that she'd have Christmas Day with her mum, which was pretty hit and miss. The range was from absolute disaster of a day to fine but boring. A boring Christmas Day was about as much as she could hope for. Tara tried to be pragmatic; it was just another day and it really didn't matter if it wasn't anything special.

James wasn't opening the shop on Christmas Eve since his parents were visiting and he had family parties to attend. The day before Christmas Eve was a weird one. Tara felt ridiculously melancholy about her stretch of time off work.

"Have you got anything fun planned for your time off?" James asked, breaking her thoughts. She'd been straightening the shelves out in the children's corner but had paused in a daydream.

"No," she said. "I'll probably laze around the house and sleep a lot."

"And you'll have Christmas Day with your mum?"

"Yeah." They'd already discussed their Christmas traditions and he'd seemed fairly surprised by her quiet Christmas with her mum. James's Christmas sounded much more lively. His whole family was going to his sister's house, including aunts and uncles and cousins and nieces and nephews.

He smiled warmly. "I'll probably be envious of your quiet Christmas after two days with my family. They're pretty loud."

"It sounds like fun," Tara said.

He checked his watch. "You can go home if you want." There was only half an hour until closing time and the shop had been quiet all day. "I've got something for you," he said, reaching under the counter.

"I've got something for you too." She'd had no idea whether or not they'd exchange gifts but had got him something in case. A set of pens with his name engraved alongside the name of the shop. And some novelty Christmas socks for some fun.

"Christmas bonus," he said, handing her a white envelope.

Tara felt like a complete idiot. Of course he wouldn't give her a gift. "Thank you," she muttered. "I've got a Christmas card for you."

Quickly, she walked into the back and pulled her

coat on. Then she grabbed her bag and took the card out while shoving his gifts to the bottom.

"Happy Christmas!" she said with false cheer as she handed him the card.

"Thanks. Enjoy your time off." He gave her a brief hug. "Merry Christmas."

She left as fast as she could. Once she got home, she sat on the couch staring into space. Reaching into her bag, she pulled out the envelope from James and looked inside. There wasn't even a card, just money. She wanted to shake herself for being such a fool.

**

Generally Christmas Eve at the Bluebell Inn was great fun. But not that year. The place seemed to be full of happy couples, and all Tara could think about was James. He was occupying her every thought and she hated the idea of not seeing him for so long.

She left the pub early and woke up without a hangover, which was odd for Christmas Day. Her mum wasn't an early bird, so there was no rush to go over to her place. Tara lazed in bed until the middle of the morning, then had cereal for breakfast before getting ready to go to her mum's house.

"Happy Christmas!" she shouted as she let herself in.

"Happy Christmas." Debbie smiled sadly but didn't get up from the couch.

"I thought you were going to put the turkey in already." Tara placed her handbag and a bag of gifts beside the table. It didn't smell like there was any food cooking.

"I didn't get one in the end." Debbie's bottom lip twitched. "I'm sorry."

"It's fine." There was always a bit of an issue about what to eat at Christmas. With just the two of them it was hard to know how much effort to go to. When Tara had spoken to her mum a few days ago they'd decided to have turkey. Since they didn't have much to fill the day, cooking a big meal was a nice distraction, even if it was only for the two of them. "What did you get instead?"

"I didn't manage to get to the shop." Debbie was staring at her hands, and tears trickled down her cheeks. "I kept thinking it's not worth it when it's just the two of us."

Tara sat down and took deep breaths. It was Christmas and they had no food to eat. She'd almost done the shopping herself but her mum had insisted she wanted to do it. The last time they'd spoken, her mum sounded fine. With each level breath, Tara told herself not to get angry.

"I hate that it's just the two of us," Debbie mumbled.

Tara's eyes filled with tears. She blinked them away. "Well, I'm very sorry that you're stuck with me," she said bitterly. "But in case you haven't noticed, you're all I've got too. But I don't sit around complaining about it."

"I'm sorry." Her mum reached for her hand. "I didn't mean it like that. It's just a difficult time of year. I should have got food."

"We can go to the pub for lunch," Tara suggested, wiping tears from her eyes. "Andy will feed us."

"I don't feel like going out. I thought maybe you could go over to Annette's. You said Sam and Josie are going over there, didn't you? And what about Max? Will he be there with his little family?"

"I think so." The twins had arrived safely into the world in November but Tara hadn't met them yet.

"I bet you'll have a great time," Debbie said. "I'm quite happy on my own."

"I can't turn up at someone else's house on Christmas Day." That wasn't really true. Annette would always welcome her. It would be so embarrassing though. Besides, she couldn't leave her mum alone.

"They won't mind," Debbie said. "Or you could go to Amber's house."

Tara shook her head. "Can't you understand how pathetic I would feel turning up to someone else's family party? What am I supposed to say, that my mum kicked me out so I have nowhere to go? Because I'd rather go and sit at home alone."

"I'm not kicking you out." Debbie sniffed loudly. "I'm sorry."

"Stop apologising," Tara snapped. "I'll see what I can find for lunch."

The best she could do was frozen pizza. After the initial shock of the lack of Christmas dinner, Tara went back to determinedly telling herself it was just another day and it really didn't matter. After they ate, they exchanged gifts and had an awkward video call with her dad late in the afternoon. Her half-brother and sister came on to say hello and happy Christmas. Tara forced herself to act cheerful as she wished them all a happy Christmas back.

As the afternoon wore on, Debbie migrated to the computer and gave up on Tara in favour of her online group. Tara lay on the couch and read the book she'd brought with her. It was a crime thriller, the third in a series. It kept her absorbed for a few hours while her mum tapped away on her keyboard.

When Tara made a move to go home it was late.

"I'm sorry about lunch." Debbie stood to hug her.

"It doesn't matter," Tara said. "I'll see you soon. Call if you need anything."

Debbie came to the door and waved her off. As she drove through Newton Abbot, Tara automatically glanced at the bookshop and was surprised to see the lights on upstairs. Puzzled, she pulled the car over. She thought James would be staying in Exeter. Should she go in and wish him happy Christmas? It was so tempting. Except he might not be alone. Maybe he had friends over. Or Olivia could be there with him. Tara almost drove away again, then paused, not wanting to spend the evening on her own. Her phone beeped and she reached into her bag for it. There was a message from James.

Are you doing a stakeout?

Leaning against the car window, she looked up and saw him standing in the window, phone in hand. Her heartbeat sped up as she tapped out a reply.

On way home from mum's. Was going to call and say hi. You busy?

She watched him read the message and waited with bated breath for a reply.

He told her to come up.

Chapter 20

"Happy Christmas!" James kissed her cheek as he held the door open. Thankfully he didn't comment on the fact that she'd been sitting outside his apartment like a crazy stalker.

"Happy Christmas," she replied. "How was your day?"

"Great. Pretty chaotic at my sister's place but it was fun."

"That's good." She smiled awkwardly, wishing her Christmas had been chaotic and fun. "I thought you'd be staying at your place in Exeter."

His eyebrows twitched. "The heating's playing up over there." He pursed his lips. "There's a pizza in the oven if you're hungry."

"Great." Pizza for lunch *and* dinner! That was fairly depressing. As she hung her coat she thought back to the first time she'd eaten pizza with James – when he'd offered her a job. "I thought you don't like to share pizza."

He smiled. "I'll make an exception seeing as it's Christmas. Plus, I don't really think I need to eat much. I ate so much today. I'm just being greedy now."

In the living room she stood by the window to

look down on the quiet street. "This place is looking better." She scanned the room. It really was much nicer than when she'd previously seen it. The kitchen was drab and old, but things were neater and looked much more homely. It felt lived in. "Do you think you might give up your place in Exeter one of these days?"

"Maybe." His gaze shifted to the floor. "I still can't quite believe Richard left me this place. And that I didn't just sell it. I actually run a bookshop." He chuckled. "It's weird."

"I think it suits you."

"I'm not sure about that." His face fell serious. "I couldn't have done any of it without you."

Tara walked over and sat on the couch. "That's not true. I don't think you really needed me at all."

"I hope you don't really believe that." His eyes sparkled as he smiled. "I didn't have you pegged as deluded."

"Anyone could have helped you," she said.

The look he gave her was so intense she couldn't hold his gaze. It was a relief when the timer beeped in the kitchen and James went to get the pizza.

"Not exactly a gourmet meal," he said as he set it on the coffee table. "But I presume you ate enough turkey dinner to sustain you for a week." She took a slice of pizza and didn't respond. "Didn't you have turkey?" he asked, watching her closely.

"We don't have a set tradition." She didn't want to have this conversation. Her Christmas celebration didn't exactly fill her with pride. "Sometimes we have turkey. Sometimes we don't."

206

"This year?" he asked.

She took a bite of pizza and chewed slowly. "This year we had pizza."

Grinning, he took a huge bite. "What did you really have?" he asked when he'd swallowed his mouthful.

"Pizza," she said. "But it had ham on it so technically I could say I had pork."

He stared at her. "Are you serious?"

"Who cares?" she said. "It's just another day. And it was only me and Mum. There's not much point cooking a huge meal for two." She was about to take another bite, but James took the pizza slice from her and dropped it back onto the plate. Stunned, she watched as he took the pizza back to the kitchen. "What are you doing? I'm hungry."

"You can't eat pizza twice on Christmas Day," he called from the kitchen. She heard the fridge open and close again. "I'll find something else."

"I'm really okay with pizza. Not everyone has some idyllic family Christmas, you know." She hadn't intended to sound as bitter as she did. "Besides, I like pizza."

Up until then she thought she'd been doing a great job at keeping her emotions in check. All day she'd told herself it was just another day and it really didn't matter at all. But the way James looked at her when he walked back into the living room made her want to curl up and cry.

"Did something happen?" he asked.

"No." She blurted out a humourless laugh. "It was a fairly standard Christmas. If I had a choice I'd skip

207

the day altogether."

"I'm sorry."

"It's fine. I'm used to it." That wasn't anywhere close to the truth. You'd think she'd be used to it, but somehow every year was a fresh disappointment.

The microwave beeped. "Come on," James said. "I'm going to make you eat at the table."

"A proper sit-down meal?" She followed him to the kitchen and pulled out a chair, curious as to what he was about to present her with. "It smells good." She bit her lip when he put the plate in front of her. "You just whipped this up, did you? A full turkey dinner in four minutes?"

"I might have to give my sister credit for that." He sat opposite her and tucked into the pizza. "She sent me home with leftovers for tomorrow. Apparently she thinks I can't look after myself and don't eat properly."

Tara was still staring at the turkey dinner in front of her. It smelled delicious.

He shot her a look. "Eat up."

Swallowing the lump in her throat, she picked up her knife and fork.

"Thank you," she said quietly.

"You're welcome."

They fell into a comfortable silence as she greedily devoured the turkey dinner. When she finished, she leaned back in the chair and stretched her legs out. "That was so good. Thank your sister for me."

"I will." He paused, an odd look on his face. "I have two really important questions, and you have to answer honestly."

"Okay," she said, hoping he wasn't about to delve into her dysfunctional family history.

His eyes narrowed. "What's your favourite flavour of ice cream?"

"That's your important question?" she asked through a laugh.

"Yep."

She thought for a moment. "Mint choc chip."

"Really?" He frowned.

"Yes. You said be honest. Are you going to tease me about my ice cream choice now?"

"No." He went to the freezer and moved things around. Tara glanced over his shoulder.

"Oh, my God." She laughed as she went over for a better look. "Your freezer is full of ice cream."

His cheeks pinked and he nudged her out of the way. "I like ice cream," he said sheepishly.

"That's a lot of ice cream. You're like a big kid."

"You can't come over and tease me on Christmas Day." He pulled a tub from the freezer and held it up. "Mint choc chip," he said proudly.

"Ooh. That's not cheap stuff either."

"Of course not. There are some things in life that are worth spending more money on."

"Ice cream?" she asked as he took two spoons from the drawer.

"Yes. You should always pay more for a good bed, good shoes and good ice cream."

She smiled as they went back into the living room. "What's the second question?"

He dropped onto the couch. "What's your

favourite film from when you were a kid? Something you feel nostalgic about."

She squinted as she thought about it. "*E.T.*"

He shook his head. "Second favourite?"

"*The Neverending Story.*"

He shrugged. "Third?"

"*The Goonies*," she said after a pause.

"Good choice." He handed her the ice cream. "You get started on that. I'll find *The Goonies*. This is a Christmas tradition for you. Every year, no matter how your day goes, you eat your favourite ice cream and watch a favourite film."

She nodded and looked at him seriously. *With you*, she wanted to say. If she could end every Christmas with James, eating ice cream and watching films, she'd never have to dread it again. He was absorbed in finding the film and was oblivious to her eyes on him.

"For someone who doesn't actually live here, you have it set up quite nicely." Tara looked pointedly at the three remotes in front of him.

"I'm here quite a lot," he said.

Tara peeled the lid from the tub of ice cream. "You don't bother with bowls?"

He raised an eyebrow. "If ice cream was meant to be eaten from bowls, they wouldn't sell it in tubs."

"That makes no sense." She put a spoonful in her mouth and groaned.

He gave her a cheeky grin. "Told you it's worth paying more for. You can't put a price on anything that makes women moan on your couch."

She playfully slapped his arm, then passed him a

spoon as he pressed play on the film. The ice cream didn't last long, and when James leaned back and ran an arm along the back of the couch, she was tempted to snuggle in beside him. Instead she moved over and lay with her head on the arm of the couch. Being so close to him felt like a test of her willpower. As the film went on, increasingly all she could think about was kissing him.

By the time the end credits came up, James was snoring gently. Tara watched him sleep for a moment before nudging him awake.

"I'm going to go," she whispered.

He stretched his neck as he blinked his eyes open. "Okay."

Her heart rate went into overdrive. It was such a struggle not to lean down and kiss him. She was certain he wouldn't complain. She was also fairly sure she didn't need to go home if she didn't want to. And a huge part of her didn't want to.

"Thanks so much." Finally, she exhaled and stood up. "You're the best boss ever."

He looked weary as he followed her to the door. She lingered in the doorway with an overwhelming urge to kiss him. It was so tempting to put all her worries and doubts aside and act on her feelings for a change.

"Thank you for the leftovers," she said sheepishly.

"You're welcome." He gave a half-hearted smile and leaned against the door frame.

"Goodnight," she said.

He watched her walk down the stairs. "Goodnight."

Chapter 21

Tara lazed in bed all Boxing Day morning and then moved downstairs to take up position on the couch. There was nothing interesting on TV so she picked up a book and stared at the page. It was hard to concentrate. She thought of James and the previous evening with him. It had been such a wonderful end to the day.

In the middle of the afternoon she got a message from Sam inviting her to join them at Annette's place. Apparently he and Josie were there, as well as Max and Lizzie with the twins. It wasn't a very appealing invitation. Too many happy couples for her liking. She politely declined. Later, she had a phone call from Amber asking if she wanted to go down to the Bluebell Inn. Again, she declined, saying she was far too comfy on her couch and had no intention of getting changed out of her pyjamas for the day.

If there was anyone she wanted to see it was James. But she knew that giving in to her desire to spend time with him would land her with problems later. There was no way things could work out between them, so it seemed cruel to start something.

At dinnertime she peered into the fridge and

wondered what James would eat since she'd eaten his leftover Christmas dinner. Before she had chance to think it through, she grabbed her phone and pressed dial on his number.

"I was just going to make some spaghetti for dinner," she said after a quick greeting. "And I was worried about you just eating ice cream all day so I thought you might want to join me ..."

There was a pause before he accepted the offer, surprise evident in his voice. He told her he'd be over in half an hour. Tara stared at the phone for a moment after they ended the call. She was part elated and part terrified. Hastily, she went upstairs to get ready. Half an hour wasn't long to make yourself look great, but in a way that also seemed like you'd made no effort whatsoever. That was the look she was going for.

When he arrived on the doorstep, she'd had a shower and put on a pair of figure-hugging jeans and a pale-blue cashmere pullover.

James shrugged off his coat and hung it on the rack. He was wearing jeans and a long-sleeved T-shirt with the sleeves pushed up to reveal his toned forearms. When he kissed Tara's cheek she got a whiff of his aftershave and realised she was doomed. The battle against her feelings for him surely couldn't last much longer. Fighting it was tiring, and she was running out of energy.

"You're a lifesaver," he said. "I'm starving and I couldn't be bothered to go shopping."

"You fed me yesterday." She walked back to the kitchen and ignored the way her heart was banging furiously against her ribs. "It only seems fair that I return the favour."

"I brought wine," he said, holding up a bottle of white.

"Perfect." She passed him a bottle opener and two glasses. "You do drinks. I'll start cooking."

It was ridiculous how self-conscious she felt. How was it possible to feel uncomfortable around him when she'd spent most of her waking time with him over the past six months? Actually, it was coming up to a year since she'd met him. It was hard to believe it was almost a year since Wendy died. That had been the first time James had made a bad day so much better.

"Can I do anything?" he asked as she chopped onions.

"No. Just relax."

"I'm quite good at that." He leaned back in the chair as he stretched his legs out.

Tara felt his eyes on her as she cooked and was glad she'd chosen a quick and easy dish to make.

"I'm not the best cook," she warned him, more to fill the silence than anything. "And I very rarely cook for anyone apart from myself and my mum, so you'll have to say it's good no matter what."

"I'll say it's amazing," he said through a gentle laugh.

"I'd appreciate that." She put the pasta in to boil and sat at the table with him. The silence made her nervous.

"Thanks for inviting me over," he said.

"You're welcome. What did you do today?"

"Not much. Usually I go out round the local pubs on Boxing Day with a bunch of friends in Exeter. I couldn't be bothered to go this year. I probably wouldn't have made it out of the apartment at all if you hadn't called."

"I probably wouldn't have got changed out of my pyjamas if you hadn't come over," she said.

"Aw. I'm honoured. You really needn't have bothered getting dressed on my account though."

"It was quite nice to have a reason to." The water was beginning to boil over, so she went and turned the hob down.

"What do you usually do on Boxing Day?" he asked.

"I don't really have a lot of traditions over Christmas and New Year." She leaned on the counter. "Usually I'm very lazy. I tend to spend a lot of time watching TV in my pyjamas. That's a bit sad, isn't it? Do I sound pathetic?"

"Depends on whether you do it because you want to or because you have no choice. I bet you have loads of invitations to do stuff."

Turning her attention to dinner, she avoided eye contact. He was right that she had plenty of invitations. But at the same time, staying home alone didn't feel like her first choice of things to do. Christmas had always been difficult, and she'd found the easiest way to deal with it was to keep to herself.

Conversation became easier the more wine she drank, and she relaxed as they ate.

"What did you think?" she asked when he finished

his plate of pasta.

"It was amazing," he said with a smirk.

"Great." She gave him a gentle kick under the table. "Now I'll never know how you really feel about my cooking."

"I think you're a good cook," he said. "And I definitely wouldn't say no if you wanted to cook for me again sometime."

"Maybe I will." She cleared the plates and left them beside the sink. "Now, I have two important questions for you."

"I presume they're deep and probing and will make me very uncomfortable."

"Absolutely."

"Go on then."

She grinned. "What is your favourite flavour of ice cream?"

His eyes locked with hers. "Mint choc chip."

She spluttered a laugh.

"I'm serious," he said.

"No, you're not!"

"I am."

"I don't believe you."

"You don't have to believe me," he said lightly. "It's still true."

She moved towards the living room, tipping her head to indicate he should follow.

"What about the ice cream?" he asked.

"I don't have ice cream." She waited for him to sit on the couch and then sat close beside him.

"You're such a tease," he said.

"I never said there was ice cream. I was only

curious about your favourite."

"You're mean. Don't ever talk about ice cream unless you're going to feed me some. What's the next question?"

Turning sideways, she pulled her legs under her. "What is your third-favourite film from your childhood?"

He leaned back, slinging an arm along the back of the couch behind Tara. "My third-favourite?"

"You can list your top three if you want."

He blew out a long breath. "It's probably going to be *E.T.*, *The Neverending Story* and *The Goonies*."

She gave him a shove, then leaned closer into him.

"Okay." He sighed. "Maybe *The Mighty Ducks*, *Back to The Future* and … *Home Alone*."

She nodded approvingly. "Good choices."

"Which one are we watching?"

"None," she said, smiling. "I don't have a fancy TV set-up like you. Unless it happens to be on TV now we can't watch it. And that seems pretty unlikely."

He looked at her TV. "Is that a DVD player?"

"Yes."

"Wow. I didn't know people still watched DVDs."

"Well they do. Stop teasing me."

"I'm fairly sure it's you teasing me with all your talk of ice cream and favourite films."

"I'm not teasing." She rested her hand on his arm, and her heart rate went through the roof. "Thank you for yesterday."

"You're welcome. I didn't really do much."

Slowly, she reached for his hand and entwined her

fingers with his. Her stomach felt like it turned a somersault. "Every time I have a bad day, you make it better."

He ran his thumb over the back of her hand. When she put a hand to his face, his features turned serious. She felt the hint of stubble along his jaw, and her heart felt like it might smash through her ribcage.

"Do you want more wine?" she asked, pulling away abruptly.

His eyebrows dipped.

"I'm going to get more wine," she said. "I'll top you up." Picking up the glasses, she hurried for the kitchen. She took the bottle from the fridge and breathed deeply. Then she jumped when James appeared behind her.

"Did you forget to open a Christmas present?" he asked, pointing to the neatly wrapped gift on top of the fridge. Tara's eyes widened. It was the gift she'd bought for him.

James looked from her to the gift. The tag was sticking up and his name was clearly visible.

"Is it for me?" he asked.

"No." She squeezed her eyes shut. "Maybe."

He reached for it but she snatched it from him.

"Let me open it," he said, laughing.

"No. It's not really for you." She put it behind her and backed away from him. He followed her, trapping her when she bumped into the counter.

"You're not having it," she said, laughing as he reached around her.

"But it's got my name on. It's mine!"

219

"It's really boring and I already changed my mind about giving it to you."

He backed off slightly. "I got you something too."

"I know. A wad of cash. Thanks."

He dragged his teeth over his bottom lip. "I got you a proper gift but I chickened out and just gave you your bonus."

She shook her head. "You're just saying that to make me feel better."

"No. I decided there was probably something in that business course about not giving employees jewellery for Christmas, so I changed my mind at the last minute."

"You bought me jewellery?"

"Yes. What did you buy me?"

When he reached for the gift again she pushed it along the counter and put a hand on his arm. Then she reached up and pulled his face to hers. As their lips met she closed her eyes and inhaled the scent of him. Their kisses were soft and lingering and wonderful.

When they finally broke apart, a smile spread over James's face. "Did you just kiss me to stop me looking at the present?"

"No," she said. "I kissed you because I'm fed up of not kissing you. You're welcome to open the gift if you really want to."

"I think I might have lost interest in it," he said, moving to kiss her again.

Chapter 22

Waking up with James felt incredible. Their legs were tangled among a mess of bedding, and Tara's naked body was nestled against his.

"Good morning," he said in a gruff voice as soon as her eyes fluttered open.

"Morning." She rested her chin on his chest as he trailed his fingers up and down her back.

"I'm supposed to open the shop in an hour," he said.

"That's a shame," Tara said. "Don't you have an assistant or someone who could open up for you?"

"It's her day off," he said. "And I'm fairly sure she's busy."

"Really?" Tara raised an eyebrow. "Busy doing what?"

He lifted his head to kiss her. "I think she said she'd be lazing around in bed between Christmas and New Year."

"Sounds nice," she mumbled against his lips.

"It does." He took a break from kissing her. "Why on earth did you tell me to open the shop today?"

"I have some bad ideas sometimes." She smiled as a wave of happiness swept over her. Her worries about the future had been put aside and it felt unbelievable. "I was thinking of doing some shopping today," she said. "I need new books."

He pushed her hair behind her ear. "Are you going to come and hang out at work with me?"

"If I can curl up in the armchair and read while you bring me cups of tea and biscuits."

"I think that could be arranged." He rolled her onto her back, making her laugh. Then he kissed her so deeply that the laughter disappeared in an instant.

When she arrived at the shop later that morning, James gave her her Christmas gift: a beautiful gold necklace with a heart pendant. She could see why he'd decided it was inappropriate. Tara spent most of the day curled up in the armchair amongst the shelves, diving into other worlds within the pages of the books. It was hard to believe that a year ago she wasn't a reader at all. Now, she felt like there were too many books and not enough time.

Frequently, she glanced at James through the shelves and thought of the previous night with him. She couldn't wait until closing time so she could have him all to herself again.

Belinda from the chemist came in at the end of the day. Her only objective seemed to be flirting with James, and Tara watched them through the bookshelves, leaning on the arm of the chair to get a better view. Belinda didn't even have any pretext for being there. You'd think sometimes she'd at least pretend to browse. When James glanced in Tara's direction she turned her attention quickly back to her book. She couldn't quite catch the conversation but apparently James was telling jokes, because Belinda was laughing a lot.

As she was leaving, Belinda caught sight of Tara.

"Hello!" she said cheerfully. "I didn't even realise you were here."

"Hi," Tara replied. "Find any good books?"

"Social visit," she said, pushing her hair over her shoulder. "Will you be in the Bluebell on New Year's Eve?"

Tara usually celebrated in the Bluebell Inn, and Belinda was quite often in there too. She shrugged. "Probably."

"I might see you there then."

"Maybe." She went back to her book.

The bell tinkled as Belinda left.

"That wasn't very friendly," James said, appearing in front of her.

"She annoys me," Tara said. "And I'm not technically working, so I don't have to be friendly."

"Were you jealous?" He leaned casually on the bookcase.

"Because she comes in here to flirt with you? And you indulge her and make her giggle like a schoolgirl? No, I'm not jealous."

There was a gleam in his eye but he dropped the subject. "I think I'll close up. Do you want to go out for dinner?" He flipped the sign to "Closed" and locked the door.

"Not really." She snapped her book shut and went to the back of the shop. He followed her into the hallway.

"You don't want to have dinner with me?"

"I didn't say that." She snaked her arms around his neck. "But I've been waiting all day to get you alone. I don't really want to go out."

He kissed her gently before leading the way up to his apartment.

They spent the rest of the week with each other constantly. When the shop was open, Tara hung around there, even though she wasn't supposed to be working. Otherwise they spent all their time in the apartment above the shop.

On New Year's Eve, she woke up at his place late in the morning. He was propped against the headboard with a book in his hand. Tara had been through a Stephen King phase and had convinced him to read *Misery*. He seemed to be hooked.

"It gives me the chills just looking at the cover of that book," she said.

"I can only read it during daylight hours," he said with a boyish grin. Putting the book aside, he scooted down the bed and wrapped his arms around her. "I really love waking up with you."

"Me too." Goosebumps ran up her arm. The past week had been wonderful.

"Do you want to come to my sister's place with me this evening?" he asked. "Kate won't mind. She always throws a big party on New Year's Eve. The more the merrier."

"I told you, I always have dinner with my mum and then go to the Bluebell Inn."

"And I'm not allowed to come out with you socially?"

She rolled her eyes but didn't really have a good response. If her friends found out she and James were together it would be a big deal. Even the thought of it made her panic. Amber would start talking weddings and babies, without a doubt.

"Let's just keep this to ourselves for now," she said. "Take things slow."

"We've hardly been apart for a week," he said. "And we've seen each other almost every day for nearly a year. Why are we taking it slow?"

"Why not? Just because we've spent a lot of time together at work, doesn't mean we have to slip straight into a serious relationship."

He frowned. "If you wanted to take things slow, maybe you should have taken me out on some proper dates rather than dragging me into bed at every opportunity."

She giggled. "It sounds like you've had a terrible week. I'm very sorry. I promise to stop dragging you into bed."

"Don't stop." His arms tightened around her as he kissed her.

She pulled away slightly. "I don't want to be one of those couples who have to do everything together. I'll go out with my friends tonight. You go to your sister's place, and we'll meet up tomorrow."

"And am I allowed to tell people we're together?"

She trailed a finger down his cheek. "Can we keep it to ourselves for a bit?"

"I suppose so. But I'd really like to tell people."

"Let's wait a little while."

He rolled onto his back and put an arm behind his

head.

Tara felt a wave of guilt. "Why don't we do our own thing this evening, and then come back here after? I've got my key for downstairs. If you give me a key for up here, I can let myself in. Then it doesn't matter what time we come back, but we'll wake up together in the new year."

He gently pushed her hair off her face and hooked it behind her ear. "That sounds good."

Tara left James's place late that afternoon and nipped home to get showered and changed before getting a taxi to her mum's house. After opening the door, Debbie hurried back to the computer in the corner of the living room.

"Terri's having a terrible time," she said, staring at the screen. Terri was in her fifties and lived in New Zealand with a guy she didn't love, but she'd decided it was better to be with him than be alone. It was sad that Tara knew so much about these people she'd never met and never would meet.

"That's a shame." Tara dropped onto the couch and picked up a magazine.

"It's a difficult time of year," Debbie said. "But Terri's usually the one to jolly the rest of us along, so when she's down it gets us all down. Everyone's trying to cheer her up."

"Maybe if you all moved away from your computers and spent more time talking to the people around you rather than a bunch of strangers on the internet you'd all be happier."

"They're not strangers." Debbie tapped away and

didn't look up. "You know they're not. I've known a lot of them for twenty years now."

Tara curled her lip. Was it really that long that her mum had been throwing all her energy into the online connections? Why couldn't she live in the real world?

"What are we doing for dinner?" Tara asked.

"I'll probably just make a sandwich later. I thought you'd be eating in the pub with your friends."

"No. I thought we were eating together."

"I don't think I'm going to be much fun this evening. I'm so worried about Terri. And Sharon's really down too. They need some support. Don't feel you have to hang around. You go to the pub and have a good time."

Tara glared at her. Her mum was so engrossed in the computer screen she didn't even register Tara's annoyance.

"I'm going to get a sandwich here, if you don't mind."

Debbie mumbled a reply. Tara went into the kitchen. Drinking on an empty stomach was a bad idea, especially given how angry Tara was. She always drank too quickly when she was angry or in a bad mood. Her mum had definitely put her in a bad mood.

HANNAH ELLIS

Chapter 23

When she arrived at the pub, Tara slipped into upbeat and rowdy mode as always. As soon as she saw her friends, she let out an excited cheer and announced she was buying shots. She was sure she'd make a great actress. Really, the last thing she felt like doing was cheering.

Since it was New Year's Eve, Amber had got her mum to babysit and had her husband, Paul, with her. Then there was Sam and Josie. So many couples. Well, only two, but it felt like a lot. It would be so great to have James by her side, but she definitely wasn't ready to make their relationship public.

She ordered five shots of sambuca, then gave Sam a nod to get him to come and help her carry them.

"Everything all right with you?" he asked. "You've not been out much over Christmas."

"I'm fine," she said. "Or I will be when I've got a couple of these down me."

They walked back to the table and she passed the shots round.

Josie shook her head. "I'm not doing shots."

"What?" Tara blinked. "Who are you and what have you done with my friend?"

"Fine." Josie sighed and put her hand on Sam's

thigh when he sat back down beside her. "I'll have one but that's it. I don't want to be hungover all day tomorrow. We're going down to Hope Cove to see Lizzie and Max and the twins."

"How are they?" Amber asked. "Worn out, I'll bet?"

"I think so," Josie said, lifting her glass and knocking back the liquid with a grimace. The rest of them followed.

"There's no way I'm drinking shots," Amber said.

Both Tara and Paul reached for the spare drink, and Tara laughed as she got to it first. The burn of the alcohol on her throat felt good. She took a deep breath and relaxed.

"What've you been up to?" Amber asked. "You've not been around at all over Christmas."

"I've been working a bit," Tara replied. "And sleeping. Just chilling out really." An image of James popped into her head and she stifled a grin.

"Did you have a good Christmas with your mum?" Josie asked.

"Yeah, it was nice. Did you all have a good time?" She knew they'd all had a great time. Josie had messaged her and sent a load of photos of them all up at Annette's place.

"It was great," Josie said.

"I'm going to get another drink." Tara stood. "Anyone want anything?"

They declined, and as Tara headed for the bar she could hear Amber launching into a conversation about how Kieron kept running away from her at the park that afternoon.

Belinda was at the bar. She greeted Tara cheerfully.

"Hi," Tara said, then caught Andy's eye and asked him for a glass of wine.

"What's your lovely boss doing this evening?" Belinda asked.

"I think he said he had a family party. I'm not really sure."

"Shame. He's such a sweetie. Is he seeing anyone now?"

"Not that I know of." Tara took a sip of the wine when Andy brought it over. She avoided eye contact with Belinda.

"What happened with the blonde woman who was hanging round for a while?"

"I don't know." Tara moved away from Belinda and returned to her friends.

She sat quietly and nodded along with their conversations. It was all pretty mundane and Tara was distracted. The mention of Olivia made her wonder if she was at the party with James. Her mind kept flicking to the day Olivia had been in the shop, flirting with James and running her hand down his arm.

Pulling her phone from her bag, she was disappointed at the lack of messages. She thought James might have been in touch. Quickly, she typed a message asking if he was having fun.

A reply came immediately. *No. There's no fun without you x*

The smile came automatically, and she felt pathetic that a simple message could have such an

231

effect on her.

"Who are you messaging?" Amber asked.

"The taxi firm." She didn't look up from her phone and went into the taxi app to order a car. There was no way she could sit around with a bunch of couples all evening. She'd go back to James's place and watch TV until he came home.

"You're not leaving, are you?" Josie asked.

"There's live music in the Golden Lion in Newton Abbot. I'm going to go and check it out."

"I thought you'd be here until midnight," Josie complained.

"Sorry."

"Are you okay?" Amber asked. "You're very quiet. What's going on with you?"

"Nothing." She looked around the pub. "It's just a bit dull in here."

"We're too boring for you?" Josie asked with a smirk.

"Yes!" Tara said jokily. "Absolutely."

"One day you'll be just as boring as the rest of us," Amber said.

Paul sat up straighter. "I'd like to jump in and say that I'm not boring."

"Me neither," Sam said, taking a sip of his pint.

"You just keep telling yourselves that!" Tara finished her wine in a long gulp, then stood and pulled her coat on. They hugged her goodbye and she wished them a happy new year before slipping away.

The taxi was already waiting for her outside, and she directed the driver to the Golden Lion pub. It was only a few minutes' walk from there to the bookshop. She didn't trust small-town gossip. There was a good chance Belinda would get the same driver taking her home, and she didn't want her hearing that Tara had gone back to James's place.

The fresh air was exhilarating too. It felt a little strange to let herself into James's apartment. She opened the door, then nearly jumped out of her skin. There was a lamp on in the living room, and James was sprawled out on the couch.

She put a hand over her heart as she closed the door behind her. "I didn't think you'd be back for hours." She shrugged her coat off and walked over to him. When he reached for her hand, she climbed on top of him and kissed his lips.

"I missed you," he said. "I thought I'd just come back and wait for you." He checked his watch. "I wasn't expecting you so soon."

"I missed you too," she said. "It wasn't much fun in the Bluebell."

He frowned and stroked her hair.

"How was your party?" she asked.

"Fine. Kate makes great food."

"I don't suppose she gave you leftovers?"

"She always gives me leftovers," he said. "Help yourself."

"I love your sister." Tara went to the kitchen. There was lasagne in a Tupperware box, and she tipped it onto a plate and put it into the microwave.

"I thought you were eating with your mum," James said, leaning against the kitchen counter.

"I had a sandwich," she said.

"Is your mum okay?"

"Fine." Tara busied herself getting cutlery out. "I didn't stay long. Her friend called from New Zealand so I left her to chat." It sounded better than saying she was spending her evening chatting to a load of depressed women in an online support group. "Who was at the party?" she asked in a bid to deflect the conversation away from herself.

"The usual crowd. Nick, who you've met, and a few people I went to school with. There were some of Kate's friends with kids too."

"Sounds fun." Tara hovered by the microwave, impatiently waiting for it to beep. "Was your friend Olivia there?"

"Yeah." He paused. "Why do you ask?"

"No reason." When the microwave beeped she took her steaming dinner to the table.

"Do you have jealousy issues?" His voice was light as he took a seat opposite her.

"No," Tara insisted. "I just got the impression she liked you."

"We went on a few dates," he said. "Ages ago."

"What happened?"

"Not much. I didn't feel like we clicked. So we ended up being friends."

"So it was you who ended it?"

"I suppose so." He stretched his legs out under the table so they rested against hers. "Nothing had really started, so it wasn't a big deal. We just stopped going out alone."

"But she still hangs around with your friends?"

"Yeah. She works with Nick and she's friends

with everyone." His lips twitched upwards. "If you'd come and hang out with my friends, maybe you'd be friends with her too."

"I doubt it," Tara said automatically. "There's something about her. I don't trust her."

James laughed. "That's a bit dramatic. You only met her a few times. She's all right."

"I'll take your word for it."

"Tell me about your exes then. If you're going to delve into my dating history I'll do the same."

"Not much to tell." She put a big forkful of lasagne in her mouth.

"Who was the last person you dated?"

She shook her head as she swallowed her food. "I haven't dated anyone in years."

"Okay." His eyebrows knitted together. "How long did your last relationship last?"

"A couple of years." She didn't like this conversation. She avoided eye contact by concentrating on her food.

"What happened?" James asked.

"We broke up."

"Why?"

She shrugged. "It just didn't work out. Can you let me eat in peace, before it goes cold?"

He leaned back in the chair and she could feel his eyes on her.

"Can you stop watching me eat?" she said. "You're making me self-conscious. I've probably got sauce all down my chin."

"Cheek," he said, leaning over and rubbing his thumb across her face.

She swatted him playfully away. "Leave me alone."

"Beer?" he asked as he peered into the fridge.

"No. I was doing shots. If I drink any more I'll feel terrible tomorrow."

"Do you want to do something tomorrow?" He cracked the lid off his beer. "The shop's closed. We could go out somewhere."

"Sounds good." She fell silent for a moment as she savoured the last mouthful of her dinner. "We could drive down to the coast. Go for a walk and get dinner somewhere?"

James nodded. "I thought you might insist on staying in. I wasn't sure if you were keeping this relationship completely hidden from the world."

After she put her plate in the dishwasher, she went and put her arms around James. "It's been a week. And you've been working most of the time. Are you really complaining that we've spent most of our time together in your bedroom?"

"I'm not complaining at all." He tightened his arms around her. "Sorry. I didn't mean to sound annoyed. I just wanted to tell Kate about us, that's all."

"Tell Kate if you want." She leaned her forehead against his, and her heart raced. It had been inevitable that things would move quickly between them. They already knew each other too well to take things slow. It made her panic, but she pushed her worries aside.

"Really?" he asked.

She nodded. "I don't want to tell Amber yet

though. She'll make a huge deal of it."

"If I tell Kate, she'll insist we go over for dinner."

Snuggling into him, she buried her face in his shoulder so he couldn't see her expression. Spending time with each other's families scared the heck out of her.

"Okay." She took a deep breath. "Just tell her to make lasagne again."

Chapter 24

Tara's phone woke her up on New Year's Day. She fought to open her eyes and banged her hand on the bedside table as she grabbed for the phone. She was alone in James's bed and the smell of bacon invaded her nostrils.

"Hello?" she said into the phone, without checking who it was.

"Hiya, love." Her dad sounded morose. Tara frowned as she sat up.

"What's wrong?"

"Your mum was calling me last night," he said. "She was in a bit of a state. Now she's not answering her phone. Can you check on her?"

"*You* could go and check on her," she suggested angrily.

"It's a four-hour drive," he snapped. "And we've got plans today. I can't disappear and let everyone down."

"No. You'll stick to letting me and Mum down."

"Will you please check on her? I'm worried about her."

"No, you're not." Her voice got steadily louder. "You feel guilty. There's a huge difference. And you *should* feel guilty."

"I can't help her," he said. "I tried. All I do is make things worse."

Tara bristled. "Leave me to deal with her then. As always. Happy New Year, Dad." She hung up and squeezed her eyes tight shut. Then she tried calling her mum but got no answer.

"Are you okay?" James stood in the doorway, looking at her with eyes full of concern.

"Yes." She went over and gave him a quick kiss. "I have to go and check on my mum." Glancing over his shoulder, she noticed the two plates at the table. "You cooked breakfast," she said with a sigh.

"Yes. What was all that about on the phone?"

"My dad claims to be worried about my mum but he's too busy with his family to do anything about it."

"His family?" James cocked an eyebrow.

"He's married with two kids."

"That's weird," James said slowly.

"Not really. Lots of people have separated parents."

"I mean it's weird that you told me you don't have siblings. But you have two?"

"Technically, yes. But I don't have anything to do with them."

"So you're not close to your dad?"

"No. I don't have a lot of contact with him." She kissed James's cheek. "I'm going to jump in the shower and go over to Mum's."

"Breakfast?" he called as she moved towards the bathroom.

She grimaced. It was already plated up, but she

didn't have an appetite and she just wanted to check on her mum. "Sorry."

"Don't worry."

After the world's quickest shower, she was ready to leave in about five minutes.

"I'm really sorry about breakfast," she said. "I'll just be an hour and then we can go out like we planned."

He handed her a square package covered in aluminium foil. "Bacon sandwiches. You can have breakfast with your mum."

"You're the best." She put a hand on his cheek as she kissed him. "I won't be long."

When her mum didn't answer the door, Tara let herself in and walked through the house, calling out as she went.

"Upstairs," the feeble voice replied.

Tara breathed a sigh of relief as she trudged up to her mum's bedroom. "What's going on?" she asked as she perched on the side of the bed. Debbie had the covers pulled up to her chin. Tears streamed down her face, leading to a damp patch on her pillow. "Dad called and said you were upset."

"I only wanted to talk to him." She sniffed. "He didn't have time."

Tara dropped her head to her hands and rubbed at her temples. She'd actually been looking forward to spending the first day of the year with James. She should have known it wouldn't be that easy.

"I miss him." Her mum's voice was choked with emotion as she sobbed into the pillow. "I miss him so much."

Tara's throat constricted and she fought off tears. "You'll be okay," she said quietly as she sat on the bed and rubbed her mum's arm. Seeing her mum so upset never got any easier. Silently, she raged at her dad. After all the hurt he'd caused them, she was sure she'd never forgive him.

Eventually, Debbie's tears stopped and she drifted off to sleep. Tara stayed on the bed, staring at her mum. Her mind drifted to an early childhood memory.

She was in a park with her parents. Tara must have only been about five. Her dad was swinging her round by her arms. Every time he put her down, she begged him to do it again. He spun her in circles for what seemed like hours, while her mum was nearby on a picnic blanket, laughing as she watched them. All three of them were laughing.

Life had been so perfect when she was five years old. By the time she was seven, everything had fallen apart, and from then on so many of her memories were her mum crying or not being able to get out of bed.

Brushing the memories aside, Tara went downstairs and got on with some cleaning. She messaged James and said she'd be longer than she thought.

It was almost three hours later when her mum emerged. The tears had stopped, but she had a blank look in her eyes, like she was a zombie.

"Are you hungry?" Tara asked.

She shook her head and went to the cupboard to

retrieve her shoebox full of photos. Tara winced. The photos were from when they lived in London and they were a normal, happy family.

"That's not going to help," Tara muttered as she backed out of the room. She sat at the kitchen table and stared at the wall. It would be so easy to walk out of the front door and leave her mum to dwell on the past alone. But that would make her just as bad as her dad.

When Tara wasn't consumed with blaming her dad, she'd sometimes let herself be angry with her mum. How many days had Tara spent sitting with her mum and waiting for her to drag herself out of her fog of self-pity? It was exhausting being around her when she was like this, and Tara couldn't help but feel resentful from time to time. She was supposed to be out with James. Her day should've been so different.

"Are you okay, Mum?" Tara asked when she ventured back into the living room.

"I'm fine," she said. "You go home if you want."

"I can't leave you like this." Tara sank onto the couch beside her. "What do you want to do? We could watch a film."

"No," Debbie said.

"How about a walk?" Tara suggested. "Fresh air might do you good."

Debbie shrugged. "Okay."

Tara checked the time as they moved to put shoes and coats on. It was already the middle of the afternoon. Her plans with James were ruined.

They wandered the countryside around the village

at a snail's pace for over an hour. It was freezing, and Tara's toes were numb by the time they got home. Her mum seemed slightly better, and after making her some pasta, Tara left her alone.

Throughout the day, she'd sent messages to James, telling him she'd be a bit longer than she thought. Then a bit longer. And a bit longer still. When she finally left her mum's house, the whole day had gone by. She drove home, got changed into her pyjamas and got into bed with a cup of tea.

Wearily, she sent another message to James telling him she was home and she was sorry, and she'd see him at work the following day. Her phone rang almost immediately. For a moment she stared at it, contemplating not answering.

When she did answer, it was good to hear James's voice.

"Are you okay?" he asked.

"Yes. Just tired."

"Do you want to come over here?"

"I'm already in bed," she said apologetically.

"Shall I come to you?"

"No." She shuffled down in bed and pulled the covers around her. "I'm tired. I'll see you tomorrow."

There was a short pause. "I'm worried about you. I'll just come over."

"No," she said impatiently. "Don't come over. I said I'll see you tomorrow. I want to be on my own."

"Okay," he said. "I just wanted to check you're all right."

"I'm fine." She felt bad for snapping at him. He

was only concerned, but she couldn't stand the thought of him coming over and seeing her so fed up.

"I'll see you tomorrow then?"

"Yeah." She wished him goodnight and ended the call. The cup of tea went cold on the bedside table as she lay staring into space. Hopefully, the first day of the year wasn't an indicator of what was to come.

Chapter 25

Tara's sleep was fitful. It was almost sunrise when she finally fell into a deep slumber. She woke in a panic in the middle of the morning and vaguely remembered hitting the snooze button on her alarm a few times. Oh, great; she was late for work. Her intention had been to go early and clear the air with James. She felt terrible for being so irritable with him.

When she finally arrived at the shop, James was crouched beside the window display with Kieron. He gave her a weak smile.

Tara went inside as Josie appeared from behind a shelf with a cup of coffee in her hand. She enveloped Tara in a big hug. "Happy New Year!"

"You look rough," Amber said. "Please don't tell me you're still hungover from New Year's Eve."

"I need coffee," Tara said cheerfully. "I'll be fine when I get my caffeine fix." She glanced at James. "Morning."

"Hi," he said quietly, then went back to watching the train go round with Kieron.

"So how was the Golden Lion?" Josie asked as they walked back to the coffee machine. "More fun than hanging out with your boring friends?"

Tara's mind drifted to the evening she'd spent laughing and chatting with James. "It was fun," she said, wandering over to the counter. There was a stack of new books piled up.

"Did you already put these into the system?" she asked James as he slowly came over, bending to hold Kieron's hand as he toddled along beside him.

"Yeah. They just need to go on the shelves."

"Sorry I was late." She tried to hold his gaze but he turned his attention to Kieron instead.

"It doesn't matter."

"So how was your night in the Bluebell?" Tara asked her friends. "Did it get any livelier after I left?"

"It was really good fun," Amber said brightly.

Behind her, Josie shook her head, then mimed falling asleep.

"I'm going to nip out for a while," James said. "Can you hold the fort, Tara?"

"Yes." Again, she tried to catch his eye, but he only gave her a cursory glance before heading for the door and calling goodbye over his shoulder.

"Is he okay?" Amber asked. "He was quiet."

"I might be in trouble for being late for work again," Tara said with a grimace.

"If you're in trouble for being late it's only because he misses you when you're not here." Josie dropped into a beanbag and fluttered her eyelashes.

"Ha ha," Tara said dryly. She knelt down beside Kieron and tickled his tummy.

"Why don't you go out with him?" Amber asked in an annoyingly whiney voice.

248

"Why don't you stop asking?" Tara said. "This conversation is really getting old."

"You know how you could put an end to the conversation?" Josie said with a mischievous grin.

"Yes!" Tara rolled her eyes. "I'll date him just to shut you two up! What a great reason to go out with someone."

"I don't get it," Amber said. "You'd be so perfect for each other."

Tara rubbed at her forehead. "Can you please shut up?"

"We'll shut up as soon as you ask him out," Josie said.

Tara was almost tempted to tell them she'd spent most of the past week sharing his bed. It wasn't worth it though. Contrary to their claims, she knew for a fact it wouldn't shut them up. They'd have far more to say on the subject if they knew she was seeing him. Although, maybe she wasn't anymore. He seemed annoyed with her.

"How's Sam?" she asked in a bid to change the subject. "And Annette, and Max and Lizzie and the babies? Tell me about everyone."

"There's nothing to tell," Josie said. "That's why we need you to ask James out so we have something to talk about."

Tara reached for a teddy from the shelf and threw it at Josie's head. "Shut up!" she growled playfully.

Kieron thought it was a great game and started throwing cuddly toys too. That set Amber off on a lecture about modelling desirable behaviour. Which in turn made Tara and Josie throw toys at her head.

Thankfully, it drew the conversation away from James, and as an added bonus made Tara laugh.

Amber and Josie didn't hang around long once the cuddly toy war came to an end. Amber wanted to get Kieron home for his nap, and Josie needed to get back to the kennels and see to the dogs. That's what she claimed anyway. Tara knew it was more a case of needing to be back in time for lunch, which Annette would have ready for her. She was quite envious of Josie's job sometimes. Mainly at mealtimes. The thought of walking dogs around the countryside in all weather wasn't actually appealing at all.

There were only a few customers over the afternoon, and Tara became increasingly anxious about James's absence. With not much to do, time seemed to grind to a halt. Her mind was whirring, so she couldn't even lose herself in a book to pass the time.

It was mid-afternoon when James finally came back. The atmosphere was tense as soon as he walked in.

"You're avoiding me then?" Tara asked.

"I had some shopping to do." He held up the bags as proof.

"But you're annoyed with me? About yesterday?"

"No." His eyebrows dipped. "Not because of yesterday. Because it occurred to me how much you lie to everyone around you."

Her stomach felt like it had plummeted down in her body. "What?" she asked quietly.

"You have so many secrets. Amber's supposed to

250

be your best friend, yet you spend more time lying to her than telling her the truth."

"So you're angry that I didn't tell my friends about us?" she snapped.

He shook his head. "You blatantly lied to them about where you were on New Year's Eve …"

"Because I didn't want them to know I was with you," she said defensively.

"But you let them think you spent yesterday hungover and never mentioned the fact that you were looking after your mum."

"Because I don't want them to know that."

"Why?" His tone was harsh. "They're your closest friends. Amber would be so upset if she knew where you really were yesterday."

"That's the point," Tara said fiercely. "I don't want her pity. Or anyone's. I didn't want you to come over last night because I didn't want your sympathy."

"It's nothing to do with sympathy." James's voice dropped to a low whisper and his features softened. "It's about support from people who care about you."

"I don't need support," she said. "And what I choose to share with my friends, and what I choose to keep to myself, is nothing to do with you."

"But Amber's your oldest friend," he said. "And I'm not sure she knows you at all."

For a moment, Tara just glared at him, not trusting herself to speak. "This is why I didn't want to get into a relationship with you," she finally said. "It's none of your business and I don't need you

251

interfering in my life."

He moved beside her and leaned against the counter. "I'm sorry," he said, taking her hand. "I don't like secrets. And suddenly I keep finding out stuff. Like you have siblings who you've never mentioned."

"I told you, I don't think of them as siblings." Pulling her hand from his, she looked away. He was right; there was so much he didn't know about her. And so much she didn't want him to know. That was the trouble with relationships; people expected you to share everything. After spending most of her life keeping secrets and telling half-truths it was hard to open up to anyone.

The bell tinkled, interrupting them. It was Rupert, the old man who liked to browse and chat but never actually bought anything. The three of them called "hello" at the same time.

"Do you mind if I go home?" Tara asked James quietly. After hardly sleeping the night before she was exhausted. She knew that as soon as Rupert left, they'd be back into another conversation about her keeping secrets, and it wasn't something she particularly wanted to discuss.

James nodded. He'd never tell her to stay. Even if the shop was busy and he needed her, if she asked to leave she was sure he'd never say no.

"Can we talk later?" he asked.

"Yeah." She squeezed his hand and went to fetch her coat.

Sitting at home alone, Tara went over the events of the last week in her head. It had been so lovely with James and she hated that things were already starting to go wrong. It was inevitable, but it hurt nonetheless.

James called her early in the evening, right after the shop had closed. Tara answered the phone with a feeling of dread.

"Do you think we can go back to being just friends without it being awkward?" she asked after a brief greeting.

He sounded surprised. "Is that what you want?"

"I thought it was what you wanted," she said.

"No." He sighed. "It's definitely not what I want. I was just annoyed. When I heard you lying to Amber and Josie so easily, I wondered how much you lie to me."

Tara pushed her knuckle to her mouth as she fought off tears. "It's not lying. I'm careful how much I share with people. There's a difference."

He was quiet for a moment. "Okay."

"Did I tell you I'm not good at relationships?" she said weakly.

"I think you mentioned it." His voice was lighter and made Tara smile.

"I'm sorry," she said.

"Me too." There was a brief pause. "You'll never guess what."

"What?" she asked.

"Rupert bought a book!"

"No way." She laughed and it was a welcome relief.

"He did!" James told her all about Rupert finally deciding to buy a book and counting out the exact money in change.

The small talk was comforting, and Tara was glad that James didn't suggest meeting up that evening. They probably both needed some space. It occurred to Tara that perhaps that was part of their problem. Jumping into spending every minute of the day together was intense.

Chapter 26

The following day Tara woke before the sun rose feeling refreshed and filled with an overwhelming desire to see James. So much for giving each other space.

Everything was quiet when she let herself into the shop. Upstairs, she knocked and then let herself into the apartment. James stirred when she went into the bedroom. Blinking, he reached for his phone and squinted at the screen.

"Am I late for work?"

"No." She knelt beside the bed, her head by his chest. "I just wanted to check everything was okay between us."

Lifting the covers, he shuffled over to make room for her. She toed off one shoe and then the other before climbing into bed beside him.

Propping herself on an elbow, she looked at him seriously. "I think I'm so used to keeping things to myself that I don't even notice I'm doing it." She trailed her fingers over his upper arm. "I'll try not to keep secrets from you." As she said it, she felt panicky. It didn't seem like a promise she'd be able to keep. For a moment she wondered why she was even there. Things couldn't work out between them.

255

She was tormenting herself and setting them both up for heartbreak.

James took her hand and kissed her palm. "Everything will be fine. We'll figure things out."

"I was thinking we should try and see less of each other." She laid her head on the pillow next to him.

His boyish grin was adorable. "You might need to explain that sentence."

"Sorry." She laughed. "That sounded bad. I was just thinking how we skipped the dating stage. We already know each other so I guess that was inevitable, but it feels like we're rushing things."

"What's the plan?"

"I was thinking we could have dinner together on Friday, and maybe go for a day out on Sunday. And other than that we don't see each other apart from at work."

He frowned. "Is that a weekly schedule or just this week?"

"Just this week," she said. "Then next week we decide if we want to go on more dates."

"So I won't see you until Friday?"

"You'll see me every day at work!"

"Do I get to kiss you at work?"

"No."

"That doesn't count then."

She bit her lip, then leaned over to kiss him. It made her insides jittery, and she decided to get out quick before she lost self-control. After one last peck on the lips she sat up and swung her legs off the bed.

"Do you ever sleep at home anymore?" She glanced around the bedroom. Clothes were draped over a chair at the end of the bed but it was otherwise pretty tidy. She hadn't heard him mention going home for a long time.

"Every night," he said with a slight twitch of an eyebrow.

"What's that supposed to mean?"

"I got rid of my other place a while back."

She playfully slapped his chest. "Now who's got secrets?"

"Sorry." There was a flash of guilt in his features.

"Why didn't you tell me?"

He exhaled a long breath. "I didn't want you to know at the time."

"Why?" she asked, narrowing her eyes.

"Because it was around the time you got a pay rise and I didn't want you to think the two things were connected."

"That was ages ago," she said. "And I'm guessing the two things *were* connected?"

"Possibly," he said. "But it really didn't make sense for me to keep paying rent on a place I was hardly using."

She laid a hand on his chest as he sat up. "You're a good boss, you know."

"I try," he said, leaning over to kiss her.

Standing, she smiled down at him. "See you at work."

***

Both of the story times were busy that week. It seemed as though the parents were desperate for indoor activities to get them through the winter months. Tara suspected the turnout would drop off again in the spring when the weather picked up. Time always went so quickly when story time was on. It was nice to have such a bustle of people in the shop, and Tara and James always had fun with the children. They knew most of them pretty well.

Apart from the odd bit of flirting, their working relationship remained the same. It was an effort not to kiss James when she arrived at work, or when she was leaving, but it meant she spent all week looking forward to the weekend.

On Sunday they drove to the coast and had a lovely long walk before stopping off for a pub lunch. They'd just finished eating when Tara's phone beeped with a message from Amber. She scanned it quickly, then put it aside and returned her attention to James as he told her about his parents' place in France in the middle of the countryside.

"It sounds amazing," she said vaguely.

"What's wrong?" he asked.

"Nothing."

"You got a message on your phone and now you look worried. Who was it?"

"Amber," she said with a sigh. "Asking if I'm feeling better."

"Were you ill?"

"No. But when you came over on Friday I told her I couldn't go to the pub because I didn't feel great." Instead of her usual Friday evening in the Bluebell Inn, she'd spent the evening cuddled up on her couch with James. "Since you mentioned me lying I realised I do it a lot, but it's not like it's malicious. It's not hurting anyone."

"But it's bothering you?"

"Yes." She glared at him. "Because you made me feel bad about it."

"Sorry," he said with a cheeky grin. "How are you and Amber friends anyway? You're complete opposites."

Tara smiled. They really were an unlikely pair. "Quite by accident," she said. "I moved to Averton when I was seven. Mum moved us at the start of the summer holidays and I didn't know anyone. Amber lived on our street. She's five years older than me, so we really should never have been friends. With hindsight, I think she didn't have many friends her own age because she was geeky and annoying." She thought of twelve-year-old Amber, who'd seemed to have the soul of a little old lady. "Anyway, she took me under her wing and treated me like her pet. Nothing much has changed."

James tilted his head to one side. "So, do you even like each other?"

"Yes." Tara reached for her phone and shot off a quick message telling Amber she was fine and having a lazy day at home. "Of course I like her."

The first few months that Tara lived in Averton, Amber had looked out for Tara when her own mother was incapable. While it should have been annoying to have a big kid bossing her around, it was actually very comforting.

She caught James watching her intently. "Amber's mum was friends with Annette and Wendy at the kennels," she said. "And Amber used to take me over there to play with the dogs. Sam and Max would be there a lot too and we'd all play together."

"Sounds like an idyllic childhood in the countryside," he said.

"Yes." Her smile faded at yet another lie. "Come on." She stood and picked up her coat. "Let's walk some more."

As they stepped out of the pub the wind whipped around them. James draped an arm around her shoulders.

"You could always message Amber and tell her you're having a day out with your boyfriend."

Tara leaned into him. "I'm not ready to tell her we're seeing each other yet."

"You won't even refer to me as your boyfriend in private!" he said jokily.

She nudged his arm away as they wandered back onto the coastal path. The view over the water was breathtaking and she stopped for a minute to take it in. "We've only been seeing each other a matter of weeks. I think you're getting carried away."

"How long until you're my girlfriend then?" he asked, his eyes sparkling in amusement.

"I don't know." She took his hand and headed for the stretch of beach nearby. South Milton Sands was a popular tourist beach in the summer months, but in the freezing weather it was deserted. Tara was well wrapped up, and it was difficult to worry about the cold when she had James's hand in hers.

"I suppose if you're not my girlfriend, I can tell you about the woman I fancy at work?"

Tara laughed loudly as they stepped onto the sand. "That sounds awkward."

"It is. Every time I look at her I think about kissing her. And she gets away with a lot – she's late for work all the time, and she leaves whenever she wants …"

Tara gave him a friendly elbow to the ribs, then turned serious. "You know you can actually tell me off for being late."

"I was joking," he said.

"But I *am* late for work a lot. And you never say anything."

"Are you complaining that you don't get into trouble for being late to work?" He pulled her hand to his face and kissed it as they wandered along the beach.

"Not complaining," she said. "Just commenting. You've never treated me like you're the boss and I'm an employee."

They reached the rocks that bordered the beach, and James leaned against them. He looked at her in amusement. "You run the bookshop," he said. She squinted, not sure if he was teasing her. "When it comes to the day-to-day running of the place, you know far more than me."

"That's not true," she said quickly.

"You're the one who stays on top of ordering stock. You remember the names of all the customers and know what they like to read. You organise and run the story times, and you track down authors and bully them into doing signings."

"I don't bully anyone," she said, amused.

261

"But you do a heck of a lot." He stared out over the water. A few seagulls hovered at the shoreline, letting out the occasional squawk. "And while I'm not saying the place would fall apart without you, it definitely wouldn't do as well as it does." He turned to face her. "So I really don't care if you arrive twenty minutes late sometimes."

She caressed his cheek as she kissed his soft lips. "I have learnt a lot about bookshops," she said when they broke apart. "But I will never understand why you employed me."

His eyebrows drew together. "I had my reasons."

"Because you fancied me?" she asked cheekily.

"I did fancy you," he said. "But that's not why I gave you a job."

"Tell me then," she prompted when he fell silent.

His gaze shifted to his feet and then back to her. "When I first heard that Richard had left the shop to me, I had this crazy idea about quitting my job and opening a bookshop."

"It wasn't a crazy idea," Tara said, shaking her head.

"Everyone else thought it was." He entwined his fingers with hers and leaned closer so they were shoulder to shoulder. "Everyone thought I should sell the place and take the money." He sighed. "Then I met you in the pub. You told me about Wendy and how she'd inspired you to quit your job and find something you loved." Tara leaned her head on his shoulder as he told his story. "It made me think maybe I shouldn't sell the shop. Then, the next morning you wandered in, and even though the place was a dump, you had a vision for it which was exactly what I'd been imagining." He paused and kissed her head. "That's why I offered you a job."

They stayed silent for a moment. Tara was touched by the story and wondered at how easily life can take you in one direction or another. If she hadn't met James that night in the pub, the past year would have been completely different for both of them.

"I'm glad you decided to give it a go," she said quietly.

"We've done pretty well with the place, haven't we?" he murmured into her hair.

Her lips twitched to a contented smile. "It's just how I imagined it would be."

Chapter 27

For the first two months of the year, everything felt perfect. Tara did her best to focus on that and not think about the future. It was the first time she could remember feeling so utterly content, and she was determined not to ruin it by overthinking things or worrying about where their relationship was heading. There was a glimmer of hope that everything might work out.

She'd even started thinking about telling people about her relationship with James. In the end he hadn't even told his sister, having decided to wait until Tara felt more comfortable.

The secrecy was feeling more and more deceitful. Strangely, Tara was more worried about Josie's reaction than Amber's. She was fairly sure Amber wouldn't care about anything other than her and James being together. The details would be irrelevant. Josie would probably dig a little deeper and ponder previous conversations where Tara had been less than truthful.

February was drawing to an end, and the sun was shining when Tara arrived at work on Thursday morning. James was already in the kitchen and she kissed him as she shrugged off her coat. Kissing him felt so natural. They avoided being affectionate in the shop, but out the back they slipped into their naturally tactile state.

Tara's phone rang. She frowned when she saw it was her mum. She'd been doing well recently, but Tara had been unconsciously waiting for her to have another slip. It was always the same pattern: she'd be fine for a while, then something would trigger her and she'd spend a few days unable to cope with the world.

Automatically, Tara turned away from James when she answered, and when she heard her mum was crying, she moved out into the hallway for some privacy.

"Calm down," she said in a soothing voice. Tears pricked Tara's eyes. "You'll be okay. Everything will be fine." Her mum tried to speak but all she could manage were heaving breaths and the occasional sob. "I'll come over," Tara said. "Just take deep breaths and I'll be there really soon."

"Everything okay?" James asked when she went back to the kitchen.

"My mum's not well." She grabbed her coat from the back of the chair. "Do you mind if I nip over and check on her?"

"Of course not."

"Sorry," she said. "I'll be as quick as I can."

"Don't worry about this place." He rubbed circles on her back. "Is there anything I can do?"

She shook her head and gave him a quick peck before dashing away. When she arrived at her mum's house, a car was parked outside with the logo for the local doctor's surgery. Tara rushed to the door. It opened as she reached it, and the district nurse, Joyce, stepped out.

"Hello." She put a sympathetic hand on Tara's arm. Tara had always liked Joyce. She knew her mum's history and would often make a house visit when needed.

"Is she okay?" Tara asked, biting her lip.

"She had a panic attack. All calm again now. She said she's not been sleeping well, so I've ordered her to stay in bed today. I tried to convince her to make an appointment with the doctor if things are getting worse, but she's resisting. Maybe you can mention it."

"I'll talk to her," Tara said.

Joyce patted Tara's arm. "Are you okay?"

"Fine. I'd better check on her. Thank you for coming."

Her mum was sitting on the couch, clutching her box of photos.

"How are you doing?" Tara asked.

"Better. Sorry to worry you. I couldn't calm myself down and I panicked."

"It's fine," Tara said. "Joyce said you need more sleep. And you should see the doctor again."

"There's nothing the doctor can do." She reached into the shoebox and pulled out a photo. "Do you remember this being taken?"

The photo was outside their old house in London. A happy family photo. "It was a long time ago," Tara said wearily.

"You should visit your dad. He said he keeps

inviting you and you never go."

"I have a busy life," Tara said.

"You're too hard on him." Her mum gazed down at the photo. "He tried his best."

"I really don't think he did." Tara's voice was laced with resentment. Gently, she took the photo and dropped it into the box with the others. Then she put the box back in the cupboard. "Why don't you have a nap and I can have a bit of a tidy up?" Tara suggested. The house was a mess again.

"The housework got on top of me," Debbie said apologetically.

"That's okay," Tara said. "I'll get started and you can finish it off later."

"That would be a help." She gave Tara a hug and went upstairs.

After sending James a message saying she'd be a couple of hours, Tara got to work cleaning. When her mum came back down in the middle of the morning she'd had a nap and seemed better.

"I was thinking," Tara said. "What about seeing the counsellor you used to go to? Angela?"

"I don't know," Debbie said with a shrug. "I feel better again now."

"I think you should call her." Tara looked at her pleadingly.

"I'll think about it."

"Will you be okay?" Tara asked. "I should get back to work."

"I'll be fine. You get off. I'm sorry for dragging you out of work. James won't mind, will he?"

"No. It's not a problem."

"He's a good boss."

"Yes," Tara agreed. "Take it easy, okay?"

"I will." Her mum hugged her again, then Tara left.

Tara had completely forgotten about story time that morning. She only remembered when she walked back into the shop and saw the crowd in the children's corner. Usually it was Tara who picked out the books and read to the children. She winced as she walked back there, imagining James panicking at being left to manage the parents and toddlers alone.

It was surprisingly quiet. When Tara did story time the little ones often wandered around and talked over her. And there'd be the hum of mums shushing their kids. Leaning against the bookcase, Tara was immediately as enthralled as the children. James was reading *Giraffes Can't Dance*. He was sitting on a chair in the corner while the kids sat on the carpet in front of him. His low voice kept them all captivated. There was one little boy, Thomas, who was generally loud and disruptive. Today he was sitting on James's knee with his head on James's chest.

Tara was overcome by a rush of emotions, and tears pricked her eyes. She loved him so much. Glancing up, James caught her eye and they exchanged smiles.

As soon as story time ended, Tara moved behind the counter to serve the parents wanting to buy books.

"Everything okay?" James asked as she scanned

the books for one of their regular mums.

"Fine." She smiled at the woman in front of her. "I think I might have to let James read in future. I've never known the kids so quiet."

"I'm sure it's just the novelty," she replied kindly. "You're both great, and the kids always love it."

"Thanks." Tara's legs buckled as a small child ran into her. She reached down and ruffled his hair. "Hi, Thomas!"

He roared at her and ran away again.

As the crowd thinned, Amber came over with Kieron on her hip.

"What happened?" she asked. "James said your mum's ill. Is she okay?"

"Yes. Nothing major. She wanted me to nip to the chemist for her." She winced slightly and glanced up at James. He didn't react to her latest lie.

"Poor thing. I hope it's not flu. It's going round."

"Just a cold," Tara said. More lies. She felt drained enough already without having to feel guilty about lying to Amber.

"I'd better get this one home for his nap." She shifted Kieron on her hip. "See you at the pub tomorrow night?"

Tara nodded and turned back to serve a customer while James wandered over to the children's corner and crouched down to talk to Grace, a cute little blonde girl. She pointed at the pictures in the board book she was looking at and he sat beside her to help her turn the page. It was an effort for Tara to concentrate on the customer in front of her.

It was early afternoon before the shop was empty

again.

"What happened with your mum?" James asked when they were finally alone.

"She had a panic attack. The nurse was there when I got there and she calmed down pretty quick."

"Sorry." James put a reassuring hand on the small of her back. "Does that happen a lot?"

"It hasn't happened for a while. She has some problems. Sometimes she's fine for ages and then it gets worse again."

"Sounds tough," he said.

"Yeah." Her chest felt tight and she moved away. "I'm just going to get a drink."

In the kitchen she filled a glass with water and sat at the table. James followed her in a few minutes later.

"Sorry," she said. "I just needed a few minutes."

"You don't have to talk about it if you don't want." He paused. "What did you think of story time? I did okay, didn't I?"

Tara bit down on her lip and covered her face with her hands. Tears streamed down her cheeks and refused to stop.

"What's wrong?" James crouched beside her and pushed her hair from her face. "Was I that bad?"

"No." She laughed through her tears. "You were great."

"Why are you so upset?"

"Because I can't have children." Her tear ducts were in overdrive, soaking her cheeks.

James pulled up a chair and sat with his legs touching hers. "I know you said you didn't want

271

kids …"

"Yes. That's what I mean." That wasn't true though, not really. It was more complicated than just not wanting kids. She swiped her fingers across her damp face. "Physically, I can. But I *won't*."

"Okay." He reached for her hand. "Why are you bringing it up now?"

"Because you're so great with kids and you'd be such an amazing dad." She looked him right in the eyes. "But I can never give you that." Her face crumpled as she lost control again. "And I'm not sure at what point in a relationship you're supposed to bring something like that up. But last time it was two years before he realised I was serious. I don't want to do that again."

The chair legs scraped as James moved closer to her. Wiping the tears away, he kissed her cheeks. "I love you," he said, taking her face in his hands. "So much."

She squeezed her eyes shut. The declaration of love didn't make her feel any better. She should've been overjoyed. But instead she was filled with a feeling of dread. He loved her. And she loved him. But she was going to lose him and it would damage her heart beyond repair.

"But you want children one day," she said as calmly as she could. "I don't. That's not going to change."

"I never said I definitely want kids."

She stared at him for a moment. "You didn't have to say it."

The bell rang in the shop. James sighed. "Sorry."

"Go," she said, squeezing his hand.

He kissed the top of her head and went back to the shop. Tara stayed in the kitchen. The tears dried up, and she stared at the wall until she heard the customer leave again. Taking a deep breath, she ventured into the shop.

"It's probably not the best time to have that conversation," she said to James.

His forehead wrinkled. "Do you want to go home?"

"Trying to get rid of me?"

"No." He rested a hand on her hip. "I just think maybe you need a break. You don't have to go home; you could go and spend the day with your mum, or sit upstairs and watch a film and drink tea. There are even biscuits up there." He twitched an eyebrow. "Stay away from my ice cream, obviously."

Breaking her rule about being affectionate at work, she leaned in and kissed him. "I might go home. If you're sure you don't mind."

"It's fine." He wrapped his arms around her and she savoured the scent of his aftershave and the warmth of his embrace. She couldn't help but think their time together was limited.

At home, she sank onto the couch. Things had been going so well, but she had a knot in her stomach and a feeling that everything was about to fall apart. It had been stupid of her to think that things might somehow work out with her and James.

All she'd done was set herself up for one almighty fall.

Chapter 28

That evening, Tara spoke to James briefly on the phone. They avoided the topic of children. It was a difficult subject to broach so early in a relationship, but theirs seemed to be progressing so quickly that it played on her mind a lot.

She had an early night in the hopes that she'd wake up feeling refreshed and level-headed. It didn't work. She woke feeling just as hopeless as she had the previous day. All her doubts about the relationship were building like a storm rolling in.

At work, she went into autopilot, but things felt strained between her and James. There was a rather large elephant in the room.

"Are you going to the Bluebell tonight?" James asked when he turned the sign to "Closed" at the end of the day.

"Yeah." Tara checked the time and sighed. "It's Josie and Sam's engagement party."

"I know." He followed her through to the back. "Josie invited me."

Tara nodded but otherwise didn't react. She'd heard Josie invite him on Monday morning. The engagement had surprised Tara. It seemed to have come out of the blue.

"Shall I come?" James said.

"If you want to," Tara said. "You are invited."

"But you'd rather I didn't?"

She unhooked her coat from the rack. "It will probably be weird," she said wearily.

"Okay." He tipped his head towards the stairs. "Will you have a drink with me before you go?"

"Yeah." She followed him up. "And you can go to the party if you want."

"But you're going to ignore me and pretend you're not in a relationship with me?"

Upstairs, Tara immediately opened the fridge and got out a bottle of wine. James reached around her for a beer.

"It's Josie's engagement party. I don't want everyone talking about us."

James didn't comment but wandered into the living room while Tara poured herself a large glass of wine. He was perched on the arm of the couch when she walked over to look out of the window.

"Is the reason you don't want anyone to know we're together because you don't think our relationship is going to last?"

She took a sip of wine. Lying seemed pointless. "Yes."

For a moment, he stared at her, then finally blinked and looked away.

"I don't want their sympathy when things go wrong between us," she said.

James dragged a hand through his hair. "That's crazy on more than one level. For a start, your friends are supposed to support you when things go

276

wrong." He looked her right in the eyes. "But why are you assuming things won't work out? I thought everything was great."

"We want different things. I don't see how two people can share a future when they want completely different things from life."

"Is this about kids?" he asked. "Because I've never once mentioned us having kids."

"You don't have to. Are you honestly going to try and tell me you don't want children one day? You told me a long time ago that you'd always imagined having a boy and a girl."

"That doesn't mean anything," he said, raising his voice.

"And when you think about a future with me, is it just the two of us in that picture?"

He took a swig of his beer. At least he wasn't going to try to deny it. "Maybe I've occasionally imagined having kids with you. I've also imagined winning the lottery and going on four luxury holidays a year. It doesn't mean it's going to happen. Or that I'll be miserable if it doesn't."

"It's not the same at all," she snapped. "I'm talking about something you have control over."

"I don't even understand why we're talking about this now. It's ridiculous."

She shook her head. "It's not ridiculous to me. The reason you don't want to discuss it is because you think I'll change my mind." She paced in front of the window. "I'm not going to wake up one day and suddenly decide I want to have kids. It's not going to happen. And I won't have kids to please someone else." Tears sprang to her eyes and she stopped pacing to gulp at her wine.

"I'm not asking you to," he said. "I would never ask you to."

"I know you wouldn't." Tears rolled down her cheeks. She brushed them away. "You wouldn't ask me to have kids, so how can I ask you *not* to have kids? I can't take that away from you."

"But you're not asking." He put his bottle down and walked over to her. "I know the situation and I choose to be with you."

He embraced her, and she rested her head on his shoulder, the tears still flowing. "I don't want to spend every day wondering if this will be the day you realise I'm serious and that a future with me is not actually what you want. And I don't want to deny you something so important."

When she pulled away, James's brow was furrowed and his eyes had lost their sparkle. "I love you," he said. "I want to be with you. That's all that matters."

"You'll end up resenting me." Carefully, she set her wine glass down on the coffee table.

He stared at her. "What are you saying?"

"I don't know." Her throat was tight and her voice thick with emotion. "Every time I see you with the kids at story time, or playing with Kieron, it kills me. I need you to be realistic. Think it through properly. Will you really be happy to not have kids?"

He turned away.

"That's what worries me," she said. It felt like her

heart was being torn apart. She so badly wanted to bury her head in the sand and carry on as though everything was fine. They'd have to face it eventually though. "I think ..." She took a deep breath. "I think it's best that we end things now. It'll only be harder further down the line."

"No." He moved quickly towards her and reached for her hand. "Don't do this. We can figure it out. Let's think things over and talk again."

"I've thought about it a lot," she said as tears spilled down her cheeks. "Talking about it will never bring us to any other conclusion. I have to go." Pulling her hand from his, she walked to the door, desperate for fresh air.

"Just wait," James said, following her.

"I'm sorry." Stopping at the door, she kissed his cheek, then touched her forehead to his. "I'm so sorry."

He shouted after her as she descended the stairs but she didn't stop. All she wanted to do was turn around and take it all back. They could stay together. If he ended up resenting her one day, so be it. Except she couldn't do that to him. He deserved so much more than she had to offer. So she kept moving and didn't look back.

***

When she arrived in Averton that evening, she lingered outside the pub for a few minutes, psyching herself up to go in. Then she pasted on a smile and lifted her chin.

279

"Oh, my God!" she said dramatically as she approached her friends. Josie and Sam were sitting with Amber and Paul. Max was there too, and Tara felt comforted by the sight of him. She hardly saw him anymore and she realised how much she'd missed him. "I did not think about a gift."

Josie paused from unwrapping the present. From the way Amber was eagerly watching it was obviously from her.

"We weren't expecting gifts," Josie said. "Don't worry about it."

"Shots!" Tara said cheekily. "My engagement gift to you is shots for everyone." She shrugged her coat off and draped it over the seat beside Max. Then she walked purposefully to the bar and ordered a round of Jäger shots.

As she slid the tray of drinks onto the table, she complimented the vase that Amber had bought for Josie and Sam.

"Is James coming?" Josie asked. "I invited him."

Tara forced a bright smile. "He said to tell you congratulations and sorry he can't make it."

"I thought he'd come," Josie said. "He seemed keen. Did you tell him not to?"

"No. He was just busy." Tara needed a change of subject. She pushed drinks over to Sam and Josie. "I'll be honest; I didn't put a lot of thought into this present."

"It's not the thought the counts," Sam said. "It's the alcohol content."

"Well in that case, I've done really well." She raised her glass, happy to have left the subject of

James behind.

Josie frowned. "I'm not drinking."

"What?" Tara's eyes widened and she lowered her glass.

"I'm on a health kick until the wedding."

"Oh, no!" Tara sighed dramatically. "Tell me you're not serious."

"I'm serious," Josie said.

Tara downed her shot, then reached for Josie's. "Give me that back then. And yours, I presume?" She looked questioningly at Amber. Paul reached for the glass at the same time, and she pulled a face when he beat her to it. She quickly downed Josie's shot. "It turns out my gift to you is getting completely sloshed. Cheers!"

Josie laughed. "Will you dance on the table later?"

"Anything for you, Josie." Tara grimaced. "Just not a vase or anything useful, obviously."

"You're in a funny mood," Amber said, rolling her eyes.

"I'm happy! It's a party."

Shaking her head disapprovingly, Amber turned to Josie. "I can't believe you're getting married this year."

"Well, we're keeping the wedding fairly simple," Josie said. "So hopefully it won't be too much stress to organise."

Max leaned close to Tara. "What's wrong?" he asked quietly.

"Nothing." The smile didn't waver and she barely moved her lips as she spoke. "I'm the most cheerful person here."

"And underneath the manic cheeriness?"

"Absolutely miserable." The grin stretched even wider.

"Thought so." He gulped the last of his pint. "Bar?"

She nodded and stood when he did. He held up his empty glass as he asked if anyone needed a drink. They all declined.

"Where's Lizzie?" Tara asked as they walked across the pub.

"At home with the kids."

"Of course." Tara rolled her eyes and shuffled onto a stool at the bar.

"I offered to stay home," he said.

"I know." Her smile turned genuine. "I always knew you'd be a great dad."

"Don't know if Lizzie would agree with you there. Everything I do is wrong."

"You guys are okay though?" she asked. "You're happy?"

He nodded. "Tired and stressed and very happy."

"I'm glad."

Max ordered a pint of lager and a glass of wine, then leaned with his elbow on the bar. "What's going on with you then?"

"Do you remember when I broke up with Joel?"

"Yeah. You called me and demanded I come and get drunk with you." They both smiled at the memory. For Tara, Max had felt like her saviour. He didn't do much, just turned up and got drunk with her for two days. But it was what she needed at the time.

"It's pretty much like that again," she said.

Max paid for their drinks and took a sip. "I didn't know you were seeing anyone."

"I didn't tell anyone."

"The guy at work?"

Tara took a deep breath, determined not to cry. She nodded.

"Sorry," Max said flatly.

"My own stupid fault," she said. "I knew it wouldn't work out. I shouldn't have started anything."

"Do you love him?" Max asked.

Tara swallowed hard. A reply didn't seem necessary.

"Can't you work it out?" he asked.

"James wants kids. I don't. I'm not sure how we work that out."

"If you love each other, it will probably work out. Somehow."

"Wow!" She slapped his arm. "Have you gone soft on me?"

He grinned. "I think I might have. It's true though."

"The reason I always liked hanging out with you was because you were never sentimental. You never told me things would be okay. I liked that."

When she slipped off the stool, he picked up his pint and followed her back across the pub. "Things worked out for me," he said. "I think everything will work out for you too."

"Of course everything fell into place for you, Mr Perfect. Why wouldn't it?"

"That's true." He flashed her a cheeky grin as they re-joined their friends.

Amber was telling Josie all about her and Paul's wedding.

"Do me a favour," Max said out of the side of his mouth. He glanced at Tara's wine glass. "Don't drink yourself into oblivion. It didn't help last time and it won't help now."

She nodded slowly.

"You'll be fine," he said confidently.

Tara wasn't so sure.

"Are you okay?" Josie asked, looking at her intently.

"Yes!" Tara said. "I was just thinking about a hen night. I presume you want me to organise it?"

Josie laughed. "If you want to."

"Of course I want to." She rolled her eyes dramatically. "Just tell me you'll stop this teetotal nonsense for the hen night?"

Amber exhaled loudly. "Not drinking alcohol is a perfectly acceptable choice. Leave her alone."

Tara exchanged a look with Josie. "I'm probably not going to leave you alone."

"I didn't think you would," Josie said, looking thoroughly amused. "Oh, I have a favour to ask you …"

"What?" Tara asked suspiciously.

"You know my best friend is a writer?"

"No." Tara shook her head. "Who's your best friend?"

"Emily. Remember we went to visit her in Oxford a couple of weeks ago?"

"I didn't realise she was your best friend. Why are we only just hearing about her?"

"We had a bit of an argument and weren't speaking for a while."

"How come?"

Josie blew out a breath. "She was dating my ex. *Is* dating my ex."

"Jack?" Tara remembered all the talk of Jack from when Josie first arrived in Averton.

"Yes."

"That's awkward," Tara said flatly.

"No, it's fine." Josie looked to Sam. "It was fine when we met up with them, wasn't it?"

"Oh, wow." Tara put a hand to her mouth to stifle a laugh. "You went on a double date with your ex-best friend and your ex-boyfriend?"

Max chuckled beside her.

"If I was next to you, I'd hit you both." Josie glared at the pair of them. "Jack and Emily are my friends. It's fine." She looked at Sam again and he put a hand on her leg.

Tara took a deep breath, surprised that she'd actually found something to laugh about. "So you have a best friend called Emily who's a writer? And you want me to stock her book in the shop I presume?"

"Yes!" Josie said, delighted.

"I'll have to read it," Tara said. "I'm not going to recommend a book if it's a load of rubbish."

Josie reached down and produced a book from her bag. Turning it over, Tara read the description. It sounded okay. Light and easy. She'd give it a go.

"I'm not promising anything," she said.

"Just promise you'll read it," Josie said. "You'll enjoy it."

"I'll read it." She put the book beside her. "Thanks."

"I invited them to come tonight," Josie said. "Emily and Jack."

Tara nearly choked on her drink. "Are you serious?"

"They're my best friends," Josie said adamantly. "They couldn't make it at such short notice but they're going to visit soon."

"Well, I can't wait to meet them," Tara said with a smirk. It sounded like a very weird situation. Only Josie would stay friends with her ex-boyfriend and the friend who'd stolen him. At least it had given Tara something to smile about.

The evening went by far easier than Tara had expected. Having Max there made it much more bearable. It was nice to talk to someone about what was going on. Max was great because she knew he would never mention it to anyone else. And he generally didn't try to offer advice, he just listened. Although, she did take his advice about not getting drunk. After the initial shots she slowed down. Getting drunk definitely wouldn't help.

She just wished she knew what *would* help.

Chapter 29

After managing to fool the majority of her friends into thinking she was fine, Tara had high hopes she could also manage a day at work with James.

She arrived on time that Saturday morning and was surprised when there was no sign of James. Normally, Tara would waltz up to his apartment and shake him out of bed if he'd overslept. She couldn't do that anymore. Sadly, she realised she'd have to give the key to the apartment back. It all felt too much. Pretending she was fine might be more than she could manage.

While she waited for James, she got herself a coffee and wandered through the shop, straightening things out which didn't really need straightening. She switched the train and the aeroplane in the window on and then turned the sign to "Open". James's absence felt odd, and she got her phone out to check for messages.

He'd messaged her asking her to open up and telling her he wouldn't be long. It was half an hour later when he joined Tara in the shop. There'd only been one customer in that time.

"Sorry," he said, inhaling a deep breath.

"Are you okay?" she asked. "You look terrible."

He was pale, and Tara ignored her instinct to put her hand to his forehead.

"I've definitely felt better." He dropped his phone beside the computer where he often left it. "I'll be okay."

"If you want to go back to bed I'm happy to hold the fort."

He went to the window and looked outside. "No. I'd feel bad leaving you alone. It might get busy later."

Honestly, apart from when they had some sort of event going on, she didn't think there'd ever been a time when they were so busy she couldn't manage alone.

"I really don't mind," she said. "I can give you a shout if it gets busy."

He rubbed his jaw and looked at her with piercing eyes. "Can we talk later? I don't like how we left things."

"I'm not sure what good it will do." She paused. "We'll still be able to work together, won't we?"

His gaze was intense. "This place is yours too. No matter what."

While she appreciated the sentiment, it wasn't true. If they couldn't work together, it was her who'd be job hunting. She nodded vaguely.

"Are you really okay on your own for a bit?" he asked.

"Yes." Actually, it would be good to be alone. She'd be busier if he wasn't around, and time would go quicker. Plus, she'd avoid the awkwardness of being around him, and the ache in her chest every ime she looked at him.

There was a steady stream of customers over the course of the morning. Even though she was feeling down, chatting to customers kept her mind off the mess she'd made of her love life. She managed to stay reasonably upbeat.

James had forgotten his mobile, and it buzzed with a call as Tara was handing over the change to an elderly woman who'd bought a selection of picture books for her grandchildren. Without thinking, Tara checked the display. Her lip curled when she saw it was Olivia. She'd never liked her, and she really didn't like her calling James. Not that it was any of her business anymore. She left the phone where it was. It buzzed again five minutes later.

"He's not answering," Tara said, glaring at the phone. "Take the hint!" Thankfully there was no one in the shop as she talked to herself.

The bell rang above the door as Belinda walked in.

"Hi," Tara mumbled. She really wasn't in the mood to deal with Belinda. Not that she ever was. "How are you?"

"Fine!" She leaned cheerfully on the counter then nodded at the buzzing phone. "That's annoying. Where's James?"

"Upstairs," Tara said idly. "He's ill."

Belinda raised an eyebrow. "Ill, or hiding in shame?"

"What?" Tara said impatiently.

"I saw that blonde woman leaving here this

morning. What's her name, Olivia? I'd call it a walk of shame except she looked like the cat who'd got the cream." Belinda stood up straighter. "I have no idea what he sees in her."

Tara froze. Her legs felt like they might give way and she clutched the edge of the counter for support. "Were you going to buy something?" she asked frostily.

"Just browsing." Slowly, Belinda walked back through the shop, trailing her gaze over the bookshelves as she went. "Bye!" she called when she reached the door.

"Bye," Tara whispered. The phone vibrated yet again and it was an effort not to throw it across the room. Calmly, Tara walked through the shelves, stopping at her favourite armchair and curling up with her legs under her. It was tempting to lock the front door. She couldn't cope with customers. Her facade was crumbling and she was running out of energy to put on a brave face for the world.

She stayed in the chair, not moving until the bell rang again. Tara worked on autopilot, making polite conversation to the middle-aged man and then hanging back while he browsed. He bought a cookbook and Tara managed to keep smiling until he was out of the door.

James came back down in the middle of the afternoon, looking marginally better than he had first thing. "Thanks so much for holding the fort. You're a lifesaver."

She couldn't bring herself to look at him. "Good night, was it?"

"No." He checked his phone and frowned. "It wasn't."

Tara stared at him, wondering if she should ask him about his little sleepover. But since they weren't together anymore, it was really none of her business who he was sleeping with. The thought made her feel sick. Quickly, she walked into the back and grabbed her coat.

"I'm going to go," she said. "I presume you're fine for the rest of the day?"

James's eyebrows shot up. "Yeah," he said slowly. "I thought we were going to be okay working together."

"We might be," she said bitterly. "But not today."

"I was hoping we could talk."

"I can't talk to you at the moment." She moved to the door, desperate to get away from him before she broke down. It was hard to tell whether she'd dissolve into uncontrollable crying, or direct all her anger into throwing things at him. She was definitely capable of either. "I'll see you on Monday," she said before making a hasty getaway.

When he called her that evening, she didn't answer. Her appetite had vanished, and she couldn't sleep that night. She didn't dare cry in case she couldn't stop. Although, surprisingly, she didn't feel like crying. There was a strange calmness to her.

When James arrived at her house on Sunday morning, she stepped aside to let him in. Eventually, she'd have to talk to him. Perhaps it was better to get it out of the way.

"I'm sorry about yesterday," he said. "I was

291

hungover and not functioning properly. But I really did want to talk to you."

Tara sat on the couch.

"I don't want us to split up," he said, standing in the middle of the room. "And it's unfair of you to make decisions for both of us. I can make my own mind up about what I want or don't want."

She stared up at him, trying not to imagine him in bed with someone else just hours after they'd split up. Finally, her tear ducts flicked back into action. She really didn't want to cry, but she didn't seem to have any control over it.

He sat beside her and reached for her hand. "I want to be with you."

"What happened on Friday night?" she asked, pulling her hand away.

His eyebrows knitted together. "I went out with friends in Exeter and got really drunk."

She studied his face, wishing she could rewind to a time before she'd set eyes on him. "Did you take one of those friends home with you?"

There was a flicker of surprise in his eyes before he squeezed them shut and dropped his chin to his chest. "How did you—"

"Belinda saw her leaving." Tara pushed tears from her cheeks. "Can you leave, please?"

"It wasn't like that." He turned to face her and reached for her hand again. "I was upset about our conversation, and I got really drunk. Nothing happened."

Snatching her hand away, Tara stood. "I can't believe you'd take her home with you. We'd only

292

just broken up."

"I got drunk and passed out." He pushed his hands through his hair. "I'm not even sure how Olivia ended up at my place. I didn't sleep with her. I promise."

"It doesn't matter." Tara paced the floor. "You're free to do whatever you want."

"I wouldn't cheat on you." There was desperation in his voice as he approached her.

"We'd already split up," she said. "It wasn't cheating because we weren't together."

"It wasn't cheating because I didn't do anything," he said firmly.

"Did she sleep in your bed?" she asked.

He bit his bottom lip and lowered his gaze to the floor. "I don't know. All I remember is dropping into bed. She woke me up in the morning and told me she was leaving."

"Were you wearing any clothes when you woke up?"

He rubbed at his temple and groaned.

"It's not a complicated question," she snapped. "Were you naked when you woke up after innocently taking another woman home with you?"

"No, I wasn't naked. I swear to you, nothing happened."

There was a part of her that believed him. But even if he hadn't slept with Olivia, things were still over between them. Tara's chest felt like it was being crushed.

"Just go," she said. "Please."

His eyes pleaded with her as he put a hand on her

arm. She flinched and glared at him.

Finally, he left.

Tara dropped onto the couch, put her head in her hands and sobbed.

Chapter 30

On Sunday evening Tara typed out a letter of resignation. She planned to hand it over without a word. If she had to actually say she was quitting – actually speak the words – she'd never manage it.

By Monday morning, she was feeling much calmer and not quite ready to give up on her dream job. The letter of resignation was tucked away in her bag. Maybe she could still find a way to work with James.

At the shop, she greeted him as usual. Then firmly told him she didn't want to talk about anything but work, and if he tried to she would walk out and most likely never come back. Thankfully, Josie and Amber arrived soon after she did and were a great distraction.

For that week and the week after, Tara managed to keep her head down and get on with work. She was cheerful with the customers, kept on top of the stock and ran the story times as usual. Occasionally, she'd glance at James and have an overwhelming desire to throw books at his head. Or to kiss him. She managed to resist both.

After two weeks of working alongside him, she felt better about the situation. They could still work together. It was awful but manageable. She smiled as Josie arrived that Monday.

"Are you okay?" Tara asked. "You're pale."

"Tired," Josie said, dropping into a beanbag. "And in need of caffeine."

"Your wish is my command!" Tara poured her a cup and went to sit with her. "Annette working you too hard?"

Josie blew on her coffee and raised an eyebrow. "She's such a slave driver."

"Sam okay?"

"He's fine. Did you read Emily's book yet?"

"Yes!" She stood up and motioned for Josie to do the same. "Didn't I tell you? I read them both and loved them. I ordered them already." She pulled them from the shelf and Josie squealed in delight.

"Thank you," she said happily.

"You're welcome. I'm happy to recommend them."

"I'm hoping Emily will visit soon," Josie said.

"Can we get her to do an author event?" Tara asked.

"Maybe. She's got a new book coming out soon."

"We could make it an evening event and have wine and nibbles."

Josie chuckled as they went back to the beanbags. "Do you ever make plans that don't involve alcohol?"

"Rarely. I can't believe you're still not drinking."

Josie ignored the comment and picked up her coffee. "Where's James?"

"Here!" He appeared from the back.

"Oh." Josie flashed a cheeky grin. "We can't talk about you now."

He smiled lightly. "I'm so sorry to interrupt you. It's rude of me really."

The bell rang as the door opened, and James crouched down, opening his arms wide as Kieron ran straight at him. James caught him and fell onto his back, then held Kieron up in the air and flew him around. When James set him back on his feet, Kieron ran away giggling and James went after him, growling as he chased him round the shelves.

"Good morning, James," Amber called.

"Hi!" he replied, then growled again.

Amber took off her coat and helped herself to a coffee. "This is better than the playground for tiring him out!"

The three of them sat quietly for a moment, listening to Kieron's giggles float around the shop.

Josie lay back on the beanbag. "I don't know how you can see him every day and not fall in love with him."

"Please just have his babies," Amber added. "You're going to be so annoyed when someone else snaps him up."

"You two are like broken records." Shaking her head, Tara moved away from them and pretended to be doing something at the computer. James crept behind one of the bookshelves and put a finger to his lips when Tara caught his eye through the books. A moment later, James jumped out at Kieron. His little laugh was adorable.

"I'm going to get back to Annette," Josie said

when she finished her drink. "Macy's been off her food and I'm worried about her. I might take her to the vet later."

"Poor Macy," Tara said. She'd always been fond of the cute little dog. "I hope she's okay."

Josie called goodbye to them all as she left.

"Do you think Josie's okay?" Amber asked as Kieron climbed wearily into her lap. A customer came in and James went over to him.

"She didn't look great," Tara agreed. "I was wondering if she's pregnant."

"Because she's not drinking?" Amber rolled her eyes.

"Not just because of that," Tara mused. "She's been in a strange mood."

"Well, I don't think she's pregnant," Amber said.

"A tenner says she is," Tara said, mostly to wind Amber up.

"I'm not going to put bets on whether or not Josie is pregnant."

"You don't want to bet against it?" Tara said with a smirk.

James walked over to them. "Looks like I wore him out."

"Yes," Amber said as she glanced down at Kieron nestled into her chest. "I think I'll take him home before he falls asleep here."

Tara stayed on the beanbag when Amber left.

"There's an email from Barbara about the book club book this month." James hovered over the computer. "Shall I leave it for you to deal with?"

"Yeah." Tara walked over and reached for the

mouse. Her arm grazed James's, and she flinched and took a step back. Then he moved as she did and they bumped into each other. They seemed to do that a lot recently.

"Sorry." He held up his hands and backed away.

A laugh escaped from Tara's lips. She'd spent the last couple of weeks being angry and upset about Olivia, but for a moment she forgot all about it. What she needed were lots more moments where she completely forgot about it, and maybe she and James could get back to being friends.

The week went quicker as she and James started to relax around each other again. Tara had just got her coat on to leave on Friday when he came into the kitchen.

"See you in the morning," she said.

"Have you got five minutes?" he asked.

She hesitated in the doorway. "Is it to do with work?"

"No." He shook his head. "I'd really like talk to you."

"I feel like things are just starting to settle down between us and I don't want to argue again."

"I don't want to argue either," he said. "But will you at least tell me you believe me that nothing happened between me and Olivia?"

"It doesn't really matter," she said gently.

He raised his eyebrows. "It matters to me."

"Okay." She tapped the doorframe. "I believe you. But it doesn't change anything between us."

"Have a drink with me." James's eyes pleaded with her. "Please. Let's talk everything through properly."

She hesitated for a moment, then nodded and followed him upstairs. As soon as she walked into the apartment she was hit with a flood of memories, and it was an effort not to walk straight back out again.

"Do you want a drink?" he asked.

"No, thanks." She sat at the edge of the couch. "What do you want to talk about?"

"There's something I can't stop wondering about," he said hesitantly as he sat at the other end of the couch.

"What?"

"Can you try not to get defensive?" He swallowed. "It's a genuine question which I would really like to understand the answer to."

Her heart beat furiously. "What?"

"Why don't you want children?"

"I just don't." She was immediately defensive as he'd predicted. "Some people don't want kids. So what?"

"I don't understand," he said. "And I'd like to."

"You can't understand," she snapped. "No one who wants kids understands people who don't want them."

"Explain it to me."

She hated how he looked at her so intently. So patiently. No one ever asked her for an explanation. They happily jumped to their own conclusions. Generally, that she was weird or that she wasn't really serious and would change her mind.

Leaning forward, she rested her elbows on her

knees. "I don't have any maternal instinct," she said. "I never had any desire to have kids. It's like I'm missing the gene that makes people want kids."

"Okay," he said slowly. "I think I understand that, but I always thought people who aren't maternal also aren't generally good with kids."

"I'm not good with kids," she said quickly. "Ask Amber."

"You're great with kids," he said. "I watch you at story time. You're maternal with other people's kids."

"It's different," she said. "I don't want my own. I'm too selfish. I can't imagine being responsible for someone else." She stared at her nails as though they were absolutely fascinating. "And sleep deprivation would drive me crazy."

"You're not selfish," he said softly.

Her gaze snapped to him. "I don't want kids. And I don't have to justify that choice to you." Standing abruptly, she crossed the room.

James caught her at the door and grabbed her arm. "I'm sorry. I didn't want you to justify it; I just wanted to understand."

"I don't want to have a baby." Her throat tightened and she gasped for breath as she was consumed by panic. "I never have and I never will."

"That's okay." He took her in his arms and she buried her head in his neck and clung to him tightly. "It's fine. I'm sorry."

"I should go," she finally said, the stubble on his jaw scratching her cheek.

"I didn't mean to upset you," he said. "Don't rush

off. We can watch a film and get a takeaway."

She sniffed and took a step away from him. His shoulder was dotted with wet patches from her tears.

"We don't have to talk," he said. "And I'll sit at the other end of the couch. I just don't want you to go home and be upset on your own."

Tara glanced at the door, then back at James. She didn't want to be on her own either. Hesitantly, she went back to the couch and curled up with her head on the arm. Tiredness seemed to sweep through her bones.

"Are you hungry?" James asked.

"No. You get something though."

She closed her eyes, soothed by the sound of James moving around the kitchen. When she woke, there was a blanket draped over her. She pulled it higher under her chin. The glow from the street lights seeped in, gently illuminating the room. She vaguely thought about going home, but she was cosy and had no desire to go out in the middle of the night. Instead, she rested her head back on the pillow and was asleep again in no time.

Chapter 31

Tara left the next morning before James woke. She couldn't face being around him first thing in the morning. It felt too intimate, and she was confused enough as it was.

When she saw him later at work, she apologised for getting so emotional the previous evening, and switched back into work mode. The shop was busy and the day flew by. She declined James's offer of a drink after work and went straight home. Maybe she should call Amber and see if she wanted to go to the pub. She'd stood her up the night before, and Amber had messaged to say Josie and Sam hadn't been going out either so she hadn't bothered herself. But a night in the pub meant forcing herself to be cheerful, and Tara decided she wasn't up to it.

In the end she drove over and spent the evening watching TV with her mum. Debbie was in a chirpy mood, so it was pleasant enough. On Sunday, Tara went over to Annette's place at lunchtime and acted surprised that she'd arrived just as Annette was sitting down to a roast dinner with Josie and Sam. It was delicious as always, and it was lovely to sit around the fire in the living room for the afternoon, chatting and joking with Annette. Josie wasn't feeling great so she and Sam left almost straight after lunch.

As Tara sat on the floor in front of the fire, the little dog Macy kept coming and putting her head on Tara's lap to be stroked. Apparently Josie had taken Macy to the vet and they'd given her medicine for arthritis that had perked her right up. It was soothing being around the dogs. Tara couldn't help but think of all the time she'd spent there as a child with Wendy and Annette. Especially when Annette brought out a plate of homemade ginger biscuits. The taste of them took her right back to childhood.

It was late in the afternoon when she left. Tara was glad she'd forced herself to get out instead of spending the day alone with her thoughts. When she drove past the bookshop, she glanced up, wondering what James was doing. She missed him so much it ached.

Tara had only just arrived at work on Monday when her phone beeped with a message from Amber. She stood by the counter, staring at the phone. She barely noticed when James walked in.

"Are you okay?" he asked, laying a hand on her arm.

"Annette's dog died," she said, finally shifting her attention from the phone. "Amber's going over to Annette's to see her and Josie."

"Poor Annette," James said.

"Yeah." Tara tapped out a reply to Amber. "I was over there yesterday and spent most of the afternoon stroking Macy. Poor little dog." She sighed. "I hate thinking of Annette being upset."

He put a hand on her back. "If you want to go over and see her, go."

She shook her head. "She's got Josie there, and Amber's going to call in. She'll be fine."

As they fell into silence all Tara was aware of was James's hand on her back. Usually she'd move away when they got too close to each other. This time she leaned a little closer. Then she turned to face him. Her heart hammered against her ribcage as their eyes locked.

Slowly, she reached up and trailed her fingers over his cheek. Then her lips brushed his. She'd missed kissing him, and even though she knew she should pull away, she couldn't bring herself to. Instead, she took a step closer and moved her lips against his, kissing him hungrily.

The bell rang over the door and they shot apart. Tara was breathing heavily as she called hello to the elderly lady walking in. Luckily, she seemed too busy scanning the shelves to notice them.

"Shout if you need any help," Tara said loudly, then she turned to James and lowered her voice. "Sorry. I shouldn't have done that."

He flashed her a smile and moved away. Tara tried to focus her attention back on the emails, but her gaze kept wandering to James. He was deep in conversation with the old lady. Tara really shouldn't have kissed him. It felt like undoing all her hard work trying to move on. Especially because all she could think about was kissing him again.

They spent the week pretending it hadn't happened, but the ache in Tara's chest seemed to get stronger every time she looked at him.

"What's the plan for the weekend?" James asked on Friday afternoon. She'd asked him for Saturday off and he'd agreed without question. It would be the first Saturday she'd had off in a long time and she wasn't exactly thrilled by the idea.

Tara sighed. "Josie's organised some sort of dog funeral that I'm supposed to go to tomorrow morning."

"A funeral for the dog?"

"They're scattering her ashes."

"Don't people usually just bury dogs in the garden?"

Tara had thought exactly the same. "Sometimes with Josie I find it's better not to ask too many questions." She continued straightening the books in the children's section. "Anyway, that's not even the weirdest part. Josie has invited her ex-boyfriend and his girlfriend, who's Josie's best friend from school."

James raised his eyebrows. "Yeah, that's weird. Is she the one whose books you ordered?"

"Yes. I'm quite intrigued to meet her. And the boyfriend, Jack. What kind of guy splits up with someone and then moves on to date her best friend?" She frowned and shook her head. "So there's the dog thing tomorrow morning and then we're all supposed to go to the pub in the evening to hang out with Josie's friends from Oxford. Sounds like a thrilling Saturday, doesn't it?"

He grinned. "If I'd realised, I could've refused to give you the day off."

"I'm still tempted to say you can't possibly manage without me." Her smile faltered slightly as she caught his eye. "I could also come in for a few hours in the afternoon if you need me to."

"Have a day off," he said. "You work too much."

"Thanks." She lifted a beanbag and gave it a shake, then set it down at the edge of the carpet, before moving on to do the same to the next one.

"Are you going to the pub tonight too?" James asked.

"No. Two nights in one weekend would be far too much. I'll have a quiet night in front of the TV and psyche myself up for tomorrow's festivities."

James looked away, then turned back abruptly. "Do you want to have dinner with me?"

"Tonight?"

"Yeah. If you're not doing anything …"

She focused on the beanbag she was reshaping. It was so tempting to agree to dinner. There was nothing she wanted more than to spend the evening with him.

"Nothing's changed," she said, finally meeting his gaze. "I was really angry about Olivia. But the reason we split up hasn't changed."

"I know," he said. "Except you made a decision for me without even asking for my opinion. You didn't even give me chance to think about it."

"So?"

"So, I've thought about it and I want to be with you. I don't care about anything else. I want a life with you, and if that doesn't involve children, that's okay."

"I just don't see how it will work out," she said sadly.

"But if you don't try, you'll never know."

Tara remembered the first time they'd met and she'd said the same thing to him. "Someone wise tell you that?"

"Very wise." He took her hand. "Let's have dinner together and figure out where we go from there."

"Okay." The pessimist in her had suddenly been overshadowed by a cloud of hope.

"Hello!" a cheerful voice called as the bell rang.

"Hi!" Tara beamed at Barbara. She called in fairly regularly and Tara always enjoyed chatting to her about the book club meetings.

"I brought you these." She held out a bunch of wild flowers. "Picked them from my garden. Just a little thank-you for always looking after me and the book club so well."

"They're beautiful," Tara said, taking the flowers. "Thank you so much. What books are you reading next for book club?"

The door opened again and James went to greet the customer. Tara was so absorbed in her conversation with Barbara that it took her a minute to pay any attention to who'd walked in. When she finally registered Olivia whispering with James by the door it felt like all the air had been sucked from her lungs. What was *she* doing there?

Tara tried her best to continue her conversation with Barbara, but her gaze kept drifting over Barbara's shoulder. The hushed conversation between James and Olivia didn't look particularly friendly. A moment later they walked to the back of the shop.

"I'll just be five minutes," James said, flashing Tara a look that she couldn't read.

"Okay," she said weakly. With a lot of effort she even managed a smile when Olivia nodded at her in greeting.

As Barbara moved to browse the shelves, Tara put in the order for the next lot of books for the book club. It was something to focus on instead of wondering what was going on upstairs.

Tara was filled with nervous energy after Barbara left. She drummed her fingers on the counter. The flowers still lay by the till, so she took them into the back to put them in water. She glanced up the stairs as she walked through the hall but it was all quiet. There wasn't a vase, but she filled a pint glass with water and fanned the flowers out in it.

Walking back through the hallway, she stopped dead at the sound of raised voices upstairs. She lingered at the foot of the stairs trying to make out words, but they were all muffled. Then it went quiet. Tara moved quickly away when the door clicked open.

She was arranging the flowers on the counter when Olivia walked past.

"Hi, Tara," she said sweetly.

"Hi," Tara mumbled, then watched Olivia walk confidently out of the shop. Glancing at the back door, she expected James to reappear any moment. He didn't, and Tara turned her attention to the customer who walked in.

When there was no sign of James an hour later, Tara sent him a message asking if he was okay. His phone beeped beside the computer. She considered running upstairs while there were no customers, but just as she thought about it the door opened and more customers arrived.

Tara avoided engaging in conversation and was glad when the couple left fairly quickly. She switched the sign to "Closed" and locked the door. It was almost closing time anyway.

There was no answer when she knocked on the door upstairs, and no reply when she called out to James. Weird. He was definitely in there. Tara wasn't sure whether to just go home, but she knew she'd only spend the evening wondering what on earth was going on. She pulled out her keys and let herself in.

James was sitting on the couch. His elbows rested on his knees, and his hands were clasped together with his head bowed over them. He glanced at Tara, then shifted his attention back to his hands.

There was a knot in her stomach. "What's going on?"

His leg bounced like a nervous tic, and she put her hand out to still it as she sat beside him. Then she pulled his face to look at her. His eyes were bloodshot and his cheeks damp.

"You're scaring me," she said. "What's wrong?"

Pain was etched in his features. "She's pregnant," he whispered.

Tara frowned, not connecting the dots. "Olivia?"

"Yes." His voice was low and gravelly.

"So?" She looked at him questioningly. Then she saw the regret in his eyes. She pulled her hand from his leg. "She's pregnant with your baby?"

"I'm so sorry." He ground his palms into his eyes.

"But you said ..." Tara let out a humourless laugh. "You said nothing happened and I believed you. I actually believed you." She laughed again, then bit her lip as tears came to her eyes. "You slept with her the same day we broke up," she said angrily. "How could you even look me in the eyes?"

"I'm so sorry." He kept his head down. "I don't even know what to say."

"You've been lying to me for weeks," she said.

"I didn't mean to."

"Of course you meant to." Her voice got steadily louder. "You were never going to admit to sleeping with her."

"I wasn't lying," he said, his head snapping up. "That whole night is such a blur."

"So you expect me to believe you were so drunk you don't remember having sex with her?"

He shook his head and looked utterly defeated. "It's the truth."

"Stop it," she growled. "Stop lying. I'll never believe anything you say to me again." Jumping up from the couch, she took heaving breaths. There was so much she wanted to say. So much she wanted to scream. Her mind couldn't form anything coherent as she struggled to comprehend everything.

In the end she didn't say anything, but turned and walked out.

311

Chapter 32

Tara was awake for most of the night, tossing and turning as she rehashed everything. She tormented herself thinking of all the good times with James: renovating the shop, walking on the beach, lazy dinners at his place. Then her mind would flick to the mess of the past month. It was no surprise to her that her relationship with James had fallen apart. The only surprise was the how and why of it.

It was almost daylight before she finally fell asleep, and only a couple of hours later when she was woken by her phone vibrating on the bedside table. There was a brief moment where she thought it would be James. Looking at the screen, she saw it was Amber and remembered she was supposed to be going over to Annette's place to scatter the dog's ashes. It had never been an appealing activity for a Saturday morning, but it was even less so now.

"Are you still in bed?" Amber asked.

"Yeah."

"You're coming to Annette's though?"

"No," she said slowly. "I've got a headache."

"Take some painkillers," Amber said. "Josie's really upset. She's expecting you to be there."

"I'll give her a call later. She'll understand."

"I can't believe you sometimes," Amber said. "Josie's your friend and she needs some support."

Tara moved the phone from her ear, tempted to hang up and switch the phone off.

"Fine, I'll come," she finally said.

"Really?"

"Yes. See you in a bit." She ended the call. As though things couldn't get any worse, she now had to go to a funeral for a dog and be sociable while she was at it.

It was an hour later when she arrived at Annette's place. She parked at the side of the house alongside Max's car. At least he might be able to cheer her up.

In the kitchen, Annette wrapped her in a big hug. Tara offered her condolences for Macy. It made Tara emotional, and she took a deep breath before heading into the noisy living room. Josie was there, sitting on the couch with her sister, Lizzie. They were fussing over whichever baby Josie had in her arms. Max paced the room with the other baby while Sam crawled around the room with Kieron on his back. Amber sat beside the fire with Charlie, the golden retriever. The poor old dog would be lost without his playmate.

Tara called hello and was met with a variety of greetings. She perched on the arm of the couch beside Josie and peered down at the peaceful baby in her arms.

"Cute," she said. "Which is which?"

"This is Phoebe," Josie said, then nodded at Max. "That's Maya."

"Twins must be a handful," Tara said. It felt like stating the obvious but she was struggling for small talk.

"Yes," Lizzie said. "It's hard work."

"Do you want to hold her?" Josie asked.

"No," Tara said, too quickly.

Amber looked up from stroking the dog. "Tara has an aversion to babies."

"Don't you like babies?" Josie asked.

"I don't dislike them." Tara really wasn't in the mood for this conversation. "She's settled though. Don't disturb her."

"She'd probably vomit all down you anyway," Max said as milky white liquid dripped down the front of his shirt. He reached a hand to Lizzie, who threw him a cloth to wipe it up.

"Have you ever even held a baby?" Josie asked, looking up at Tara.

Tara gazed down at the tiny little bundle of joy and felt her chest tighten. "Yes," she said quietly.

"She held Kieron when he was a baby," Amber said. "When I forced him on her!"

"I prefer kids when they're a bit sturdier." Tara stood and headed for the kitchen. "I'm going to see if Annette needs help."

Annette was pulling a tray of biscuits from the oven.

"Need a hand?" Tara asked.

"You can start taking drinks through." She tipped her head towards a row of steaming coffee mugs.

Tara went back into the living room, dodging around Sam. "Careful, Kieron," she said. "We've got hot drinks. You might need to tie your donkey up outside." Kieron's giggles filled the room.

"I'm a lion," Sam said, roaring.

"I could've sworn you were a donkey," Tara said, chuckling and moving out of the way when he pretended to bite her leg, much to Kieron's delight.

Almost as soon as they'd finished their drinks, Josie ushered them all outside. They were going to scatter the ashes under the big oak tree beside the barn. Josie's friend Emily was supposed to be there with Jack, but apparently they'd been held up and wouldn't arrive until later. Josie didn't want to wait for them. It was all a bit weird anyway. Surely they didn't actually want to be around to scatter the dog's ashes. They were probably arriving late on purpose.

It took a while for Lizzie and Max to get the babies organised and in the double buggy. Lizzie kept snapping at Max to find various items – dummies and blankets and who knows what. Tara wanted to point out that they were only going to the end of the garden, but she didn't think it would go down well.

As they made their way down to the old oak tree, Tara fell into step with Amber.

"I can't believe you dragged me out of bed for this," she whispered. Kieron was ahead of them, on Sam's shoulders.

"Josie appreciates you being here," Amber said. "And you'd already taken the day off work."

Tara's stomach lurched at the thought of work. It was never going to be the same again. If she could

316

even go back. She wasn't sure she could cope with being in the same room as James. How could he sleep with someone else? She bit her lip and focused on her breathing. It really wasn't the time or place to fall apart.

"Josie's quiet, isn't she?" Amber remarked. "She doesn't seem herself."

"Probably morning sickness," Tara said mischievously.

"She's upset about Macy," Amber said with a slight shake of the head. "Try and be a bit sympathetic."

"It was Annette's dog," Tara said. "I don't know why Josie's so upset." She fell silent as they caught up with the rest of the party by the barn. Sam lifted Kieron from his shoulders and passed him to Amber, then put an arm around Josie, who looked like she was about to burst into tears.

Annette was holding it together much better. She cheerfully told them all the tale of the day she and Wendy got Macy, and a few anecdotes about the feisty little dog. The other dog, Charlie, stayed by her side the whole time.

As soon as she began pouring out the ashes, Josie let out a loud sob and then cried hysterically, burying her head into Sam's chest. The rest of them exchanged glances. The atmosphere was terrible.

Tara leaned in to whisper to Amber as they set off back to the house. "That was a dramatic reaction for a dog that didn't even belong to her. It's probably all the pregnancy hormones turning her into an emotional wreck."

Amber swatted at Tara's arm in reply.

Back at the house, Annette fussed over everyone, offering drinks and snacks as always. When Amber said she was going to get Kieron home for his nap, Tara excused herself too.

"You're coming out tonight, aren't you?" Josie asked as they lingered in the kitchen saying their goodbyes.

Tara gave her a big hug. She felt like she'd done her duty and was keen to avoid having to spend an evening being sociable. All she wanted to do was go home and hide in her bed. Her mind wandered constantly to James and Olivia. The only positive she could find to focus on was that she hadn't told anyone about her relationship with James. At least she didn't have to endure the humiliation of everyone knowing the situation.

"If you're not feeling up to it," she said to Josie, "we don't have to."

Josie's face was blotchy from crying. "I really want you to meet Emily and Jack. And I want you to talk to Emily about a book signing. She's a bit shy about stuff, but if you ask her I'm sure she'll go for it."

"We'll be there," Amber said decisively. "Usual time?"

"Yes." Josie gave her a hug. "Thanks."

"See you later then," Tara said as brightly as she could.

Driving through Averton, Tara was tempted to go straight to the pub. She checked the time before deciding it was a bad idea. Going home also didn't

318

seem like a good idea. There was too much alcohol in her cupboards.

In the end, she called in at her mum's house. She was happy to see Tara and was surprisingly upbeat. The box of old photos was out on the coffee table again. Glancing round the room, Tara noticed that the framed photos on display had been moved around. Sometimes Mum would swap the photos around, claiming that if you kept the same ones up for too long you got so used to seeing them that you didn't notice them anymore. Tara always felt that not noticing them was a blessing. If it were up to her she'd collect up all the photos and hide them away.

"You could put up some recent photos," she suggested. "It can't be healthy to live in the past so much."

"Actually, Angela said it's good. She thinks you need to be able to reflect on your past in a healthy way."

"How's it going with Angela?" Tara asked. Her mum had mentioned the last time she saw her that she was having sessions with the counsellor again.

"Really good," Debbie said. "It's amazing how much it helps to talk things through."

Tara flopped onto the couch and mumbled a vague agreement. Honestly, she didn't agree. An image of James flashed into her head and she pushed it aside. If she could avoid thinking about him she would. Unfortunately, she didn't have as much control over her thoughts as she'd like. The one thing she could control was talking about him. Or not talking about him.

She rested her elbow on the arm of the couch and propped her head up, trying to ignore the way her mum flicked through the box of old family photos. Going home and being alone seemed like a good option all of a sudden.

"I'm never quite sure how much you remember from when we lived in London," Debbie said.

"Enough to know I don't want to think about it," Tara said tersely. "Can you please put the stupid box away?"

"Look at this one." Her mum ignored the request and held up a photo. "You were so cute."

"I don't understand how looking at these helps. Surely you should focus on the future not the past."

"Have you spoken to your dad recently?" her mum asked, ignoring her again.

"No."

"You should. Why don't you go and visit him?"

"Why doesn't he visit us?" she asked. The conversation was old and stale.

"Because he thinks you don't want him to."

"Well, at least he got that right."

"He said he emails you and you don't reply."

Tara tensed. Why on earth were her divorced parents such good buddies? "He emails me photos of his family, and tells me how great his kids are. Like he wants to rub my nose in it that we weren't good enough for him."

"That's not true. He just doesn't know what to say to you. You could make more effort."

Tara pulled her legs up onto the couch and dropped her head onto the arm. "Can we change the subject, please? Things are bad enough already without you wanting to rehash the past."

"You might feel better if you talked to him properly. Or me. You can always talk to me."

Tara pulled a cushion over her head. In the blackness, all she could think about was James. A feeling of utter hopelessness washed over her. Her mum patted her leg and mumbled something about making sandwiches, leaving Tara alone with her thoughts.

If she weren't so devastated, she might be able to laugh at the irony of breaking up with James because she wanted him to have kids, only for her to now be furious at him for getting someone pregnant. It felt like there was a brick in her chest when she thought about it. He'd actually slept with someone else. She'd told him she wanted him to have kids one day, and now he was going to. Perhaps she should have specified she meant a little further in the future than nine months.

Her lungs fought for air, and she moved the cushion from her face and turned on her back, trying to relax her throat enough to get oxygen to her chest.

"What's going on with you?" her mum asked five minutes later as she put a plate of sandwiches on the coffee table. "You said things were bad enough already. What's wrong?"

"Nothing." She swung her legs round and smiled at the cheese and pickle sandwiches. There was something very comforting about her mum making her favourite sandwiches for her. "Everything's okay," she said. "I was over at Annette's this morning. The dog died and Josie was really upset. It was a weird morning, that's all."

"How's Annette?"

"She seemed okay."

"It must be hard for her without Wendy."

"Josie and Sam are there a lot," Tara said.

When Tara finished her sandwiches, Debbie picked up a section of Tara's hair from her shoulder. "I can give you a trim, if you want?"

"Okay." She felt like doing something radical. "Maybe you should chop it all off."

"No," Debbie said firmly. "You'll have to find another hairdresser for that. I'd cry cutting your beautiful hair off."

Tara had always kept her hair long, but she was suddenly tempted to make some changes. Cut her hair off, find a new job, maybe move to a different country. Change was very appealing.

It was relaxing to sit in her mum's kitchen and have a haircut. Her mum being present enough to look after her couldn't have come at a better time. She regaled Tara with tales of her clients. It made a refreshing change from her mum talking about the people in her online circles.

Late in the afternoon, her mum asked Tara to go out for a walk with her. Apparently, she was trying to spend more time in nature and do more exercise. Tara declined, checking the time and realising she needed to go home and change if she wanted to be on time to meet Josie and her friends in the pub.

She'd just got into her car when she realised there was really no need to get changed for an evening in

322

the Bluebell Inn. Mainly she realised that driving home involved passing the bookshop, and she was worried she might fall apart and not make it out of the house again.

She called out to her mum who'd started walking down the road. She told her she was going to head straight to the pub and would leave her car where it was and collect it the following day.

"I can drive over in the morning and pick you up," Debbie said. Wow, she really was doing better. Often, she couldn't manage to plan more than an hour ahead.

"That would be great," Tara called, then set off on the short walk down to the village. Maybe a night out would perk her up.

Chapter 33

t felt like her body was pinned to the bed. Tara squinted at the daylight that streamed in through the gap in the curtains. A night out had definitely *not* perked her up. Perhaps she should stop tempting fate by thinking things couldn't possibly get any worse.

Drinking alone before the others arrived hadn't been a good idea. She was in a foul mood by the time Amber arrived, and had launched into an angry rant as they stood together at the bar. She'd really gone on, waging bets on Max and Lizzie getting divorced and Josie being pregnant. Unbeknown to Tara, Josie's friends Emily and Jack were standing right beside them and overheard the whole thing. The evening was pretty awkward after that. As far as first impressions went it was about as bad as it could've been.

When Tara finally dragged herself out of bed, it was a surprise to find an email from Emily. Attached was a digital copy of her new book. Tara had offered to help with marketing in a bid to redeem herself. She'd thought Emily was just being polite when she'd said she'd send her a copy. Opening the file on her Kindle, Tara went back to bed to begin reading it. Historical romance wasn't her favourite genre –

though she'd yet to decide what was; it changed depending on her mood. She found herself enjoying the book nonetheless and was thankful for the distraction.

There was a possibility she would have stayed there until she finished it if it weren't for the doorbell ringing. She peeked out of the bedroom window. If it was James, she'd ignore him. When she'd checked her phone at the end of the previous evening there was an onslaught of messages from him, and she'd hidden her phone away in a drawer. Thankfully it was her mum on the doorstep.

"What are you doing here?" she asked as she opened the door. It was a pleasant surprise. Her mum hardly ever came over to visit her.

"I thought you wanted a lift to get your car." She handed over a bunch of tulips.

"Thank you." Tara went to the kitchen in search of a vase.

"They're a lovely colour, aren't they?" Debbie said, following her. "I bought myself a bunch too. They brighten the place up."

"They're gorgeous." Tara arranged the purple flowers in the vase. "I forgot all about my car."

"You didn't answer the phone so I thought I'd just come over."

"I haven't even looked at my phone this morning," she said. "Do you want a drink?"

"Tea, please. I've been to the bakery too. I brought croissants."

Tara felt a wave of emotion as she took the paper bag from her. Her mum was in such a good mood.

They sat together on the couch, eating the croissants and chatting amiably. Then Tara went for a quick shower and got dressed before they drove back to her mum's house.

She didn't stay at her mum's but got straight in her car and headed home again. On the drive, her thoughts turned to James. If she intended to keep her job she couldn't keep avoiding him. Sadly, she realised she might need to seriously think about job hunting. It was hard to imagine how she could keep working with him.

When the thought of leaving her job felt too much, she took a deep breath and decided she'd go and finish reading Emily's book. It would be a good distraction. Then she had an idea. If she had a project to throw herself into at work, maybe she could face going in.

From what she'd read of Emily's new book, she was confident it was just as good as her previous ones. Definitely good enough for her to promote at the bookshop. They could have a launch party for when it released. It was just the sort of project Tara needed to throw herself into. All Tara had to do was convince Emily that she wasn't a horrible person who made a habit of gossiping about her friends behind their backs.

Turning the car around in the next driveway, she headed back the way she'd come. From the conversation the previous evening, Tara knew Emily and Jack would be at Annette's place, having lunch with Josie and Sam. Nobody would be at all surprised by Tara gatecrashing a meal at Annette's house.

***

On Monday morning, Tara dragged herself out o
bed and determinedly got ready for work. When
she'd split up with James on her terms she'd
intended to keep working at the bookshop. So she
still could. That's what she kept telling herself. I
was only when she grabbed her phone as she was
leaving the house that doubt crept in. She paused by
the door, reading the messages from James that
she'd been avoiding looking at over the weekend.
He was sorry and he wanted to talk were the main
themes.

On the walk to work, she told herself working
with James was manageable. She had Emily's book
launch to organise, so she intended to throw hersel
into that.

In the end it had been easy to persuade Emily to
come for an event at the bookshop. The afternoon at
Annette's place had been surprisingly enjoyable. I
was much more relaxed than the first time she'd met
Emily and Jack. After getting to know them better
the fact that Jack was Josie's ex didn't seem as
weird as it previously had. He and Emily were a cute
couple, and if Josie didn't have an issue with the
situation, she supposed no one else should.

Tara arrived at the shop early, intending to be
immersed in organising Emily's book launch by the
time James came down. Her plan was to cultivate a
new and entirely professional working relationship

with him. Eventually, she'd stop being angry with him, and her feelings for him would dissolve. He'd move on and have his little family with Olivia, and Tara would go back to her plan of being a happy singleton with a job that she loved.

It seemed like a great plan until she looked in the window of the bookshop and saw James was already downstairs. He was standing at the counter, leaning casually as he stared at the computer. Tara felt faint. Taking a step back, she put a hand on the wall, sure she was about to pass out.

How on earth had she thought she could continue working with him? There was no way in the world her plan would work. She was furious with him. And she loved him so much.

Quickly, she tapped out a message to James saying she wouldn't be at work that day. She sneaked a look through the window and watched him stand up straighter as he read the message. He pushed a hand through his lovely hair, then began typing out a reply. Tara didn't want to read any more messages from him. She messaged Amber and Josie telling them she was ill and wouldn't be in the shop that morning. Hopefully they hadn't already set off for the usual Monday morning coffee.

Before James's message came through, she switched her phone off and headed home. She didn't go inside, but climbed straight into her car and set off for the coast. A change of scene might do her some good.

She felt better as soon as the sea air hit her lungs. She stood for a few minutes looking out over the harbour at Dartmouth. The ferry boats chugged across the River Dart, and the sails of the yachts moored in the harbour tinkled gently as they bobbed. Seagulls hopped along the small stretch of beach between the boats lying on the wet sand.

After a few minutes taking in the picturesque view, Tara walked back the way she'd come and nipped into the bakery, from where the scent of fresh bread wafted out into the street.

Outside the Bookshelf Tara paused, thinking of the last time she was there. It felt like a lifetime ago.

There were no customers in the shop. Tara grinned as she held up the paper bag from the bakery. "Did someone order a chocolate croissant and a cream cheese bagel?"

"Tara!" Deirdre rushed over and threw her arms around her. "It's so lovely to see you. We often talk about you."

"I'm sorry it took me so long." She kissed Darren's cheek and handed over the treats. "I should have been to visit sooner."

"Don't worry," Darren said. "We know how it is. Running a bookshop keeps you busy."

"Come and tell us all about it," Deirdre said, pulling Tara further into the shop. It felt amazingly familiar. Tara had only spent one day there but it felt so homely.

"How's it all going?" Darren asked, then took a large bite of his croissant.

"The shop's done really well," she said. "I was so worried that we'd fail, but the place is plodding along nicely."

"I knew you'd make a go of it," Deirdre said. "Darren wasn't convinced but *I* knew it. You had a look in your eye that day you were here. Absolute determination. Nothing was going to stop you. I knew you'd overcome any hurdles."

Tara beamed at the compliment, then without warning her eyes filled with tears. She put a hand to her face as a sob escaped her. "I'm sorry," she said quickly.

Deirdre was beside her in an instant, a reassuring hand on her back leading her to the armchair in the corner. Tara sat down and Deirdre perched on the arm, gently rubbing Tara's back as she cried.

"I'm so sorry." Tara took a deep breath and tried to compose herself.

Deirdre gave her a tissue, and Tara wiped her eyes, feeling utterly pathetic. By the time she'd calmed down, Darren was in front of her with a cup of tea. She blew on it before taking a sip. It was sweet and surprisingly comforting.

"Do you want to talk about it?" Deirdre said, laying a concerned hand on her shoulder.

"I think I might have to leave my job," she said, wiping the remaining tears from her cheeks.

"But I thought the shop was doing well," Deirdre said. "And you enjoy it, don't you?"

"I love it," she said. "I don't want to leave." Sniffing, she looked from Deirdre to Darren, who seemed to be waiting for the rest of the story.

"I fell in love with the boss," she said. Admitting it out loud gave her a strange sense of relief. She'd never told anyone how she felt about him. Not even him.

"Doesn't he feel the same?" Deirdre asked.

"He does," she said. "It's complicated though. We can't be together. And I'm not sure I can still work with him. It's too hard."

"That sounds like a difficult situation," Deirdre said gently.

"It's a safe space here." Darren perched on the other arm of the chair and patted Tara's knee. "Anything you need to get off your chest, just go ahead."

Tara took another sip of the tea. She wasn't even sure how to explain. "We were together for a little while," she said slowly. "And everything was great. But I didn't think it was going to work so I ended things."

"If things were going well, why would you break up with him?" Deirdre asked.

"Good question," Tara said with a sigh. "Because I've got issues," she added under her breath.

"There's more to this story, isn't there?" Darren asked.

Tara nodded slowly. "I don't want children and I know he does. That's why I ended it. But I was starting to think things might work out anyway. Except … now things definitely won't work out."

"Why?" Deirdre asked.

Tara took a deep breath, not sure she could force the words out. "Because his ex-girlfriend is pregnant with his baby." God, it sounded so ridiculous. Her life was like a soap opera.

Darren inhaled deeply. "Well, that is a bit of a

pickle."

"So he got back together with his ex-girlfriend?" Deirdre asked.

"No." Tara sank further into the chair. "As far as I can gather it was a one-night thing after we broke up. Or so he says."

"Perfect," Darren said, standing up.

"Is it?" Tara asked, taken aback.

He bobbed his head. "He gets a kid for the weekends, and you don't have to worry about him being childless for you. Seems like the perfect solution to me."

Deirdre gasped and reached out to slap his arm. "You can't be serious?"

"I don't know what the problem is," Darren said, looking genuinely puzzled.

"What about the fact that he cheated on her?" Deirdre said.

"Did he?" Darren looked at Tara. "I thought you'd broken up?"

"We had," she said weakly. "I think."

"See," he said to Deirdre with a triumphant tone. "They were on a break."

"Oh, will you stop!" Deirdre shook her head and looked at Tara. "His favourite TV show is *Friends*. He can barely go a day without quoting Ross Geller. And, by the way . . ." She glared at Darren. "Ross was out of order and you know it. Poor Rachel had every right to be furious."

"Well, if she didn't want him to sleep with someone else she shouldn't have broken up with him," Darren said.

"But if he loved her he'd have been thinking about how to win her back, not off jumping into bed with someone else!" Deirdre argued.

"He was upset." Darren sighed heavily. "He wasn't thinking straight."

"Well, that's a fine excuse." Deirdre clicked her tongue and glanced at Tara. "Bloody men!"

Tara watched in amusement as Deirdre and Darren continued the lively discussion. She had no idea if they were talking about Ross and Rachel or her and James but it didn't matter; it was very entertaining.

They only stopped when customers entered the shop. After that the subject didn't come up again. Tara kept thinking she should leave, but whenever there was a lull between customers Deirdre got chatting about books. She was impressed by the change in Tara. It was hard to believe that it wasn't much more than a year ago that Tara was there with almost no knowledge of books at all. Now she could chat all day about literature. Which she did, in the end.

She also told Deirdre all about the author events she'd held, and about Emily and her books. Though Tara was starting to think she may have to back out of the launch party. She'd feel bad – Emily had seemed excited about it.

The day flew by. When Tara wasn't chatting to Deirdre about books, she was curled up in the chair reading a book that Deirdre recommended. After such a bad start to the day she was pleasantly surprised by how it had ended up. Closing time came around far too soon.

"You don't want to go home, do you?" Deirdre asked as though reading her mind.

"You were right," Tara said, looking at Darren. "It's a safe space. I feel much better just being here."

"Stay the night if you want," Deirdre said.

Tara's eyebrows shot up. "At your place?"

"No." Darren chuckled. "Here! There's an apartment upstairs. We used to rent it out but we had a problem with the last tenant which put us off. It's been empty for a few months."

"It's got a sea view," Deirdre said. "It's good for the soul."

"I shouldn't," Tara said. "I've already put you out enough."

"It's no trouble," Deirdre said. "In fact, Darren has a dentist appointment in the morning, so if you stayed and gave me a hand in the shop tomorrow it would be a great help."

"That's a good idea," Darren agreed.

Tara was certain they were just being kind, but it was a tempting offer, and after a moment's hesitation she took them up on it.

The apartment had a separate entrance, so Tara had to go out of the shop and in the front door beside it, then straight up a steep staircase which led to a small landing. There was a bedroom, a bathroom and a living room with a kitchenette. It was basic but pleasant enough. And the front window looked out over the estuary. The view was wonderful.

Deirdre was right about the sea view. It was good for the soul. After a short walk down to the harbour for a fish and chip supper, Tara spent the evening sitting by the window, reading. Occasionally, she glanced out of the window at the people on the street below or gazed at the lights shimmering on the water. It was wonderfully peaceful.

She vaguely thought about turning her phone on to check the messages, but she'd managed to tuck her problems in a far corner of her mind and she didn't want to draw them out again. So she kept it switched off and enjoyed the feeling of being disconnected.

Unsurprisingly, her sleep was disturbed, and it was an effort to get up when her alarm went off. It would be rude not to be in the shop first thing, even if she was sure Deirdre had only asked for her help to make her feel useful.

It was another pleasant morning in the Bookshelf, and when Darren suggested she move in upstairs and help them on a permanent basis she was almost tempted to take him up on it. She couldn't hide forever though. Driving back to Newton Abbot that afternoon made her feel weary.

Hiding a little longer would have been nice.

Chapter 34

The downside to hiding away with your phone switched off was turning it on again to all the messages and missed calls. Most were from Amber, but one or two were from Josie and James. The messages had a common theme: where was she? Tara felt a wave of guilt for ignoring her friends. With a sigh, she sent Amber a message reassuring her she was fine, and then sent an almost identical message to Josie. It was no surprise when her phone rang a moment later.

"Where have you been?" Amber asked.

"In bed, ill," she said. "Sorry. My phone died and I couldn't find the charger. It was in the car."

"I almost came over," Amber said. "I was worried."

"I'm fine," she said brightly. "Sorry to worry you."

"I'm glad you're okay," Amber said. "I bet James was lost without you at work for two days. Are you going in tomorrow?"

"Yes." That was the plan. Hopefully she'd make it through the door this time. "I'm sure he managed fine without me."

"What was wrong with you anyway?"

"Just a cold," Tara said, hating the lie. Part of her wanted to tell Amber everything. The trouble was she'd told so many lies it was hard to unravel them all. It would take a lot of explaining. And Amber wouldn't understand.

"I'm glad you're feeling better. I'll probably see you later in the week."

"Yes," she said. "Thanks for calling."

With her phone still in her hand Tara contemplated messaging James to tell him she'd be back at work the following day. A lump formed in her throat as she thought about him. She swung between being furious with him and feeling sorry for him. He'd looked such a mess the last time she saw him. In the end she messaged him and said she was okay. That was all she could manage, and she wasn't even sure it was true.

On Wednesday morning Tara was outside the shop again. This time she didn't hang around, just marched straight in.

James looked up from the computer and stared at her. "Hi."

"Hi." Tara walked straight past him and hung her coat in the back, then took a deep breath and went back to him. "Sorry about the time off," she said confidently.

"It's fine." He stood up straighter, swallowed hard. "I wasn't sure if you were coming back."

"Neither was I." She went over to rearrange the beanbags. "Would it have been better if I'd stayed away?"

"No," he said quickly. "I'm glad you're here."

"Good. I met up with Emily Winters the other day. Josie's author friend. I told her she could have a launch party here for her next book." She pummelled the green beanbag into shape. "That's okay, isn't it? I thought we'd make it an evening event."

"It's fine," James said. She felt his eyes on her the whole time but couldn't bring herself to look at him.

"I'll start organising it. I'll need to make some promotional materials. Posters and flyers. Can I use your laptop and do those this morning?" She'd intended to bring her own laptop but had been too preoccupied to remember much that morning.

"Yeah. It's upstairs."

She glanced at him. "Can you get it? I'll work in the kitchen."

"You can work upstairs if you want. It's comfier."

"I'd rather work in the kitchen." There was no way she could go up to his apartment. It was full of memories, both good and bad.

"I'll fetch it," he said.

As soon as he was out of the room, Tara clutched a shelf and inhaled deeply. It was so hard being around him.

He was back too soon and held out the laptop to her. "I'm sorry," he whispered as she took it.

"I know you are."

"I hate that I hurt you. I wish I knew what to do to fix everything."

Again, she found herself feeling sorry for him. Because she knew what he said was true; he *was* sorry, and he clearly felt terrible.

"I'm not sure what to say," she said slowly. "And I don't know if I really can work with you. But I can't stand the thought of losing this place as well as you."

He nodded, and the pain in his features was hard to witness. "I'm glad you're here," he said again.

"I'm going to get on with this." Holding up the laptop, she walked out the back door and into the kitchen.

It was fairly absorbing work designing posters and flyers. She got creative and spent far more time on it than was necessary. When she finished them, she sent them straight over to Emily for her opinion and to get her to confirm the date before she started promoting it. A reply came quickly to say Emily loved the promotional materials and the date worked fine.

The launch would take place the following Friday. Emily would come down from Oxford for the weekend, and Josie had said she wanted them all to go wedding dress shopping with her the same weekend so Emily didn't have to make a separate trip for it.

There wasn't a lot of time for Tara to organise it, but she hoped there'd be a good turnout nonetheless. She would organise drinks and nibbles, and Emily would prepare a little something to say. She seemed nervous so Tara reassured her, saying she could talk as much or as little as she wanted. She knew most people would be happy just to meet the author and get a signed book.

Next she emailed Barbara, attaching one of the flyers and asking her to forward it to the members of her book club. There would no doubt be a good showing from them. She posted about the event on all the bookshop's social media pages and then trawled Facebook, looking for any appropriate groups to post in. Mostly, she was just avoiding joining James in the shop.

When she finally ventured back out, James was chatting to a middle-aged man in the crime section. Tara wandered the shop, looking for something to do. Other than straightening a few books she couldn't find much.

"I might make a sandwich," James said after the man left. "Do you want one?"

"No, thanks," she said automatically.

James headed for the door. "Are you sure?"

No, she wasn't sure. She wasn't really sure of anything.

"Okay," she said. "I'll have a sandwich. Whatever there is."

She wasn't even hungry. Her appetite had vanished since Olivia's revelation. She had to eat though.

Fifteen minutes later, James came back.

"Food's in the kitchen," he said. He must have eaten already. Tara was glad he'd assumed she'd want to eat alone. The kitchen was far too small a space to be in with him.

She didn't know whether to laugh or cry when she took a bite of the sandwich. It was cheese and pickle. She chewed slowly. Then her throat constricted with emotion and she almost choked as a sob came out of nowhere.

It was the longest lunch break she'd ever taken as she sat at the table with her head in her hands. Why couldn't she have a simple life like everyone else? All her friends fell in love, then got married and settled down to live happily ever after. It should be so easy.

Finally, Tara pulled herself together and went back to the shop. She thanked James for the sandwich without even looking at him. They had some customers throughout the afternoon, mostly the chatty types who hung around for a long time. As long as there was someone else was in the shop, things were bearable. It was when she was alone with James that it was a struggle.

Over that week and the following one, Tara did everything she could to avoid being alone with James. She made sure she always had a job on hand for the times it was just the two of them: she'd remember she had to talk to Andy at the Bluebell Inn about borrowing glasses for the launch party, or she'd go and talk to someone at the community centre about borrowing chairs. She used the chair excuse a few times, claiming the person she needed to talk to was difficult to get hold of. Actually, she'd sorted the chair situation out with a five-minute phone call and her trips out involved wandering around the block a few times.

Tara was slightly concerned about what she'd do after the launch party when she didn't have so much work to do, or pretend to do. She'd have to find nother project to throw herself into.

***

On the Friday of the launch party, Tara was busy all day. She drove to Averton to collect the wine glasses and the bottles of Prosecco Andy had ordered for her, then she made a few trips back and forth to the community centre to collect the chairs.

She slipped straight into upbeat and excitable mode when Josie and Emily arrived late in the afternoon. Emily seemed fairly anxious, and Tara used it as an excuse to crack open the wine. It would help curb Emily's nerves and hopefully calm Tara down too.

James appeared just after Tara had made a toast to Emily and her new book. When he came over to meet Emily and have a drink with them, Tara was trying so hard to be cheerful she felt borderline manic. Josie was unusually quiet too, so Tara felt alone in her task to keep the energy up. Although there was a chance Josie just couldn't get a word in with Tara's endless chatter.

Part of her wished James would disappear upstairs and leave them to it, but it was his shop. It might seem odd if he wasn't there. He was helpful with setting the chairs up and filling wine glasses as people arrived.

After Tara introduced Emily, she stood at the back of the crowd. It was a great turnout. There weren't enough chairs, but people didn't seem to mind standing. Emily got into her stride after a couple of

343

minutes and chatted confidently about her writing career.

Tara's attention kept shifting from Emily and landing on James. He was standing against the wall near the back door. The midnight-blue shirt he was wearing was one of her favourites. Her gaze lingered on him as he watched Emily intently. As though he felt her watching, he turned and caught her eye. Quickly, she shifted her attention to Emily and ignored her racing heart.

After that it was hard to focus on anything Emily was saying. There were some questions at the end and then a hearty round of applause. Tara went over to Emily and thanked everyone for coming and encouraged them to stay and get their books signed by the author.

There were a few people waiting to buy books. Tara was about to go and serve them but James got there first. She caught sight of Belinda making a beeline for her through the crowd but couldn't get out of the way quickly enough.

"I heard about James and his ex," Belinda said quietly.

"What are you talking about?" Tara asked. How would Belinda know?

Belinda twirled the wine glass in her hand. "I don't get it," she said. "He's lovely. What does he see in Olivia? Is it me, or is she a bit mentally unstable?"

"I don't really know her." Tara's gaze drifted to James, chatting and smiling with customers.

"Surely he's just marrying her because of the

baby?" Belinda said. "Do you think she got pregnant on purpose to trap him? I wouldn't put it past her."

"What?" Tara flicked her eyes to Belinda. "Who said they're getting married?"

"Olivia did."

Tara shook her head in confusion. "When did she say that?"

"She was in the chemist last week. We got chatting." Belinda sipped her drink. "Oh, I'm not supposed to tell anyone. Sounds like it's not common knowledge yet. She said they're waiting until after the baby arrives to get married."

"If no one knows, why are you telling me?" Tara snapped.

Belinda grimaced. "Sorry. I assumed you'd know."

"You need to stop gossiping so much," Tara said tersely. "Mind your own business for a change."

Belinda rolled her eyes and sauntered away, no doubt to find a more appreciative audience for her gossip. Her words swirled around Tara's head. She must have got it wrong; there was no way James was marrying Olivia. They were having a kid together, but they didn't have a relationship beyond that. Or did they? Tara had been so busy trying to avoid talking to James about it that she was now left with no idea what was going on. Maybe they'd decided to give it a go for the sake of the baby.

"Are you okay?" Josie asked, sidling up beside her.

"Yes!" She beamed. "Emily was great, wasn't she? You'd never have known she hates public speaking."

"I knew she'd be fine as soon as she got going," Josie said. "Thanks for organising it all."

"My pleasure," she said brightly. "Are you okay? You're quiet this evening."

"I'm great," she said.

Tara didn't quite believe her, but they were interrupted by one of the ladies from Barbara's book club, so she didn't get chance to dig deeper.

By the end of the evening, Tara was exhausted. It had been a success; all of the books had sold and Emily seemed to be on a bit of a high.

When Tara hugged Emily goodbye outside the shop, she felt a little emotional. Emily had helped Tara get through the last couple of weeks without even knowing it.

"Do you want a lift home?" Josie called from beside her car.

Tara dithered for a moment. She was tempted to go back and talk to James and find out if what Belinda had said was true.

"Yes, please," she finally said. The chat with James could wait. She was too tired and emotional to try and have a rational conversation.

Chapter 35

In the hopes of clearing her head, Tara walked into work on Monday morning, mulling over the events of the weekend as she went.

Wedding dress shopping with Josie had been a disaster. It was a stark reminder to Tara of all the things she would never have. In a bid to stay upbeat she'd consumed the best part of a bottle of fizzy wine at the dress shop and had only been vaguely aware of Josie's strange mood.

It was in the pub on the Saturday evening that Josie finally broke down in tears and told them about her recent miscarriage. Tara felt awful – not just because Josie was so upset but for all the time she'd spent teasing Josie for not drinking.

There was no sign of James when Tara arrived at the shop. She'd only been there a few minutes when knocking at the window drew her attention. She turned to see Emily waving at her.

"I thought you'd be on your way back to Oxford by now," Tara said, smiling widely as she let her in.

"I am," she said. "I just wanted to come and say thank you again for Friday."

"You're welcome," Tara said. "Have you got time for a coffee?"

Emily accepted the offer. She gushed about the shop again as they moved to the coffee machine.

"How's Josie?" Tara asked as she poured the drinks.

"I'm not sure." Emily frowned. "I think it probably did her good to talk everything through. I can't believe she'd been keeping it to herself."

Tara could absolutely understand Josie keeping it to herself. As the queen of dealing with things privately, Tara had no problem relating. It was good that Josie had finally opened up though. Maybe Tara should do the same and tell someone all of her problems. But she couldn't see how it would help her situation.

They moved to sit in the beanbags and chatted about Josie for a few minutes, sharing their concern for her. Then Emily cautiously manoeuvred the conversation to James.

"Is it true what Josie says about him being in love with you?" she asked.

Tara blew on her coffee. Her instinct was to change the subject, but she couldn't help but think about Josie sharing her problems. Emily was easy to talk to, and it felt somehow easier that they weren't close.

"Sometimes Josie gets things back to front," she finally said.

It took a moment for Emily to digest the information, then her eyes widened in surprise. Tara spent the next ten minutes telling Emily how hard it was to work with James. She calmly told Emily the worst-case version of events: that James was engaged and they were expecting a baby. It was as though she was preparing herself for that eventuality. If she could say it aloud, she'd be able to cope when James confirmed it was true.

Emily was a good listener and didn't pass judgement, but commented on how difficult it must be.

"How on earth do you manage to work with him?" she asked. "Don't you want to leave?"

"I've had my letter of resignation in my bag for a while," Tara said. "But if I leave I won't see him anymore. This way I still get to see him." And even though seeing him every day might feel like torture, she couldn't quite imagine the alternative – not seeing him at all.

When Emily tried to tell her everything would work out in the end, Tara sighed and took their empty mugs to the counter. "Sorry to dump all this on you," she said.

Emily wrapped her in a hug. "If you ever need someone to talk to, you can always give me a call."

"Thank you," Tara said, though she thought she'd done enough talking to last her a while. "Josie and Amber don't know any of this," she added quickly.

"I won't say anything," Emily promised before thanking her again for the book launch party.

Tara stood at the door, watching her leave. When she turned, James was walking out of the back. He looked slightly puzzled.

"Amber and Josie aren't here?" he asked. "I thought I heard voices."

"It was Emily. She called in to say thanks for the

launch party."

"I presume she was happy with it? It went well, I thought."

"Yeah, it was great."

She nodded at a beanbag in an invitation for him to sit down. It would be easier if she knew exactly what was going on. She had so many questions to ask, but she was scared to hear the answers.

"Are you and Olivia together?" she finally managed.

"No."

She forced her gaze to his face. "Really?"

"I love you," he said. "I don't want to be with anyone else."

It shouldn't be such a relief to hear, but it was. "What will you do about the baby?" she asked. "Share custody?"

He leaned forwards and buried his face in his hands. "I've no idea. I can't actually believe this is happening." He sighed. "It's not what I want. I don't know what to do."

"You're not tempted to marry her and be a happy little family?"

"No." His features were intense. "Of course not. I don't want to be with her. Somehow I'm going to have to figure out how to co-parent with her, but that's all." He stood up and paced. "That sounds insane. It feels completely surreal."

"You'll get used to the idea," she said.

"I hope so. At the moment it makes me feel sick. I always thought becoming a father would be something exciting. This is just a mess." He leaned on the bookcase. "You know I'm sorry, don't you?"

"Yes." She really did feel sorry for him. It was far easier to be angry with him, but no matter what he'd done, nothing had turned out well for either of them.

"I love you," he whispered.

She bit her lip. "Don't say that."

"It's true."

"It doesn't matter. It's too complicated between us. It always has been." She turned and caught his eye. "And you hurt me."

"I know. I never meant to. If I could go back and erase that night I would. I still don't even know what happened."

"Olivia's pregnant," Tara snapped. "I think it's fairly clear what happened."

Silence descended. Tara's phone buzzed in her pocket. She checked it; Amber was worried about Josie and was going to see her. So neither of them would be over that morning. Tara would be alone with James. All day. Suddenly it felt impossible. She walked to the counter and drummed her fingers on it. "I really want to work here, but I don't think I can be around you all the time. It's too hard."

He remained by the shelves, watching her intently. "What do you suggest?"

"Give me the shop," she blurted out.

"What?"

Quietly, she pondered for a moment, but the more she thought about it, the more it seemed like the perfect solution. "Most of the time we don't both need to be here. Let me work alone." She studied his face. He looked pained, but that seemed to be his default recently.

"No," he said. "I can't leave you to do all the work while I … What would I do?"

"I don't know." She stared at her fingers as they tapped the counter. It did seem like a weird request. But when she thought about being around him every minute of her working day, she knew it would only be a matter of time before she broke. It was too much. "Please," she said. "It's the only way I can imagine staying here." She so badly wanted to continue working there. Losing James was bad enough; she couldn't face losing the shop too.

"Okay." He swallowed as he walked over to her. "We can try it for a couple of weeks. I'll stay out of the way during quiet times."

"Thank you."

"It feels weird though, leaving you to do all the work."

It did seem like an odd kind of punishment. He got to hang around not doing much while she ran the shop. But as far as she was concerned, she got the best deal. "I'm quite happy doing all the work," she said. "I like being busy."

He nodded and made for the door.

Tara called him back. "Just to warn you, Belinda knows about the baby. She also seems to think you and Olivia are getting married. So you might want to have a word with her if you don't want rumours flying all over town. Though it might already be too late."

He let out a low growl and headed for the front door. "I'll go and talk to her. Thanks for the heads-up."

Tara watched him go, feeling marginally better. Working alone was a great idea. She wasn't sure how well it would work out, but if it meant she didn't immediately have to start job hunting, it was a relief. She liked the idea of running the place alone.

It went surprisingly well. The first week was a bit awkward. James kept arriving downstairs to check everything was okay, and he'd linger until Tara glared at him impatiently. He didn't seem to like the arrangement at all. Tara loved it. Her favourite part of the week had always been story time, but that soon changed. Those were the times James was in the shop. Watching him play around with the kids felt like someone reaching into her chest and squeezing her heart. She missed him so much.

Sometimes, she even found herself thinking about what Darren had said when she visited the Bookshelf. James would have a child while she had her childfree life. Except she wouldn't be childfree. There'd still be a child in her life, and it would be a constant reminder of James's night with Olivia.

"Where's James?" Amber asked one Monday morning, a few weeks since they'd started the arrangement of him not being around unnecessarily.

"Out for a jog," Tara said. She'd passed him on her way in. He'd taken to jogging most mornings. She wasn't sure what he did with the rest of his time but he'd stopped hanging around so much.

"We hardly see him anymore," Josie said. "I thought he was avoiding us."

353

"We just re-jigged the hours we work so we're not both here unnecessarily."

"I always thought you just liked spending time together," Josie said cheekily.

Tara forced a smile. "It makes more sense. If he's paying me, he doesn't need to be here all the time too."

"If you're not working together all the time, maybe you can finally get together," Amber said as she reached over and wiped Kieron's snotty nose. "Wasn't that the issue, you can't date each other because you work together?"

"No." Tara sighed. It was tempting to tell them about Olivia being pregnant so they might finally stop asking about her and James. The trouble was, she wasn't sure she could make it through the conversation without breaking down in tears. "Men and women can just be friends, you know?"

"If you're definitely not interested in James, maybe you should date someone else." Josie looked at her eagerly, like this might be her new project.

"I don't need a man," Tara insisted. "I have a great job, and a nice life. I'm perfectly happy. Leave me alone."

"Can we set her up with someone at your wedding?" Amber ignored Tara and looked to Josie.

"That's a good idea," Josie said. "Weddings are a great place to find someone. I might invite someone for you."

Tara sipped her coffee. "Please don't. I intend to spend your wedding drinking and dancing." There was no way for her to avoid this wedding, so she

354

was going to have to grin and bear it. At least she already had a dress – the one she'd bought for Max and Lizzie's wedding.

"I'm going to invite a hot guy for you to dance with," Josie said firmly. She had a look in her eye as though she were hatching a plan. "That's how I met Sam. I spent all of Lizzie's wedding dancing with him."

"Do you know someone you can invite?" Amber asked.

"I know the perfect guy." Josie had a mischievous glint in her eye.

"Don't," Tara said. "I mean it. I don't need romantic complications in my life. I'm serious," she said sternly.

Josie smiled into her coffee. "We'll see."

Conversation turned to wedding plans, and Josie spent twenty minutes filling them in on the latest developments.

James came in the back way at some point and appeared in the shop not long after the girls had left. He had a stack of business cards, which he set on the counter beside their own cards.

"What are those?" Tara picked one up. "Since when do we advertise other businesses?" She registered the information on the card. It was for a web design company and included James's details.

"Since I set up another business," he said. "Feel free to pass them out."

"You set up a second business?"

"You stole my job." His tone was gruff and she was taken aback. Was he really angry at her?

355

"Besides, child support won't pay itself, will it?" He turned to go back upstairs.

"Are you annoyed with me?" she snapped, stopping him in his tracks. "Because I'd argue you brought this on yourself." He leaned his head against the doorframe. Tara swallowed the lump in her throat. "Do you want me to leave?"

"No," he muttered. "I'm sorry. I shouldn't take it out on you. You're right; I brought it all on myself."

She moved closer, hating that he wouldn't look at her. "The web design stuff is a good idea."

"Yeah." Finally, he forced a smile. "I got sick of sitting up there contemplating the mess I'm in."

It was hard to see James looking so defeated. And she couldn't help thinking it was partly her fault. If she'd have let him love her without putting so many obstacles in the way things would be completely different.

"Things will probably work out okay in the end." Tara remembered Max saying the same to her. And Emily too. It wasn't advice she'd usually give, but she really wanted it to be true.

"You really believe that?" he asked, looking deep into her eyes.

"I don't know," she said sadly.

Chapter 36

Just as it had the previous summer, business tailed off in August. They stopped offering the story time for the school holidays. It wasn't worth it. Tara also didn't set up any author events. With so many people away on holiday it was hit and miss as to how many people would turn up, so instead they relaxed into a quiet month.

As time went on, Tara felt an increasing sense of concern for James. He'd lost weight and he'd lost his spark. When he was around her, he kept conversation neutral, only talking about work. Tara missed him more and more each day.

James came into the shop for half an hour every day while Tara had a lunch break. He also came down late in the afternoon to take over for the last couple of hours so Tara could go home. After initially wanting to be around him as little as possible, she gradually craved his company and hung around when he came down at the end of the day. He wasn't his usually chatty self, though.

"When's the baby due?" she asked one afternoon in the middle of August.

James was leaning over the computer and looked up in surprise. Generally, Tara never brought up the subject.

"I don't know," he muttered, then went back to the screen.

She let out a laugh and walked over to him. "You're having a baby and you don't know when it's due?"

"November, I suppose."

"You suppose?"

"Yes."

Tara was tempted to walk out and leave him to his bad mood. She didn't want to leave though. Whatever he was going through, she wanted to be there for him.

"But you don't know for definite?" she asked, feeling as though she was poking a bear. "That seems like the sort of thing you should know."

He clicked on the mouse and ignored her.

"Fine. Don't talk to me. I'll see you tomorrow."

"How can I talk to you about this?" he said fiercely. "Do you actually want to hear it?"

She took a deep breath and nodded.

James stood up straighter. He looked exhausted. "Is there any chance you could stay and close up?"

"Yes," she said automatically. It was unusual for him to ask her to work extra hours, but she really didn't mind.

"Thanks." He walked out the back. Tara hesitated before following him into the hallway.

She called out to him and he stopped at the foot of the stairs, one hand on the bannister.

"What's going on?" she asked.

"Olivia isn't speaking to me."

"Why not?" In the past Olivia seemed to hang off his every word, and Tara had often pondered Belinda's remark about her trapping James.

"She wanted us to move in together," he said. "When I made it clear there wasn't going to be anything between us she got annoyed. So *she's* angry with me, *you're* angry with me, and my sister is disgusted with me." He leaned heavily on the bannister. "I'm not even sure how I got myself in this mess."

Without thinking, Tara walked over to him. He tensed as she snaked her arms around his waist. She buried her head in his neck and felt him relax as he hugged her.

"I miss you," he whispered into her hair.

Her chest ached. She missed him too. So much. They stayed in the tight embrace until they were interrupted by the tinkle of the bell over the door. Tara kissed his cheek and went back to the shop. There were a few more customers before she closed up for the day. James startled her when he walked quietly into the shop just as she'd flipped the sign on the door.

"I'm sorry for snapping at you," he said. "You shouldn't be the one to bear the brunt of my bad mood."

"I don't like seeing you like this," she said. "I want you to be happy. I always did."

"It feels fairly unachievable at the moment."

"You need to figure things out with Olivia," she said. "Make an effort with her. If you can't be amicable now, things will only be more difficult later."

He gazed at her in a way that made her heart race. "Will you have dinner with me?"

She shook her head. "I can't."

"Why not? Nothing is ever going to happen between me and Olivia."

"But you're going to have a baby. And I don't want to be involved in that."

He slouched against the counter. "I don't want this either." He scanned her face as though measuring her reaction. "That's awful, isn't it? I'm worried I'll resent the child forever."

"You won't." She smiled lightly. "As soon as you hold it you'll fall in love, and everything that felt like a mistake will make perfect sense and you won't regret any of it."

"I hope you're right."

She fetched her bag from the kitchen and wished him goodnight before she left. It was amazing that she could still manage to talk to him. There was a time when she thought her heart would break every time she looked at him.

What she hadn't considered was that at some point she was bound to bump into Olivia again. When the door to the shop opened on a Wednesday afternoon in late August, Tara automatically smiled at the customer. Olivia was wearing a bright yellow sundress which showed off her swollen belly. Tara couldn't take her eyes off it.

"Hi!" Olivia said brightly. "How are you?"

"I'm okay, thanks. How are you?"

"Hot and uncomfortable. But otherwise fine." She

owered herself into a chair and stroked her belly. "I houldn't really complain."

"Still a little while to go," Tara said. Her hands elt shaky and her mouth was dry.

"Yes. Too long. I'm certainly not one of those omen who relishes every minute of pregnancy. I'm ure she'll be worth it though."

"It's a girl?" Tara felt like someone had kicked er in the gut.

"Yes. We haven't decided on a name yet."

"I'll go and find James for you," Tara said bruptly. Her legs felt weak as she walked up the tairs. It didn't take James long to come to the door.

He looked at her in concern. "Everything okay?"

No. Nothing was okay. She wanted to go inside nd lock the door. Lock them both away and stay ith him forever.

"Olivia's downstairs," she said. "I probably hould have sent her up." Her brain hadn't really een functioning at full capacity.

James's eyebrows shot up and he followed Tara ack down.

As soon as they walked into the shop, Olivia eamed at James. "Come here," she said quickly, eaching for his hand. She pressed it against her elly. "Can you feel it?"

"Yeah." James looked about as uncomfortable as ara felt.

Olivia looked at Tara over his shoulder. "Sometimes I'm sure she's going to break my ribs. he kicks so hard. Do you want to feel?"

"No, thanks. I was actually about to leave." She

looked at James, desperately needing to get out c
there. "Is that okay?"

"Yes. It's fine."

"Could you possibly stay longer?" Olivia askec
"I was hoping to steal James away for a little while.
She turned to him. "I thought we could go out fc
dinner and chat everything through like yo
suggested."

"I have plans," Tara said, heading into the bacl
There was no way she was staying at work so the
could go out on a date. "Bye," she called over he
shoulder.

The tears hit as soon as she was away from then
In the kitchen she grabbed her bag and stopped t
take a breath. Then she hurried out of the back doc
so she didn't have to walk past them again.

James called her a couple of hours later.

"I'm sorry," he said. "I didn't know she was goin
to come to the shop."

"It's fine."

"It's such a weird situation," he said hesitantly
"I'm not even sure how this all happened an
Olivia's so unpredictable. She's talking to me agai
but—"

"I can't do this," Tara blurted. She sank onto th
couch. It felt like everything was falling apart. He
world, her heart, everything. "I can't do thi
anymore. I was fooling myself that I could still wor
at the shop, but I can't."

"Don't say that."

"I mean it. I don't think I can work with you," sh
said. "I'm so tired of it all."

"What can I do?"

"Nothing."

"I want you to stay." He sounded desperate. "Take a few days off. You've been working so much. Maybe you just need a break."

"Yeah." She swallowed hard. A break wasn't the answer though. What she needed was a fresh start. She needed to move on from James.

"Have a long weekend," he said. "We can talk next week."

"Okay." It was Josie and Sam's wedding that weekend, so at least she had some distraction. "I'll talk to you next week." She ended the call without saying goodbye.

The evening drew on and she couldn't find the strength to move from the couch. As she stared at the wall, her mind kept coming back to the same conclusion: it was time to move on.

Chapter 37

It was hard to think any further ahead than the weekend. Sam and Josie were getting married and Tara needed to focus on that. She did a great job of being the life and soul of the party on Friday for Josie's hen night. Tara had decided the only way to get through it was to turn up with a load of alcohol and novelty hen night games. It all felt pretty pathetic, but the rest of them got quite into it and had a great time. Tara found that pretending to be upbeat and happy was the way to get through the weekend.

The weather was perfect for the wedding. Blue skies dazzled overhead and there wasn't a cloud in sight. The reception took place in a marquee on Annette's lawn. It all seemed very fitting, and Tara was thrilled for Josie and Sam.

"Are you okay?" Josie asked, appearing behind Tara as she stood near the house looking out over the party.

"Yes." She'd paused for too long and got lost in a daydream. "Just getting a bit emotional." She dabbed at the corner of her eye and then lifted her wine glass. "Too much of this stuff."

"Sorry, I didn't manage to get you a date," Josie said cheekily.

"Thank goodness you didn't. I actually thought you were going to try and set me up with someone."

Josie grimaced. "To be honest I invited someone but he didn't turn up."

"Are you serious?" Tara laughed then blew out a breath. "There's no hope for me, obviously."

"There's always hope."

"You look amazing, by the way." She looked at Josie's traditional wedding dress. It suited her perfectly.

"Did you see my shoes?" Josie lifted the bottom of her dress to reveal a pair of baby-blue Converse.

"I like them," Tara said in amusement as they moved to join the party.

"What are you so happy about?" Josie asked as they reached Jack and Emily.

Jack was laughing uncontrollably. He pointed over his shoulder. "The old guy thinks Emily's a porn star."

Tara snorted a laugh as she looked at Graham. He was Annette's neighbour and had been in the shop the previous week, asking for Emily's erotic fiction, which he'd heard she wrote under a pen name. It was a rumour Tara had started in the pub one night when she'd had too much to drink.

"He got his words mixed up," Emily said. "He thinks people who write erotica are called porn stars."

Emily had been outraged when she'd heard about the rumour, but she soon saw the funny side. Gossip travelled even faster than Tara thought. Everyone was talking about it.

"He's drunk," Tara said. "He'll tell everyone you're a porn star by the end of the evening."

It was amusing how flustered Emily was by it all. She went bright red when Annette came up behind her just as she was talking loudly about porn stars. The laughter was light relief for Tara. The sun was beginning to set and soon she'd be able to slip away unnoticed.

"Don't look now." Josie swung on Tara's arm. "Your date just arrived."

"What?" Tara's smile evaporated at the sight of James walking up the drive. "What's he doing here?"

"I invited him," Josie said proudly. "I didn't want to say anything because he wasn't sure he could make it. I knew he'd turn up. Just get together with him, will you? I know you like him. It doesn't matter that he's your boss."

"Josie!" Tara snapped as tears pricked her eyes. "You don't know what you're talking about." She'd almost made it through the day and now she was going to fall apart. She strode down the path, determined to get rid of James.

"What are you doing here?" She grabbed his arm and swung him round the way he'd come. "You need to go."

"Josie invited me."

"Well, she shouldn't have. And you shouldn't have come."

"I need to give them a card at least." He held up the envelope.

"I can give it to them."

He stopped on the path. "Can we talk? I need to speak to someone, and you're the only person I want to talk to."

"Not here," she said. "Please just leave."

James glanced over her shoulder at the party. "Dance with me?"

She shook her head sadly but didn't resist when he took her hand and led her over to the dance floor. Tara smiled at Max, sitting near the dance floor rocking one of the twins in his arms.

The music was appropriately slow, and she draped her arms around James's neck as he drew her to him. He looked so good in his crisp white shirt. It reminded Tara of the first time she'd seen him in a shirt, before the bookshop was even open and he was going to a meeting at the bank. Her fingers trailed over the hair at the base of his neck. She leaned closer and inhaled the scent of him.

It would be the first and last time she danced with him. And maybe the last time she saw him. She knew it was time to move on. Her future was completely unknown, but she knew James couldn't be in it. As the song came to an end, her arms tightened around him. It was so hard to let go.

His mouth brushed her ear. "I love you," he whispered.

A lone teardrop rolled down her cheek and she took a deep breath. Then she forced herself out of his embrace and led him out of the marquee and away from the party.

"I mean it," he said when they reached the gate at the end of the driveway. "I love you."

"I'm not coming back to work," she said. "I thought I could keep working there but I can't. It's too hard. I can't see you with Olivia. It kills me."

"I'm not with Olivia," he said angrily.

"Maybe you should be," she said through tears. "That way your kid wouldn't grow up in a broken home."

He stared at her. "Lots of kids grow up with untraditional families. It doesn't mean they're unhappy."

"But some of them are," she cried. She knew that all too well. "I'm going to leave and you should be with her." She sounded hysterical but she didn't care.

He paced, then stopped and pushed his hands through his hair. "I don't even know if it's my baby."

"What?" She wanted to laugh but instead she just cried harder.

"I don't remember sleeping with her." His eyes narrowed. "How can I not remember that? And Olivia's vague about the due date and keeps telling me the doctor thinks it will probably be early and most babies in her family are born early. But she won't let me go to any appointments with her, and she gets cagey if I ask too many questions."

Tara gripped the fence. "If you really believe it's not your baby you should be speaking to Olivia, not me."

"But what if I accuse her and I'm wrong?" He looked at her desperately. "I don't know what to do."

"You're asking the wrong person," she said, as calmly as she could. She couldn't let herself consider that he might be right, because if it wasn't his baby they were back to square one. Her excuse for not being with him would disappear. But she still couldn't be with him. What she needed to do was stick to her plan of moving on. She didn't need James in her life. She'd be perfectly content alone. It would have been so much simpler if Belinda had been right about him marrying Olivia. If he was with someone else, it would make it easier to move on.

"I don't have anyone else to talk to," James said. "And I want to talk to you."

"But I don't want to talk to *you*," she said fiercely. "I don't want anything to do with you."

He stared at her, and the sadness in his eyes broke her heart. Slowly, he moved around the gate, then paused. "You were right. I should never have come here. I thought maybe you still felt something for me but I guess I was wrong."

As his gaze bored into her, it took all her strength not to admit exactly how much she loved him.

Eventually he continued to his car. The headlights lit up the country road and then faded as he drove away. Tara could hardly catch her breath as she leaned against the gate and quietly sobbed. When Emily hurried over to her a moment later Tara completely fell apart, ranting about how James was going to be with Olivia and the baby. Because that's what she needed to tell herself. She needed him to move on, so she could do the same.

With tears still streaming down her face, she

asked Emily to make an excuse for her. There was no way she could re-join the party. Instead, she walked towards the village, ordering a taxi as she went. When she reached the pub, she sat on the bench outside.

It was all over.

No more bookshop.

No more James.

Just a flood of tears.

Chapter 38

When Tara arrived in Dartmouth on Monday morning it was with only a small suitcase. She'd spent the previous day moving things from her house to her mum's. The furniture belonged to her landlady, so moving was relatively easy. It was fairly liberating to be able to pack up everything she owned in the space of a day. She intended to collect the rest of her things from her mum's house when she was settled. Her mum was worried about her, but Tara had done her best to reassure her that the move was a positive step.

The sea air was lovely as she walked the quaint narrow streets. It would be nice to see Deirdre and Darren again. She was almost at the Bookshelf when her phone rang. She pulled it from her pocket, expecting it to be James. He'd called several times the previous day but she hadn't answered. She grimaced at Amber's name flashing on the display. She'd forgotten to tell her she wouldn't be in the shop for Monday morning coffee.

"Where are you?" Amber asked when she answered. "Come and let us in. We're on the doorstep."

"I'm not there," Tara said, surprised by her

373

composure.

"James isn't here either. We can't get in."

Tara kicked her toe on the pavement. "I don't work there anymore."

"What?" Amber laughed.

"I quit."

"Are you serious?" She mumbled something away from the phone, presumably relaying the conversation to Josie.

"Yeah." Tara continued walking.

"Are you at home? We'll come over."

"No." Tara winced. "I don't live there anymore." She'd sent her landlady an email but would follow up with a call later.

"What on earth are you talking about?"

"I need a change. A fresh start and all that."

"I don't understand." There were muffled voices and then Josie telling Amber to put the phone on speaker.

"Are you messing around?" Josie said cheerfully. "You went home with James on Saturday, didn't you? I bet you've not left his bed since. Just come and let us in."

"No." Tara reached the Bookshelf and found a nearby bench to sit on. "I left my job and my house."

"How gullible do you think we are?" Josie asked. "Where are you really?"

"Job hunting," she said. "And flat hunting."

The silence was punctuated by Kieron babbling.

"You quit your job?" Josie asked.

"Yes."

"Is everything okay?" Amber asked.

"What happened with you and James?" Josie said quietly.

"You might need to work on your matchmaking skills," Tara said as lightly as she could.

"You're worrying me," Josie said.

"Me too," Amber called. "Just tell us where you are and we can come and meet you."

"We'll catch up another day," Tara said. "Don't worry. I'm fine, but I really have to go."

"Tara you're scaring me," Amber said quickly. "Explain properly."

"I already did." Tara moved towards the bookshop. "I'll call you back later. We can talk then. Give Kieron a hug for me." She hung up. They could talk all day and get no further with the conversation. And Tara needed to focus on getting her life together, not falling apart even more.

Deirdre greeted her with a warm hug. "How is everything?" she asked. "Did you sort things out with James?"

"I'm afraid not," Tara said as she hugged Darren. "And I've got a huge favour to ask you ... I was wondering if the apartment upstairs is still empty."

"You need somewhere to live?" Deirdre asked.

"Just for a little while," she said. "Until I sort myself out."

"You're welcome to the place," Darren said. "Stay as long as you want."

Relief washed over her. "You can charge me whatever you were charging the last tenant. I'm going to start job hunting straight away so money shouldn't be a problem."

"Nonsense." Deirdre shook her head. "You're our guest."

"I can't stay for free," Tara insisted.

"You can help us out in the shop," Darren said. "That kills two birds with one stone. You've got yourself a job and a place to live all at once. When do you want to move?"

"I've got my stuff in the car," she said sheepishly.

***

Over the next few weeks Tara had numerous phone calls from Amber and Josie. They were keen to come and see her, but she kept putting them off until they finally accepted that she needed some space and stopped asking.

As well as helping out in the bookshop, she found a part-time job at a local pub. Darren and Deirdre were friends with the landlord and set it up for her. It was only a few hours to cover the lunch rush, but the extra bit of money was helpful. When she wasn't there she was in the bookshop, or wandering along the coast, or sitting in the window of the apartment and watching the world go by.

Her mum embraced her in a tight hug when she ventured back to Averton a few weeks later.

"I would've come to see you," Debbie said in the hallway. "I'd like to see your new place."

"I know," Tara said. "But I wanted some time to settle in and get my head together."

"And you're okay?"

"Yes." She took her mum's elbow and guided he

to the kitchen. "I have a favour to ask you. And I know you're going to say no, but I'm going to nag you until you give in so you may as well just say yes to start with."

"What?" Debbie chewed on her lip.

"Cut my hair."

Debbie lifted a section to inspect the ends. "It doesn't really need a cut."

"Cut it to my chin," Tara said, pulling a chair into the middle of the room.

"No!" Her mum laughed as though Tara had said something insane.

"Please. I'm getting my hair cut and I'd rather you do it. No one else has ever cut my hair." Tara smiled. "I'm thirty years old and my mum is the only person who's ever cut my hair."

Standing behind her, Debbie ran her fingers through Tara's hair. "I always liked it long."

"Me too." She craned her neck to look at her mum. "But I want a change. Please."

Debbie let out a resigned sigh and went to fetch her scissors. For the next half an hour her dark hair fell all around her, carpeting the kitchen floor.

"That's not really to my chin," Tara said when she looked in the mirror.

"I thought you said shoulders." Her mum flashed a cheeky grin.

"I suppose it's fairly dramatic anyway. Thank you."

"You're welcome. Go and sit down. I'll clean up the floor and make us a cup of tea."

Tara did as she was told. The living room was

377

neat and tidy, and her gaze was drawn to an old family photo. She stared at it for a while, then picked it up for a closer look.

"You can take it if you want." Her mum came in with drinks, startling her. "I've got so many."

"I haven't got any." It occurred to Tara that it was unusual not to have any photos on display. James had a few family photos at his place, with his parents and Kate. And a couple of silly photos of his friends on nights out. Tara had been trying so hard not to think about James, but he'd pop into her head with no warning at all.

"Take it with you," Debbie said again.

Tara placed it back on the shelf. "It looks nice where it is."

"Are you seeing Amber while you're here? She's worried about you."

"Have you seen her?"

"Yes. She called in the other day."

Tara sat heavily on the couch. "I'm meeting her and Josie in the pub later. And Sam."

"That'll be fun. You can sleep here if you don't want to drive back tonight."

"Thanks, but I'll only meet them for an hour then head back to Dartmouth. I'm working tomorrow."

"Do you remember when we used to drive to Dartmouth for ice creams when you were little?"

"Yes." Tara grinned. "I liked to watch the boats."

"You'd sit all day watching those boats."

"My new apartment overlooks the water, so I get to watch the boats whenever I want."

"It sounds wonderful. I'll come and visit soon

You're definitely staying there?"

"Yeah. I like it."

"What about James?"

Tara shifted in her seat. "I'm sure he'll manage without me. He's probably already got a replacement."

"I doubt that," her mum said quietly. "What happened between you two?"

"It's a long story. And I'm trying not to think about it."

Her mum patted her knee. "What do you want for dinner?"

"What's the choice?"

"Omelette and chips?"

"Or?"

"Or you go hungry!"

"Omelette it is then." She smiled as her mum went off to cook. At least one of them seemed to be doing well.

HANNAH ELLIS

Chapter 39

Walking into the Bluebell Inn felt odd. Tara was self-conscious when she joined Amber, Josie and Sam. She knew she had to offer some sort of explanation but it was hard to know what to say. They spent a few minutes excitedly chatting about her new haircut, and she loved how they were obviously trying to act like nothing had happened. Clearly they all thought she'd had some sort of breakdown. Maybe she had.

"How's the new place?" Sam finally asked.

"It's great," she said. "It's lovely to live by the sea. You'll have to come and visit now I'm settled."

"That would be nice," Amber said. "I'll bring Kieron to look at the boats."

"He'll love it," Tara said.

Josie was far too quiet. She'd been staring into the bottom of her glass, stirring the ice cubes with the straw. "I'm sorry," she said, looking up at Tara. "I should never have invited James to the wedding."

"It doesn't matter," Tara said. "It wasn't a big deal. I'd already decided I was leaving."

"I don't understand what happened," Josie said. "I always thought you liked him really."

"It wasn't meant to be." She hoped she could

381

breeze through the conversation and put it to bed once and for all. "And it was too awkward working together. So I left. It's not a huge deal."

"I feel so guilty," Josie said. "I don't know why I thought inviting him to the wedding was such a great idea. Everyone told me not to."

"Stop worrying about it," Tara said. "It's over and done with. Let's talk about something else. I can't stay long and I don't want to spend the whole time talking about me and James. Tell me what's going on with all of you. How's Kieron?"

"He's great," Amber said. She chatted about how he'd had a growth spurt and had outgrown all his clothes. The subject change was welcome and Tara relaxed as she enjoyed catching up with her friends.

When Tara stood to leave an hour later she promised to keep in touch.

"Dartmouth is hardly any further than Newton Abbot," Sam said as he hugged her. "You can still come over on Fridays."

"Maybe," she said. She knew she wouldn't. It was time to make proper changes in her life, not just keep plodding along as she always had.

***

It wasn't long until she saw Amber again. On Monday morning, Tara woke in a daze as the phone buzzed around the bedside table.

She grunted as she answered.

"I was thinking I could bring Kieron to visit you," Amber said. "We could make a new Monday morning tradition. Or are you working?"

"I'm not working." She smiled into the phone. "And I'd love to see you and Kieron." She gave Amber the address and promised to look out for them.

It was lovely showing Amber her new apartment and the bookshop. They walked down to the waterfront and got takeaway coffees to drink while Kieron threw stones into the water from the small beach.

"I'm worried about you," Amber finally said. Up until then they'd been doing a great job of sticking to small talk, but Tara had known there'd be questions eventually.

"You don't need to be," Tara replied. "I honestly think this change will end up being good for me."

"James doesn't look too good."

Tara bent to pick a stone and threw it into the water. "You've seen him?"

"At story time," Amber said.

Of course. Tara hadn't even considered what a mess she'd left James in by leaving work without notice. "He'll be fine," Tara said.

"You're not going to tell me what happened, are you?"

Tara inhaled a lungful of salty air. Part of her wanted to explain but it felt so overwhelming. Reliving it all would be too painful; she'd have to say how James had got someone else pregnant. The words were too hard to speak. For a moment Tara was transported back to the wedding and James saying he wasn't sure it was his baby. He'd sounded so desperate.

"It's okay," Amber said. "You don't have to talk about it if you don't want to."

"I'm sorry," Tara said. "One day I'll explain everything. But I think for now I need to focus on moving forward. Please don't be angry with me for keeping secrets."

"I'm not." Amber put a hand on her arm. In fairness, Amber never really got angry with her about anything. It was probably why they'd stayed friends as long as they had. Amber had the patience of a saint. "But make sure you let me know if there's anything I can do."

"I will." She bent to help Kieron find stones. He giggled every time they splashed into the water.

Amber came to visit her every Monday morning after that. It was always lovely to see her and it added a bit more structure to Tara's week. She still missed James constantly. His phone calls finally stopped, and she wasn't sure whether that was a good thing or a bad thing.

It was another month before she went back to Averton again. She spent a Saturday visiting her mum and then Annette. In the evening she met up with Sam and Josie in the Bluebell Inn. It was pleasant enough but she didn't stay long. She was just leaving when Belinda called out to her.

"How are you?" Belinda asked, hugging her as though they were long-lost friends. "I haven't seen you in so long. What happened with your job?"

"Oh, you know, time for a change."

"I had no idea you were planning on moving."

Tara couldn't help but smile as she imagined Belinda hearing the news. It was the sort of gossip she thrived on. "It was a spur-of-the-moment thing," she said.

"Your old boss misses you," she said. "He's turned into a real miserable old devil since you left." She paused. "At least that Olivia's not on the scene anymore. Some women are awful, aren't they? Poor James. There's no wonder he's grumpy, really."

"What are you talking about?" Tara said, wrinkling her nose.

Belinda's eyes widened. "Didn't you hear? It turned out it wasn't his baby. That horrible woman just said it was. There ought to be some punishment for that."

The noise of the pub suddenly fell away. "How do you know this?" Tara asked, stunned.

"I saw James last week, and I asked when the baby was due. He snapped at me. But I suppose I can't really blame him. He's got a lot on his mind."

"Yes," Tara mumbled. "I've got to go. Nice to see you."

"You too." She grinned and Tara fled out of the door. Sometimes Belinda had her uses.

It played on Tara's mind the whole drive back to Dartmouth. When James had mentioned his suspicions at the wedding she'd dismissed them completely. Now she felt terrible for not even considering the possibility. Olivia had tricked him. How could she play games with people's lives like that?

385

When Tara got back to the apartment she paced the living room with her phone in her hand. She wanted to call James so badly. But by calling him, was she playing games too? It wasn't like she intended to go running back to him. All she wanted was to hear his voice and make sure he was okay.

The phone rang for a while, and she thought of hanging up several times before he finally answered.

"Hello?"

"Hi," she said quietly. "Sorry, I know it's a bit late."

"It's fine," he said. The sound of his voice made Tara want to get in the car and drive over there. She'd never known she could miss someone so much.

"I just wanted to see how you're doing," she said. "I saw Belinda. She told me about Olivia and the baby."

"I presumed you'd hear eventually."

"You should have called."

"There didn't seem to be much point since you don't answer my calls." He paused. "And I didn't think you'd be interested."

She sank onto the couch, hating how bitter he sounded and feeling unbelievably guilty. "You didn't even sleep with her, did you?"

"No," he said quietly.

"I'm so sorry."

He sighed. "It's hardly your fault."

"I know, but I feel like I should have suspected something."

"Why would you?" he said. "It took *me* lon

enough to figure it out."

"What happened? Did she just admit it?"

"No." He let out a humourless laugh. "There were several arguments. Eventually I said I wanted a paternity test. Then she admitted everything."

"Sorry."

"I should go," he said. "It's late."

Tara nodded and tears streamed down her cheeks. She wanted to stay on the phone and chat to him, but she knew she'd given up that privilege.

When they ended the call, she sat for a long time wishing everything had been different.

Chapter 40

Winter in Dartmouth was fairly miserable, which suited Tara down to the ground. She didn't hear from James again, though she thought about him every day. If it weren't for Deirdre and Darren keeping her spirits up she was sure she'd have gone mad. She spent a couple of hours in the bookshop most days. Occasionally they put her to work, but generally they didn't actually need her to be there. It was just a nice place to spend time, and they were such lovely company.

Working in the pub wasn't much fun, but it killed some time and earned her a bit of money. The landlord promised there'd be more work in the summer if she was interested. Seeing as Deirdre and Darren refused to take any money for rent, Tara wasn't particularly concerned about her finances. She didn't need much.

December came around quickly, but Tara couldn't muster any enthusiasm for the festive season. It made her think of James even more than usual. And the shop too. She missed working at the Reading Room. Hopefully James would decorate the windows for Christmas.

On Christmas Day she drove over to her mum's

house armed with everything they needed for a turkey dinner. Of course, Debbie was already cooking and they had far too much food. Tara managed to get most of what she'd brought into the freezer. It was actually pretty enjoyable cooking with her mum.

They were exchanging presents when Debbie suddenly left the room.

"Something came in the post for you," she said. "I almost forgot."

"Interesting," Tara said as she took the package. Her heart rate increased as she recognised the handwriting as James's.

"Open it then," Debbie said, snapping her out of her trance.

Tearing at the paper, she pulled out a collection of DVDs.

"They're old ones," her mum said. "You used to love *E.T.* when you were a kid."

"Still do," she said looking down at the six DVDs. All the ones they'd listed as their favourites.

"Who sent you those?"

"James." She pulled out a card and opened it up. *To Tara, Happy Christmas! With love, James.* It was short and sweet, but the sight of his handwriting, and knowing he still thought about her, made her head spin.

"Are you still in touch with him?" her mum asked

"We haven't spoken for a while."

"You'll have to give him a call."

"Maybe."

When she got home that evening, she unpacked

her bag of gifts onto the coffee table. She intended to curl up on the couch with a tub of ice cream and one of the DVDs James had sent. In among the gifts was a framed family photo that usually had pride of place on Mum's shelf. She'd been trying to get Tara to take it for ages and had obviously sneaked it into her bag. Tara stood it up beside the Christmas card from James, then hastily reached for the DVDs before she got too emotional.

As she watched *E.T.* she greedily devoured far too much ice cream and thought of calling James. Or at least messaging him to thank him for the gift. A few times she even had her phone poised in her hand. She didn't dare though. What would it achieve? Finally, she was beginning to get over him. That was what she needed to focus on. The photo her mum sneaked into her bag was helpful too. It was a good reminder that things would never work out for them.

***

Time was supposed to heal, but after Christmas Tara seemed to feel worse with each passing week. It was a cold and wet Tuesday in February, and Tara's thoughts were on James again. She'd given up on trying not to think about him. Tuesdays and Thursdays were especially bad because she couldn't help but imagine him reading for the kids during story time. She thought about him animatedly reading to the sea of little faces gazing up at him. It always brought a smile to her face. And usually tears to her eyes too.

That particular afternoon she was walking along the harbour, getting a breath of fresh air after a shift at the pub, when her phone vibrated in her pocket. She debated whether or not to look at the message. It meant taking her hands out of her pockets, and her fingers were numb enough as it was.

Curiosity got the better of her, and when she saw the message was from James, her heart rate soared. He'd sent a picture of the children's corner at the Reading Room. There was a caption with it: *Story time got a bit out of hand today. Whose idea were beanbags?*

Tara zoomed in on the photo. The little polystyrene balls were all over the place like a blanket of snow. The children sat among them looking delighted.

Tara's shoulders shook as she began to laugh. By the time she sat down on a nearby bench, her laughter had turned to tears. It took a few minutes for her to calm herself down.

Back at the apartment, she lay on the couch and stared at the photo of the Reading Room. Then she swiped through her phone, looking at photos of James. The photo of the bookshop made her realise it wasn't just James that she missed. They'd built the bookshop up together and it had become like home to her. It was one of the few places that she felt connected to. It was late when she reached for her keys. She still had a key for the shop. Filled with an overwhelming desire to curl up on a beanbag, she got in her car and drove over to Newton Abbot.

The shop was dark when she pulled up. She

shouldn't go in. Why had she even come? It felt like she was being drawn back.

With the dim light from the street, she navigated her way to the back of the shop, then turned on a light. Beside the light switch on the back wall hung an array of framed photos. James had talked about making a photo wall a few times but never got round to it. Now, Tara was faced with pictures of her and James with all the different authors who'd visited. There was also a photo of the two of them on the day the shop opened, standing in the doorway about to cut the ribbon.

Tears ran down Tara's face as she was bombarded with memories. Dragging herself away from the photos, she went to the children's corner. The beanbag she sat in was even more comfy than she remembered. It was bittersweet being there, and more tears filled her eyes as she thought of James just upstairs.

She hadn't been there long when she heard a noise. The back door opened and light flooded in. She felt light-headed at the sound of James's questioning voice.

"It's just me," she answered quickly, worried he'd call the police.

His brow was furrowed when he came over to her. "What are you doing here?"

"I missed the place," she said, wiping furiously at her damp cheeks. "I just wanted be here for a few minutes."

For a moment he stared down at her, then he reached for her hand and pulled her up. His touch sent goosebumps up her arm. He looked at her intensely. "Come and see what I did upstairs."

Following him up to the apartment felt like the most natural thing in the world. He was so calm, as though catching her sneaking around was completely normal. Being around him was wonderful. Except somewhere in the back of her mind, she knew she'd have to say goodbye soon, and the thought of it made her feel sick.

"Wow." She looked around the living room and kitchen. "It's gorgeous." The old kitchen had been replaced and the living room completely refurbished. It was bright and airy and perfect.

"The kitchen only went in a couple of weeks ago," he said. "The new bathroom's being fitted next week."

"It's amazing. I can't believe it's the same apartment."

"I'm happy with it." He took a couple of bottles of beer from the fridge and handed one to Tara. She followed him to the couch and sat beside him. They clinked the bottles together and took a sip. "I had some extra money from the web design work and thought I'd do something useful with it."

"I love it," she said. There was a short silence, and her heart went into overdrive at being so close to him.

He smiled cheekily. "You really missed some fun at story time today. Little Rosie managed to get the zip all the way open before anyone noticed. There were balls and kids everywhere."

Tara chuckled. "Sounds like chaos."

"It was. And kind of fun." He laughed and then his features grew serious. "I kept wishing you were there." He put his beer on the table and turned to face her. "I miss you. All the time. I don't know why you're here and I don't really care. I started to think I wouldn't see you again."

"I miss you too," she whispered. When he leaned into her, butterflies took flight in her stomach and she knew she couldn't resist if he kissed her.

His hand on her cheek made her skin tingle.

"I miss you so much," she said. "But—"

"Let's not do buts," he said, caressing her cheek. His lips were so close to hers that his breath tickled her skin. "I miss you. You miss me. That's enough."

When his lips brushed hers, she felt like she would melt into him. Her arms wrapped around him and the gap between them disappeared as the kisses became frantic.

James pulled back, and she panicked, thinking he was going to stop. "Do you want to see the bedroom?" he asked with his forehead against hers.

"Yes." She sighed with relief. "I'd love to."

***

It was dark when she woke in James's bed. Her instinct was to flee. All the effort she'd put into distancing herself from him had been undone in a few hours. His arm was draped across her chest. The weight of it could have been stifling but instead it was comforting.

"I need to go," she whispered as she nudged him

off her. Tempting as it was to sneak out, she couldn't bring herself to do it.

"No," he muttered, pulling her closer. "It's still dark. Stay a bit longer."

She didn't need any more persuading and murmured her agreement. A moment later James was fast asleep again, snuggled so close she could feel his shallow breaths on her neck. Tara lay in the darkness, trailing her fingers over the fine hairs of his forearm.

The next time she opened her eyes, the room was bright. There was a lamp on beside the bed.

"Morning," James said. He was in front of the mirror buttoning up his shirt. His hair was damp and the fresh scent of shower gel permeated the air.

"Hi." She pulled the bedding over her.

"I have to go to work," he said. Their eyes met in the mirror and his gaze lingered.

"Me too." She paused, watching him straighten his collar and feeling a huge amount of guilt. "I'm sorry. I shouldn't have just turned up here."

"You can turn up any time you like." He dragged his fingers through his hair to style it.

"I don't want you to think …" She trailed off and pulled the sheet tighter around her.

He walked round the bed and sat beside her. "You don't want me thinking you're staying? Or that this will be a regular occurrence?"

"I really shouldn't have come," she said.

"I'm glad you did." He reached for her hand and laced his fingers with hers. "You're always welcome here."

"I don't want you waiting around for me."

"I'll always wait for you," he said softly.

She shook her head and shot him a stern look. "I'm not coming back. This was a mistake. You should get on with your life."

"You don't get to make all my decisions for me. If I want to wait for you, I can." He leaned over and kissed her forehead.

She smiled sadly. "Persistence doesn't always pay off, you know."

"I'm hoping patience might." He kissed her again, this time catching the edge of her lips. "I'll call you." She was about to protest but he was gone before she could argue.

When Tara left she slipped out of the back door. The drive back to Dartmouth was awful. It felt like she was going the wrong way. Maybe she should turn around and go back to James. If she told him everything – all the stuff she kept buried away – maybe he'd understand. Maybe they could be happy together.

Inhaling deeply, she brushed the thoughts aside. She was content in Dartmouth. Life was pleasant and stable, and that was all she needed. It was enough and she should be thankful for it.

Chapter 41

The weekend went slowly. All Tara could think about was James, and she kept glancing at her phone, wondering if he might call. A few times she was tempted to call him but she resisted.

On Monday morning, she got up early and drove over to Averton. She put her phone on speaker and called Amber on the way.

"I'm going to come to your place for coffee for a change," she said. "Is that okay?"

"Of course," Amber replied. "Is everything all right?"

"I'm not sure. I'm on my way to see Josie. Did you know she's upset with me?"

"No." Amber sounded puzzled. "She hasn't said anything to me except that she was worried about you. Why?"

"Her friend Emily called me last night and had a go at me. She said I've upset Josie."

"That's weird."

"Yeah. I feel bad. I haven't been in touch with Josie much since I left." Josie had had another miscarriage before Christmas and all Tara had managed was a few messages. She really should have been more supportive. They'd met up a couple of times in the pub, but there'd always been other people around so they hadn't had a proper chat.

"Emily was probably overreacting," Amber said. "I'm sure Josie's fine with you."

"I'll go and find out. Then I'll come and see you guys."

"Brill," Amber said. "See you later."

Tara pressed end on the call and focused on the road. When she pulled up at Josie and Sam's place ten minutes later there was no one home. She set off for Annette's instead.

"You just missed her," Annette said, wrapping Tara in a warm hug. "But if you hurry down to the barn you might catch up with her. Otherwise she'll be off roaming the hills with the dogs."

"I'll see if I can find her." Tara turned to hurry down the path. "I'll come back for a cuppa in a bit."

There was no sign of Josie in the barn, so Tara headed round the back and hopped the fence Standing at the top of the hill, she cupped her hands around her mouth and called out for Josie as loudly as she could. It was fun to shout so loud. She did i again and then laughed. A dog barked somewhere down in the valley, and Tara marched in tha direction. At the bottom of the hill she hopped across the stepping stones to get across the stream then reached down to pet the familiar golde retriever.

"Hello, Charlie," she said, ruffling his fur. "Hello boy." A couple of other dogs bounded over, an when Tara looked up Josie came into view too.

"What are you doing here?" she asked.

"Looking for you!" Tara embraced Josie tightly. It was so good to see her.

"Are you okay?" Josie asked.

"I don't know," Tara said honestly. "But I'm worried about you. Emily called and shouted at me. She said I'd upset you."

"Oh, God." Josie rolled her eyes. "When did she get so feisty?"

"I think she might have been drunk," Tara said.

"Shall we walk back to my place for a cuppa?" Josie said.

Ten minutes later they were settled on the patio chairs in Josie and Sam's back garden.

"You didn't upset me," Josie said. "I was upset because you seemed angry with me. Sam kept saying you weren't, but you've been so distant since I invited James to the wedding ... I didn't know what to think."

"I was never angry with you," Tara said. "I had no idea you thought that."

"It seemed like everything was fine until I invited James to the wedding. If I hadn't invited him ..."

"It wouldn't have made any difference," Tara said quickly. "Things were a mess long before that."

"Why?" Josie asked. "What happened?"

Tara sighed. "It's such a long story."

"You can tell me," Josie said.

Tara sat quietly for a moment, watching the dogs sniff around.

"I love him," she said quietly. "But it's never going to work out between us."

"Why? It's always seemed like he loves you too."

Tara let out a long breath. "Because he wants kids and I don't."

"So he said he doesn't want to be with you?"

"No. He wants us to be together. But I know it won't work."

"Surely if you love each other you can work it out."

Tara wrapped her hands around her coffee mug and stared down the garden. "It's not enough," she said. She thought of her parents and how happy they'd been when Tara was small. They'd loved each other so much, but it didn't stop them from falling apart.

"I'm sorry," Josie said. "If I'd known I'd never have teased you about him."

"You're not allowed to feel bad for teasing me," Tara said. "It was my fault for not telling you. And I've teased you for far worse."

"That's true." Josie smiled.

"How are you?" Tara asked with a slight tilt of the head.

"I'm okay." She reached down to stroke Charlie, who lay beside her chair.

"Really?"

Josie shrugged. "It's not been the easiest of times but I'm getting through it."

"I'm sorry I've not been around much."

"It's fine. I wish you would come back more though. I hate that you deal with everything alone. You can always talk to me, you know."

"You've got your own problems to worry about," Tara said.

"Yes," Josie said. "And I have Sam to share them with. Who's helping you?"

Tara forced down the lump in her throat. "I'm fine."

"I'll call you more," Josie said. "I kept thinking you wanted to be left alone."

"I think I did for a while." She stood and hugged Josie tightly. It felt good to have a proper chat with her.

***

The rest of the day went by in a blur. Tara spent half an hour with Annette, and then went to see Amber before driving back to Dartmouth for a shift at the pub. After that she called into the Bookshelf. She was exhausted when she finally went back to the apartment. She got straight into her pyjamas and settled down in the armchair with a book. When her phone rang, it took her a moment to drag her eyes from the page. It was James.

"Hi," she said hesitantly.

"Hi. I just wanted to call and see how you're doing."

"I'm okay." She turned the book over and rested it over the arm of the chair. "How are you?"

"I've been better. I miss you."

She screwed her face up but didn't reply.

"I thought I could come and visit you," he said. "I'm just not a hundred per cent sure where you are. Amber said Dartmouth, but it would be helpful to have a more exact location."

"Don't visit me," she said. "I don't want to see you."

"I don't believe you," he said softly. To be fair, it was about the least convincing lie she'd ever told. Of course she *wanted* to see him. She shouldn't though.

"Things will never work between us," she said firmly. "Please just stop. This is exhausting."

"Stop running then. Come back to me."

"I can't. I'm sorry." She pressed end and then turned her phone off. When she reached for her book again, all she could do was stare at the pages. The words no longer made sense and her brain wouldn't focus on anything but James.

The following week seemed to be the slowest week ever. Every moment felt unbearable, and every day Tara was tempted to get in her car and drive back to James.

It was Sunday afternoon when he turned up at her place. When the doorbell rang she thought it might be Deirdre and Darren calling in with some home baked goodies and hurried downstairs to open the door. Then she just stood, staring at James.

"Can I come in?" he asked.

Tara glanced over her shoulder. Her heart was racing and she didn't know what to do. It was hard to think clearly around James.

"No," she finally said. Her apartment in Dartmouth contained no memories of him and she'd rather keep it that way.

"I really want to talk."

"We can go for a walk," she said. "I could do with some fresh air." Grabbing her coat and keys, she stepped outside and pulled the door behind her.

"This is where you work?" he asked, tipping his head toward the bookshop.

"Yes. Sometimes." She waited while he peered in the window. Amber had obviously kept him informed.

"It looks nice."

"We can walk down to the water," she suggested, ignoring his remark. Having him there was too hard. Because all she wanted to do was slip her hand into his and stroll down to the waterfront. It was a beautiful day. The air was crisp and the sky was bright blue. They could walk for miles by the water, stopping now and then to exchange kisses. She blinked the thought away. It would be best if she got rid of him as soon as possible.

"I've never been to Dartmouth before." He looked up at the houses as they walked.

"It gets busy in the summer," she said. "It's fairly quiet at this time of year." Even given the chill in the air, there were a few people strolling along the front.

"I can see why you like it." They paused at the road, waiting for a car to crawl by before crossing. The gentle tinkle of boat masts floated on the breeze, mixed with the intermittent screech of seagulls.

They walked in silence for a few minutes then stopped at the next available bench.

"I told you not to visit," Tara said flatly.

"I missed you," he replied as though that were reason enough.

"Did Amber tell you where I was?"

He pushed his hands into his pockets and bunched his shoulders up against the wind. It reminded Tara of the first time they'd met and he'd walked her home in freezing temperatures.

"Your mum told me," he said.

Her eyebrows rose. "You were talking to my mum?"

"I went to ask her where you were. We talked for a while." He paused, and his features softened. The way he looked at her made her nervous. "She told me about your brother."

Tara closed her eyes. She was aware of nothing but the way her heart thumped against her ribcage and the sound of blood rushing in her ears. She flinched when he laid a hand on her arm.

"You shouldn't be talking to Mum." Her eyes flicked open. "You have no right snooping around asking questions."

"I only asked where you were," he said gently. "The rest she just told me."

"You've probably upset her," she snapped. "She doesn't like to talk about it."

"She said it's you who doesn't like to talk about it."

"I don't even remember him." Tara shot up from the bench. "I need to check Mum's okay."

"She's fine." James grabbed her hand but she snatched it away. "Tara, wait ..."

"No." Her vision misted with tears, and she turned and pushed him squarely on the chest. "Why are you here? I left to get away from you. I don't want to be with you. Just go."

"Talk to me," he said, hurrying after her as she marched purposefully away. "Stop shutting everyone out and talk to me."

"Just go," she called behind her. At the apartment, she fumbled with the keys. Stopping, she took a deep breath and wiped the tears from her eyes. James stood beside her, his head tilted to one side.

"Can I come in?" he asked when the key finally clicked in the lock.

"No."

"Please."

"No," she said fiercely. "I don't want to talk to you."

He looked at her with pleading eyes. "Please let me come in."

"Stay away from me," she growled. "Stay away from my mum." Her hands were shaking as she slammed the door. Her throat was so tight she could hardly breathe. Somehow her legs took her up the stairs, and she inhaled ragged breaths as her lungs cried out for air. Pulling the framed photo from the drawer, she hugged it to her and sank onto the couch.

Gradually, her throat relaxed and her lungs began to work again. She thought about calling to check on her mum but she knew James was right; Debbie wouldn't have been upset by a conversation about the past. It was Tara who couldn't cope with it.

Her fingers trailed over the photograph, landing on the plump cheeks of her sweet baby brother. In the photo, six-year-old Tara gazed down at the adorable little boy who she loved with all her heart. Back when her heart was still whole.

Chapter 42

It felt as though Tara had only just fallen asleep when she was rudely awoken by the doorbell ringing incessantly. Her phone was buzzing around the bedside table too. She really didn't want to get up. Sleep was lovely. She just wanted to sleep. Squinting at the phone, she groaned. It was Amber. She assumed it was also Amber at the door.

"I'm coming," she said into the phone as she stumbled out of bed. "I'm awake. Please stop ringing the bell." Finally, the annoying ringing stopped. Tara threw her phone aside and padded down the stairs. Her eyes protested to the brightness when she opened the door.

"Don't worry me like that," Amber said, pulling her into a hug.

"Like what? Why were you worried? It's early. I was asleep." She smiled at Kieron as they moved past her and up the stairs.

"James called me. He said he'd upset you. He's really worried about you. It made me worry too."

"I'm fine," she said.

At the top of the stairs, Amber tugged Kieron's coat off. "Are you really?" she asked. "Honestly? Because I don't think you are."

Tara led the way to the living room. She struggled to find anything to say. Pretending she was fine was too hard.

Amber emptied out a bag of toys onto the living room floor for Kieron. Crouching, Tara ran a hand over his soft hair then sat beside him.

"Will you tell me what's going on?" Amber said, sitting on the couch. "James sounded really upset. He's worried about you. I didn't even know you two were still speaking."

"We're not. Well, we shouldn't be. I saw him last week, and then he turned up here yesterday."

"And what did he say to upset you so much?"

Tara reached for one of Kieron's cars and gave it a push to roll it over to him. "It's fairly complicated."

Amber's shoulders sagged. "So you still don't want to talk to me?"

"It's not that I don't want to," Tara said quickly. "But it's such a long story and you'll tell me I'm being ridiculous."

"When have I ever said that to you?"

"Every time I say I don't want kids." Tara focused on the toy plane in her hand.

"I didn't say it's ridiculous. To be honest, I never thought you were being serious."

"Well, I was serious," she said firmly. "And can't be with James because I don't want kids. Even though I love him. So that's why I never wanted to get together with him, and why it all went wrong when I did get together with him." She stood up, her throat clogging. Tears dripped down her cheeks. "S

410

you can tell me I'm ridiculous now if you want. Or I can tell you *why* I don't want children."

She went over to the drawer and pulled out the faded family photo.

"Here," Tara said, shoving the picture at Amber, who sat in a stunned silence. "That's why."

Amber's eyes darted from Tara to the photo. "I don't understand."

"I didn't know babies could die." Tara sank onto the couch beside Amber and stared at the photo. "I was six years old and I thought only old people died. And then he was gone."

"You told me you didn't remember your brother," Amber said, sniffing loudly. "You said your mum never fully got over it but it didn't really affect you."

"I couldn't talk about it." Tara leaned onto her knees and buried her face in her hands as she cried quietly. When they'd moved to Averton Debbie had decided it would be best if they didn't talk about Reuben. She'd said it would upset people so it would be easier not to mention him. Tara was quite happy with the plan. Her mum always got upset when Tara mentioned him. Except it only lasted about a year. After that, Debbie changed her mind and decided they should talk about him all the time, to everyone. Tara quickly learned it was easier to tell people she didn't remember her brother than deal with their awkward sympathy. Eventually, her mum realised that no one really wanted to talk about dead children, so she found her online support network instead.

"I'm so sorry," Amber whispered, rubbing Tara's

back. "I wish you'd talked to me."

"I thought you'd say it was a long time ago and I should get over it." She wiped furiously at the tears and wished she could stop crying. "*I* think I should get over it. But we were a normal happy family, and then Reuben died and Mum had a breakdown. Dad left. Everything fell apart, and I can't stand the thought of going through that again."

"He had a virus, didn't he?" Amber said. "It was just one of those freak things."

"Yes. He was perfectly healthy and then he caught a virus. And you think it was a freak thing and it's really rare. But it's not. Kids die every day. My mum has about twenty friends and they all lost kids. And all of them are broken. My mum is broken."

"I don't know what to say." Amber rooted around in her bag until she pulled out a packet of tissues. "I'm so sorry."

Tara swallowed hard and took a tissue.

"What about James?" Amber asked. "What did he say?"

"He said he doesn't mind not having kids. But didn't want him to give that up for me so I left. He only found out about Reuben yesterday when he went to ask my mum where I lived. I shouted at him and told him to go away."

"So you love James? You've been in love with him all this time?"

"Yes."

"You should be with him."

"I can't," she said. "If I'm alone I don't have anyone to lose. James makes me want more and scares me so much."

"You seem miserable," Amber said. "Are you going to spend your life being miserable so you don't risk getting hurt?"

Tara managed a small smile. "You're dying to tell me I'm being ridiculous, aren't you?"

"No." Amber dabbed at her eyes. "Definitely not." She wrapped her arms around Tara and hugged her tightly. "What will you do? I want you to be happy."

"I want to be with James." Tara pulled out of Amber's embrace and sat up straighter. "I'm just scared I'll freak out and mess it up again. And everything seems to go wrong for us. Maybe it's just not meant to be."

"I don't believe that," Amber said.

"I'm so torn." Tara smiled at Kieron as he brought her a cuddly toy. "Part of me wants to go back to Newton Abbot and be with him, and part of me thinks I'll end up getting hurt. And hurting him."

"You're already hurting," Amber pointed out. "Both of you. How much worse could it get?"

Tara frowned. "You should spend some time with my mum on one of her low days. Then you'd see how bad things could be."

"You and James would be happy," Amber said. "I'm sure of it."

"Because you're a born optimist." Tara shook her head.

"Don't say it like it's a bad thing," Amber said with a grin.

"Sorry." Tara sighed and flopped back on the couch.

413

Amber squeezed her hand. "I like it when you talk to me instead of pretending everything is fine."

"Me too, actually." It was surprisingly good to talk it all through. "I'm so tired. I swear I'll go straight to sleep after work today."

"We can go and let you have a nap if you want."

"No." Tara stood. "I'll have a quick shower and we can go for a walk before work."

It was a beautiful bright day and the fresh air felt therapeutic. Just what Tara needed before her shift at the pub. The day went by fairly fast, and she was sitting on her couch that evening when James called.

"Hi," she said, answering immediately.

"Hi." He sounded surprised. "I didn't think you'd answer. Are you okay? I've been worried about you."

Tara pulled her legs under her. "I'll survive."

"That's good to hear."

"Sorry about yesterday. You caught me by surprise."

"It was my fault," he said. "I shouldn't have blurted it out like that. Of course you'd be upset."

"I don't usually talk about it," she said. "It was a long time ago."

"I can't imagine what that must have been like."

"Pretty crappy," she said. "Is it okay if we talk about something else?"

"Of course." There was a short pause. "How was your day?"

She told him about her shift at the pub and the regulars who she knew pretty well. Then he told her about the bookshop and the customers. It was lovel to hear about it even though it made her miss her old job. They chatted for a while, and when they ended the call neither of them mentioned meeting up. Tara was glad. There were no expectations, which was exactly what Tara needed.

Chapter 43

James called Tara again the following evening. Then they spoke on the phone every evening for the next two weeks. Mostly they chatted about their days or other mundane stuff. Occasionally she'd tell him some snippet about her childhood and how awful life had been after Reuben died. A couple of times she talked about her dad and how much she resented him moving on with his life.

Being able to talk to Amber about everything was a relief too, and Tara was annoyed with herself for not having opened up before. Everything felt easier when she talked it through. Just being able to say out loud how much she missed James felt good. She even mentioned him to Annette when she was over for a visit one Saturday.

"What happened with you two?" Annette asked, handing Tara a cup of tea.

They moved to the living room and Tara stopped to look at a photo of Annette and Wendy. They beamed into the camera, so young and carefree.

"I don't want children," she said calmly. "James says he'll be happy without children but I worry he'll change his mind." She took a deep breath, then sipped at her tea. "I spent so long thinking I was

417

destined to be alone it's hard to let myself imagine anything else."

"If he says he's happy without children, then I don't see what the problem is. Surely that's his choice to make."

Tara took a seat on the couch. "I'm scared he'll end up miserable because of me. And mostly I'm scared he'll change his mind and leave me."

Reaching down, Annette stroked Charlie, who lay at her feet.

"I would've liked to have children," she said slowly. "I gave up on that dream when I decided to be with Wendy. She did the same for me."

"It's a bit different," Tara said, leaning her head back on the couch.

"Not that different," Annette said firmly. "Neither of us ended up miserable. We were very happy, just the two of us."

Tara stared into the fireplace, silently contemplating. Annette made it sound so simple.

"We had the kennels, of course," Annette said idly. "That was our baby. I think you need to share something you both love. You and James have got the bookshop and each other. That should be enough."

Tara stared ahead, unblinking. "Maybe it is," she whispered.

"Don't tell me my little talk worked?" Annette chuckled. "I was trying to think of what Wendy would say to you. But you're usually so stubborn; didn't expect you'd pay any attention to me rambling on."

Tara rubbed at her eyes. "I want to be with him. I'm just scared of everything going wrong."

"Wendy would tell you to go for it," Annette said.

"And what do *you* think?" Tara asked.

"I think you should give it a try."

Tara took a few sips of her drink, then stood and bent to kiss Annette's cheek. "I need to go," she said. "Sorry to rush off."

"Are you going to see James?" Annette asked happily.

"Maybe later. First I need to talk to my mum."

***

Debbie was just stepping out of the house when Tara pulled up. "I was just going for a walk," she said brightly. "Do you want to come?"

"Yes." Tara hugged her mum. A walk sounded perfect.

"I love spring." Debbie linked her arm through Tara's. "All the pretty flowers are coming out. It's lovely."

Debbie was chatty and lively as they walked. Tara always felt better when her mum was doing well. When they got back to the house, Debbie went to get drinks and Tara impulsively sought out the shoebox of old photos.

She was staring into the box when her mum came into the living room. "I do remember him," Tara said. "It was just easier not to think about any of it."

"I thought that too for a while." Debbie put two glasses of water onto the table and sat beside her. "It eats away at you though." She trailed a finger over the photo. "And he deserves to be remembered."

Tara nodded but felt too emotional to speak. Eventually her mum took the box away from her. "We can look at them another day," she said, wiping the tears from Tara's face.

"Are you still seeing Angela?" Tara asked.

"Yes. Just a couple of times a month but it helps."

"I thought I might talk to her," Tara said with a shaky voice. It had been such a relief to talk about things with Amber, and it made Tara realise how much she'd bottled up over the years. It might do her good to talk to a professional.

"That's a good idea. I'll give you her number." Debbie went to the desk and wrote the details down. "You'll like Angela."

Tara took the piece of paper and tucked it in her pocket. "What happened with you and Dad?" she asked sadly. She had the urge to unravel her jumbled childhood memories.

"I was angry with him." Her mum sat down and stared at her hands in her lap. "After Reuben died he focused on you. He was determined to make everything okay for you. He could still laugh with you and I hated him for it. Every time he smiled or laughed I was furious with him. We argued a lot. Then I decided I needed a fresh start. Somewhere new where I didn't have to deal with sympathetic looks every day." She reached over and squeezed Tara's hand. "I should never have taken you away from him."

"But he let you?" Tara said tearfully.

420

"I begged him. Told him it was for the best. He only ever wanted what was best for us. He visited every weekend at first. Until I asked him not to. I hate that you blame him."

"I thought he gave up on us. Just went away and got a new family."

"No." Debbie shook her head. "It wasn't like that. He was devastated. Neither of us knew how to get through it."

"Do you still love him?"

"Yes. In a way. For a while I was bitter about him moving on with his life. But now I'm glad he did. And I know he still cares. I can call him at two o'clock in the morning and he'll always answer."

"I should get in touch with him," Tara said wistfully. Her dad had always tried to connect with her but she'd shut him out. She'd got pretty good at shutting people out.

"He'd like that." Debbie patted Tara's hand. "I'm going to make us some dinner. I've got chicken in the fridge."

Tara felt emotionally drained when she finally left her mum's house. She couldn't stop thinking about her dad, and on impulse she pulled out her phone as soon as she got in the car.

"Hi," she said when he answered. "It's me."

"Hello, love." His voice sounded uncertain. "Is everything okay?"

It was sad that he thought there must be a problem for her to be calling. "Yes," she said. "How are you?"

"I'm fine," he said slowly.

"Good. I was thinking about coming to visit you sometime. If that's okay?"

"Of course it's okay," her dad said. "Any time."

"Sorry to call out of the blue," Tara said.

"I'm glad you did."

"I wanted to say I'm sorry." She pushed her head back into the headrest and swallowed the lump in her throat.

"You don't have anything to apologise for."

"I think I do." Tara tapped on the steering wheel. "I can't talk properly at the moment. But I'd like us to."

"I'd like that too," her dad said. "Are you sure you're okay?"

"Yes." She wiped tears from her cheeks. "I think might be."

Chapter 44

It was just after closing time when Tara arrived at the Reading Room. She hovered on the doorstep, fingering the key in her pocket. After a moment she rang the doorbell.

"Hi!" James beamed down at her from the upstairs window.

"Hi," she said, craning her neck. Her stomach fluttered at the sight of him.

"Did you forget your key?"

She pulled it out of her pocket and held it up to him. "Can I come up?"

"Yes." He glanced over his shoulder. "Just walk slowly. I might need to tidy up."

She chuckled as she put the key in the lock. The shop smelled wonderfully familiar and Tara took her time walking among the shelves, then stopped in front of the photo wall and let the memories wash over her. It was her favourite place in the world.

The door to the apartment was open and Tara stepped inside. James walked from the living room with his hands full of mugs.

"It's not too much of a mess, is it?" he asked when she followed him into the kitchen. The table was strewn with papers, and his laptop sat in the

423

middle of it all.

"Erm …" She raised her eyebrows.

"Well, I'm running two businesses. I don't really have time for cleaning."

"You're still doing the web design?" He hadn't mentioned that during their phone calls.

"Yeah."

"Why?"

He put the pots down and turned to face her. "I needed to keep busy." He stretched his neck. "I might have taken on a bit too much."

"I'm sorry," Tara said. "I didn't mean to leave you in such a mess."

"You didn't."

"Liar." She crossed the room to him, suddenly certain she knew where she wanted to be. He looked slightly taken aback when her hands landed on his collar and she pulled him close. "Did I ever tell you how much I love you?"

"No." A smile broke slowly over his face. "I don't think you did."

"A lot." She touched her forehead to his. "I love you so much."

"I love you too," he said, running his hand through her hair.

"I have two questions for you," she said, drawing back ever so slightly.

"Deep and probing, I presume?"

She brushed a thumb over his neck. "Can I come back and work for you?"

His shoulders tensed. "What's the second question?"

"I'd rather you answer one question at a time." She had a mild panic that she'd left things too late. Except he'd been calling her every evening for weeks. Surely he wanted the same as she did.

"I think you working for me again would be weird," he said slowly.

She shook her head. "It'd be different this time," she said. "I want us to be together. When you found out about Reuben and came to Dartmouth, I panicked. I thought you wanted to fix me and try to convince me that babies don't usually die and that everything would be okay—"

"That wasn't my intention," he said, talking over her. "I have no idea what you went through. But when I spoke to your mum everything made more sense – why you're so guarded. I only wanted to see you. I didn't have any plans other than that."

"I know." She trailed her fingers along the back of his neck. "But it made me realise that I do need to fix things. I've spent so long not dealing with my emotions, and now I'm trying to work through things properly."

"That's good."

"Yes. I want to make some changes ... and I really want us to be together."

His lips twitched into a smile. "What's your second question?"

"You still haven't answered the first one. I really want to come back to work."

He took a deep breath. "I don't want you to come back and work for me." Surprised, Tara tried to take a step back, but he tightened his arms around her. "It was always weird you working for me."

"No, it wasn't." She gave a slight head-shake. Why was he grinning?

"You can come back to work," he said, his features turning serious. "But I'll sign half the bookshop over to you. You'll be co-owner, not an employee."

"What?" She spluttered out a laugh. "No. It's yours."

"If it weren't for you, there wouldn't be a bookshop. It's always been both of ours. I want to make it official."

Tears stung her eyes. "You can't …"

"It's non-negotiable." He cupped her face in his hands and kissed her lips. "What's the second question?"

She pulled out of his embrace, trying to digest his words.

"The suspense is killing me," he said.

She paused for a moment and looked deep into his eyes. "Will you marry me?" she whispered.

"What?" His eyebrows knitted together.

"I still don't know about kids," she said quickly "It was never really that I don't *want* children. But the thought terrifies me and I don't know if I can ever get past that."

He pulled her closer. "I told you, I want you Nothing else matters."

"I know. But—"

He put a finger to her lips. "Did you really just as me to marry you?"

"Yes. And now I see why it's traditional for me

426

to ask. It's no fun waiting for an answer."

"I was hoping you were going to ask if you could move in," he said. "But I was really only expecting you to ask me on a date …"

She bit her lip. "To be honest, at the start of this conversation I *was* only planning on asking if I could move in with you. But I really want to marry you."

He frowned. "You can't just propose out of the blue."

"I just did," she said lightly.

"There's supposed to be a ring." He moved purposefully away from her.

"Where are you going?" she called as he disappeared into the bedroom. "You didn't answer the question!"

A moment later he returned with a silly grin on his face. Then he held out a red velvet ring box.

Tara's hand shot to her mouth, and her eyes filled with tears as he opened it to reveal a perfect diamond ring.

"Yes," he said. "I will marry you."

Her vision was blurred with tears as he slipped the ring onto her finger. "How long have you had that?" he asked.

"Quite a while." He brushed the tears from her cheeks. "You're really staying this time?"

"Yes." She kissed his lips. "I'm exactly where I belong."

The End

Other books by Hannah Ellis

The Cottage at Hope Cove (Hope Cove book 1)
Escape to Oakbrook Farm (Hope Cove book 2)
Summer at The Old Boathouse (Hope Cove book 3)
Whispers at the Bluebell Inn (Hope Cove book 4)
The House on Lavender Lane (Hope Cove book 5)

Always With You

Friends Like These
Christmas with Friends (Friends Like These book 2)
My Kind of Perfect (Friends Like These book 3)
A Friend in Need (Friends Like These book 4)

Beyond the Lens (Lucy Mitchell Book 1)
Beneath These Stars (Lucy Mitchell Book 2)

Made in the USA
Monee, IL
14 July 2020